Miriam Wakerly

Shades of Appley Green

A Modern Village Novel

Published in Great Britain in 2012 by
Strongman Publishing
Woodland Edge, St Catherine's Road,
Frimley, Camberley, Surrey GU16 9NN

A CIP catalogue record for this book
is available from the British Library.

ISBN 978-0-9558432-2-8

Printed and bound by
The Atlas Print Group
a United Kingdom Company

Many thanks for your support
in reading this book before publication,
Jane, Tessa, Carole, Margaret and Steve.
You know who you are!

Characters

The story focuses on Steph Perriman and her inner circle of friends and family; but living in a village, as she does, it is inevitable that she brushes with the wider community.

Key People

Faith	Steph's daughter
Barnaby	Steph's son
Jackson Jeffrys	A retired architect
Greg Mason	Steph's boss
Giles Perriman	Steph's father
Molly Perriman	Steph's mother
Lucas Richardson	Father of Steph's children
Ted Devonish	Deceased benefactor

Minor Characters

Jason	Estate agent
Mia	Jason's wife
Tracy	Jason's lover
Heather	Speech Therapist
Nora	Specialist Nurse
Tony and Babs	Owners of *Gemstones* shop
Lettie	Next-door neighbour
Richard	Steph's ex-husband
Gloria	Computer expert
Sheena	Babysitter

Incidental

Joshua and Sam	Schoolboys
Nick	Simulac Executive
Adina	Hairdresser
Brodric McTavish	Office bully
Liz Burns	Joshua's mother
Astrid and Arthur	An elderly couple
Angwyn	Lettie's husband
Sue and Eddie	American couple
Estebel/Essie	Jackson's daughter
Carole	Steph's aunt
Natalie	Ted's daughter

You may spot a few others with a walk-on part or off-stage.

Prologue

Once revered as the landed gentry, the Devonish family and their patronage to the village of Appley Green go back many generations. Within recent living memory, the very approachable Ted Devonish was well known as the local landowner and farmer, wealthy but generous to a fault. He recognised some of the changes that had taken place in the village during his lifetime, not all good, and decided to leave a sustainable legacy that might do something to help.

He had a philanthropic vision and, before his sudden tragic death, identified a spiky, capable young woman as the right person to make it happen, initially for Appley Green.

Steph Perriman always remembered how he singled her out and put his trust in her. She would never let him down.

Nestling quietly in a middle-England wasteland of sandy heath, Appley Green straddles the boundaries of two counties south west of London. The old manor house and estate of the Devonish family sit on the southern outskirts; their farmland lies further west, where the soil is fertile and workable.

Appley Green's new clusters of housing, schools and community buildings fall mostly within Hampshire, while the nucleus of the village with its little shops and beloved Green are historically rooted in Surrey. Nobody is entirely sure how this came about. At times its unclear identity of mixed post codes causes confusion; but seems to be so tightly bound in knots of red tape that both villagers and the authorities have rightly long assumed that attempts to unravel it might result in chaos.

Dear Reader, I hope you are happy to suspend your disbelief, for in truth, Appley Green is entirely fictitious though in some ways typical of many villages in the area. The small town of nearby Bloomstock is also an imagined place.

1

Every year since her daughter was five years old, Steph had read aloud to her a special page from her old Diary. Even long after Faith was perfectly able to do this for herself, it had become something of a tradition, a birthday ritual. It was to remind her who she was, who her real father was.

As she was about to leave for school, Faith casually remarked, "So, tomorrow I'll be able to read the *rest* of the Diary – *at last*."

"What?"

"You always said – when I'm grown-up I can see the whole thing. Until then I wouldn't understand …"

Steph blinked. Sixteen! Is she an adult?

"Oh … When you're eighteen, I meant, or twenty-one."

"That's just mean!"

"I'll have to read it through to see what I wrote. You know, it's…" She struggled to find the words. This had taken Steph by surprise, much to the amusement of her teenager, who went off to school, swinging her bag, clearly thinking she had also swung the argument.

Steph knew she must park this domestic issue somewhere in her overcrowded head until her working day was over.

For today, she was going to see Jackson, her favourite elderly 'client', as *Special Support for Seniors*, or

1

SSS, called them. This was not going to be an easy ride – for she must sit down with Jackson to broach the dreaded subject of residential care.

After his usual warm welcome, they sat down together in the study of his spacious and quite famous house designed by himself as a young man. Though built in the 1950s, it was of an earlier minimalist style that had inspired him as a boy and led him to become an *avant-garde* architect of celebrity status. This was the room where he still preferred to spend most of his time alone, even though his degenerating eyesight prevented him from reading the dusty books that lined its walls. His gnarly, arthritic hands, with blue veins like ropes, stopped him from tending his beloved garden; stiff legs would no longer propel him around the many rooms without him leaning heavily on a frame; and his poor hearing kept people away, for a conversation was near impossible and made visiting Jackson a very wearing, exhausting exercise. All this he endured through a veil of pain and tendency to freeze.

On her previous visit last week she had tried to explain to him what Skype was about and how simple it was to use – if you had a computer, or the right type of mobile phone, and he had neither. He had adult children, now in their sixties: a daughter in Scotland, a son in Australia and another son in South Africa; so they saw him rarely. Children could be cruel.

"Busy lives" he would say, with an engaging smile, difficult to produce through the Parkinson's 'mask', and no trace of bitterness. "All done so well, you know." But he saw them maybe once a year if he was lucky. "And two more great-grandchildren this year, another one expected next month," passing across with a shaky hand a couple of photos of grandchildren taken, he said, last year sometime.

She wondered if the far-flung locations of his family were an unintended consequence of the adventurous spirit he and his wife had fostered in their upbringing. Today, before she handed him brochures and costings of local Homes, he fondly described their off-the-beaten-track treks and holidays of a more exploratory nature than the average family package holiday, eyes shining as he recalled memories of Peru, Zambia or the furthest reaches of New Zealand. He talked and she listened.

His distant daughter and sons probably pictured him leading an independent life in the village filled with bridge parties, golf, still writing his books on architecture, and giving talks to Rotary clubs and WI groups, driving around from town to town with his camera hanging round his neck, permanently at the ready. He was not one to cause worry. They would have no idea how quickly the unhappy marriage of Parkinson's and arthritis had trapped him inside a body that would not do as it was told.

Later that morning, Steph managed to prick her finger hurriedly fixing a small poster to the Appley Green village notice board with drawing pins. Still upset from her visit to Jackson, her eyes were swimming, unable to focus properly, 'not fit for purpose' her boss, Greg would have said, she thought grimly. Anger lent her the strength needed to pierce the laminated sheet and now bloody fingerprints crawled across it like something out of a crime scene.

"Oh hell," she muttered, pulling a tissue from her denim jacket pocket, lightly spitting on it, thus replacing one bodily fluid with another. She hoped nobody was watching – or listening! Fortunately it was quiet, a mere smattering of people wandering past, probably on their way to the village shops just beyond the Green with its criss-crossed paths and rush-fringed pond, where swans were allegedly building a nest. As an Appley Green resident she was reminded of how lucky she was, belonging to a village not blighted by the throb and fumes of through-traffic. Locals generally stuck to an unwritten code that the able-bodied should walk or cycle to local amenities when possible.

As ever, she had a long list of things to do today. Yes, tomorrow would be Faith's sixteenth birthday and Steph knew she must somehow find a minute to visit *Gift Goodies Galore* for a little special something to go with the main present she had already secretly bought online. For the rest of the year her daughter was far from spoiled, and Steph loved to see the utter delight shining from her girl's face when she opened up surprise parcels. Hopefully Faith's joy would be contagious – she needed to catch some of it for herself. No doubt about that.

The truth of the matter was that each year Faith's birthday revived bittersweet reminders that, apart from the annual Diary reading, she kept to herself. Where had the years gone? How much had happened since, and how lacking she was in what life had then promised to deliver, apart from her two precious children. They were indeed 'the sunshine of her life', as the song goes.

But today, as she wrestled with her task, such reminiscences were not the main cause of her bad temper, though they did compound her mood. No, it was leaving poor old Jackson the way he was, so alone and so unable, with the words of Greg, her boss, still annoyingly ringing in her ears from a meeting they had months ago. "Staring at a screen all day … paedophiles … porn …

4

identity theft ... fraud ... unreliable information ... threats to personal and national security ..." On and on and on, he would go, relentless, never it seemed to Steph, acknowledging proven benefits of using the Internet. He had made it clear he would not condone encouraging the elderly to use technology. 'Playing with fire' was another of his choice metaphors.

Why did Greg have to be such a technophobe? He seemed so unreasonably resistant, she suspected he would never change. He had done very well thank you very much all his life without relying upon a computer and did not intend to start now. Of course, he was not unique in this; she had met one or two like him before, but as manager of their quite new, not-for-profit charity, *Special Support for Seniors*, he seemed unaware that he actually could not fulfil his role without being computer literate. It was only because of social connections that he had secured the part-time job, slipped into it more as an altruistic retirement project, seeing it as a 'people-job'. "No need for admin or paperwork," he would say with what she perceived as a smug smile as if he had at last found his nirvana – not that he was Buddhist, as far as Steph knew.

Defying Greg in this way, her job could be on the line, but she had tried everything else to help her client Jackson, getting him to sample special fitness classes and day centres, taking him library books and DVDs. Other charities and clubs did their bit too, offering coffee mornings and coach-trips to Hampton Court Palace, Windsor Castle, the Royal Horticultural Society Gardens at Wisley or even Brighton beach. Such things, frankly, fell some way short of what he really needed; in fact, outings were way beyond him.

Having polished off the notice to a sheen, she stood back to read it, to see it as others in the village would view it for the first time: *People of Appley Green! Even if you've never used a computer before, come along and Google! Learn how to find new friends, information and have fun! At least give it a try. Friday, 13 May 7.30 pm in Saviour's Hall. And – it's free!!*

So now it was time to move on: sometimes it was necessary to do what you know is right, and suffer the consequences. That was her conclusion.

Ah! Friday, the 13th! "Oh, great," she groaned. So absorbed with the risks of her venture, she failed to spot it before. Maybe that would account for the ready availability of Saviour's Hall at short notice. It was used for all kinds of activities from fundraising bring and buys; amateur dramatics and choirs; yoga; playgroups; to consultation meetings about their French twin-village. It was just too bad; hopefully possible recruits would not be put off by superstition.

She had left out contact details, to avoid her name being associated with it by *everyone* in the vicinity. She was the one paying for the notice-board space and organising the class, but she didn't want phone calls. People would see it as another village activity on offer and drift along – or not, as the case may be. The curious, the lonely, the bored. No, maybe that was unfair. Was the Greg negative mindset rubbing off on her? Surely it would lure thirsty minds, socialites, fun-loving freethinkers. Hmm. Who was she kidding? Most of those in that category would already be up and running, browsing, booking, downloading, searching ... She vaguely but cheerily waved across the road to a village newcomer, being walked by two exuberant Portuguese Water Dogs and an impossibly cute Bichon Frise.

Then she stared and blinked. How could she have been so dumb? What a blunder! In haste, she had left out the name of the sponsors, who would be expecting the publicity. She must go back home pronto to amend the poster, insert their company logo and print it off. But for now, she would leave this one as it was.

She heard shuffling footsteps behind her and swung round. Two lads were standing there. She vaguely recognised one of them, Joshua, son of Liz Burns, primary schoolteacher who had taught her son, Barnaby, a few years ago.

"Hi," she said, wondering why they were not both at school. They both looked down, staring at their shoes, examining the dusty ground where grass was worn away by the footfall of schoolchildren. The village had fought fierce battles to keep their schools and they had successfully hung onto their primary and a small comprehensive. Children from nearby hamlets and the outlying commuter sprawl easily made up the numbers. But how sad, noted Steph, that kids are reluctant to look people in the eye, unless they know them. So different from when she was a child living in a village near Guildford; even in twenty or thirty years, things had changed. She understood the stranger policy drummed in from an early age, but it was something she often sought ways to soften.

Her poster was not aimed at their age group; the two lads were looking at it now and smiling, or sniggering perhaps. She guessed their amusement was close to a scoff, but it might help to have all ages come along. She wanted to encourage senior citizens, of course, but would do well to avoid ending up with a patently 'oldie' class, for silver surfers only.

"Shouldn't you be at school?"

"We're on our way to a human geography project – meeting up in the graveyard."

"Euw! You don't believe in ghosts, do you?" She acted out a shiver. "Better get a move on then! Oh! Before you go, boys, are you any good on computers?" she asked, with such a feigned casual air she felt sure they would see through it instantly.

Of course, they nodded. In a flash of inspiration, Steph decided to cut to the chase, aware of the time and knowing they could be reported missing and she must get back home. But a quick chat could be a few minutes well invested.

"Could you come along and help?" She nodded in the direction of the notice board. "Show people how to do things?"

They shrugged and looked at each other, their mouths twisting with embarrassment. Steph put them out of their misery.

"Well, think about it. OK? We could do with some youngsters like you to show us how it's done."

"We might do," said Joshua. "Need to check out what else is going on, though. Don't we, Sam?"

Sam shrugged. "Who'll be there?" he asked.

"I've really no idea," replied Steph, truthfully.

"Well, what's it for then? Who's putting it on and stuff?" said Joshua, sounding impatient.

Steph had to skirt round a totally honest answer which would have been, *It's to get elderly people who struggle to get out – for one reason or another – to get back to the human race, find a social life and reach distant families through a computer screen.* No, this was not a good selling point to achieve a balanced mix of people. She would need to get some younger people involved too, or it would be like having a choir composed entirely of people who truly could not sing. She must capitalise on this opportunity to pull in a couple of schoolboys. Skip a generation; it was well accepted that grandchildren usually hit it off with grandparents. How could she induce them? She thought quickly. If they took to it they could persuade others … her mind was racing, carried along on a wave of enthusiasm.

"If you could help out a bit as 'coaches' I could give you a reference for when you need one, maybe looking for a job in a few years, or going to university?"

This prompted nothing but blank looks. Quick rethink. They were only a couple of years older than her son Barnaby, much too young to be lured by the promise of meeting girls there. Maybe she had scared them off – after all, she guessed they were only about thirteen. She had proper technically qualified Trainers coming from the IT company helping her out for free, but these two disconcerted boys did not know that.

"Maybe you could assist the guys from Simulac. They're lending the …"

Sam and Joshua suddenly came to life like ignited kindling, eyes bright, faces flickering with interest.

"Simulac?" They exchanged knowing glances. "What time do you want us there?"

2

Steph drove back around Appley Green, with her windows open so she could feel and breathe the warm pine-scented air of early summer; then along a minor road to her cottage in Furzey Terrace, on the west side of the village. Sunlight was filtering through the overhanging silver birches, squirrels playfully darted about on the verge recklessly close to the wheels of her car. It was a perfect day, bright enough to lift the spirits and yet all she could think about was if she should call in again on Jackson. Really, this was all about Jackson. Even she could see that, as clear as day. The disturbing question that kept bobbing up like a cork in a bucket of water, as fast as she pushed it down, was why? Why was she so affected by him? She saw plenty of struggling seniors but somehow drew upon inner resources to support them with relative detachment and a cool head.

At least today she could feel a welcome warmth as it teased leaf buds all around the village to unfurl their springtime shades of fresh green: from acid-lime to olive-sage. Steph was filled with hope that this summer would be a good one. She judged she could just fit in editing the poster before an afternoon meeting, depending on how quickly she could get Nick from Simulac to email the logo to her. Frustrated at the lack of time, she could not imagine how she would conjure up the few minutes needed to go to the gift shop so she could give Faith her entire birthday package before she went to school, as she normally did …

As she drove back to her cottage, associations with the honeyed past flooded into her head again, triggered by Faith's earlier expectations regarding her Diary. How could she find time to read through the whole thing? She would have to be firm. Surely eighteen was the socially normal 'coming of age', wasn't it? Just because she could legally have sex or a tattoo, did not mean she was mature enough to understand complicated emotional stuff. She was not even sure she could face reading those pages herself, let alone expect her daughter to cope.

She tried to focus her mind on the present, but the hopelessness she felt at leaving Jackson kept bubbling up. Logically there was a long list of folk who could benefit from *Special Support for Seniors*. Its founder, Ted Devonish, knew what he was talking about.

But with Jackson, the need to help him was compelling, insistent. It sometimes even kept her awake at night. He deserved so much more than the life he was forced to lead. Perhaps it was because he had always been a do-er, a person who made things happen, with immense creative energy, a big wheel indeed, and a selfless philanthropist.

"I always knew that when I retired and had the time," he told her one day, as they sat chatting over a cup of tea and stem-ginger biscuits, "I would want to help others. Oh dear, Stephanie, does that sound a bit patronising? A bit holier than thou?" So self-deprecating, he was such a lovely man, but in no position to be able to help others now. He chuckled through the discomfort he must be feeling, as she witnessed his medication begin to wear off. It was time to take another pill, she could tell by the tremor in his right hand that lay 'at rest' on the table and the rigid expression that had crept across his features. He would benefit from slow-release medication administered in a steady stream. Might stem cell therapy be available within his lifetime, she wondered? Could he benefit from surgery for deep brain stimulation? There was no definitive cure for Parkinson's yet they could do wonders these days. She had to trust his medical team to do the best thing for him.

In the past few months his speech had weakened and it was becoming a strain for both him and any listener. It tore her to pieces to watch him fail, to see a man's dignity betrayed as his life disintegrated. Yet she could see his mind was alert, with no sign of dementia, his fingers could operate a keyboard and a mouse ... and he could live for years yet.

"Hi sweet-pea," Steph called out, as she could see her daughter's blazer and school bag strewn on the sofa.

Faith's voice responded from upstairs. "Be down in a minute."

Steph opened up her laptop to update the poster, also taking a closer look at the Simulac website. She hoped Faith would not bring up the subject of the diary again. Not now.

Steph had been highly suspicious of Simulac at first but assumed the charitable service they offered was good PR for them, more effective than paying for advertising. She had found their high-tech website, softened by a community policy to 'give something back' and 'make a difference'. Even better, she pulled up a page that explained that, in addition to free training, they also put people who need computers – perhaps disadvantaged youngsters, disabled or elderly people – in touch with offices or other donors of used hardware. It was obvious to Steph this would be vital for her project to work. They seemed ideal: local, did all the electronic safety testing and, anyway, she did not know of anyone else.

Scrutinising their site now for more information, she saw some computer games marketed by Simulac, which would explain the sudden burst of enthusiasm from Joshua and Sam when they heard the name.

Faith came clattering downstairs into their small living-room where Steph sat with her laptop on the dining table.

"Just popped home for my mobile. Left it in the loo."

Steph looked up with a teasing smile. " Not *in* …"

"No-o. On the shelf."

"I suppose you can't see your way through the rest of the day without it?" Actually, she was the one who actively encouraged her daughter to have her mobile on her at all times and Faith knew that.

Faith just gave a little good-natured shake of her head as she pulled on her blazer and grabbed her bag. "Uhuh. Anyway must dash – double maths this afternoon."

"Have you had …" the front door slammed "… lunch? Ah well, I'll take that as a yes."

Steph stared at her screen. This poster … it was all wrong, she thought. It's not in the right language to reach the people I want to read it.

She should make it more general. *Have a go with computers – don't be shy*, she typed in. Perhaps she should not even mention 'computers' at all. Some of those who had never even switched one on or had no concept of how to use one, would be immediately put off. How could she have been so dense? 'Google' wouldn't mean a thing to the very people she really wanted to be at the training sessions.

She imagined she was Daphne with the fluffy white hair like a dandelion clock; or wry-humoured chatterbox Iris, waiting for new hips and knees; old Eric who had to give up his allotment last year and staunchly refused to even use a mobile phone – or Jackson. Even Jackson, an artist and an intellectual, was not of the computer age.

She sat back, detaching herself, again trying to see the words through others' eyes: *Would you like: 'pen-friends' abroad or even down the road? without using a pen! to see your grandchildren, near or far, every day? and chat to them? to have groceries, meals, music and much more delivered to your door?*

She pushed her shoulder length blonde hair behind her ears - its layers had an annoying habit of flopping forward - and stared at the screen. Maybe there were too many words. If she were elderly and living alone, would she be seduced by these concepts? Of course some of them, frail with arthritis; or wary of having an angina attack, would be unable to even walk as far as the notice board. That was the point. But perhaps by word of mouth it would reach them. She was doing a house-to-house leaflet drop too. There would be those who have no grandchildren, or never listen to music. Steph sighed. She could fiddle with this forever striving to achieve perfection.

The word 'computer' must go in there now, she decided, reinserting, *'Have a go with computers – don't be shy'* at the end. Gently does it. It would be unfair to lure people along unwittingly. She hoped she had the balance right now, quickly amending the matching leaflets and printing off a small supply while making, then munching a hastily prepared peanut-butter sandwich, as the ham seemed to have been already taken.

The amended publicity also had the advantage of giving little away to 'other people' about the true nature of the classes. If it reached Greg's ears that she was setting up computer classes she'd be stuffed! At least she would never be one of those employees sacked by email!

Her subterfuge was not on a scale likely to rock national security, but it did give her a small adrenaline rush. Greg would know about it eventually – once she could jubilantly prove to him the 'evidence-based' (blindingly obvious) benefits of her project. If he remained stubbornly unconvinced by results she would present her case to a higher authority (whoever that might be) – or resign.

The edits took longer than planned; so Steph dashed to her next appointment before replacing the notice. There would be no time to get this one laminated, she thought, slipping it inside a transparent plastic folder. She was meeting up with two medical professionals: a specialist nurse and a speech and language therapist, at the big District and General Hospital in Bloomstock. She had some referrals for them, people who would gain from their expertise. On her way home later that afternoon she would fit in a client visit and somehow find time to take in some leaflets to the Citizens Advice Bureau in Bloomstock, Appley Green library, *Hair and Now* who have a special deal for pensioners, and the village Post Office that had just changed hands.

She would have no time today to stop and introduce herself to the new young couple who had taken it over from Mr and Mrs Patel, but this was definitely on her mental to-do list. Tomorrow, Faith's birthday she reminded herself, she would drop by a couple of nearby village community centres and a retirement home where she was visiting some residents, after which she would print off more leaflets to take to neighbouring villages and a local town that fell within her patch. Less likely that people from outside Appley Green will travel in though ...

And she must fit in Faith's presents too. Life was a rush.

3

Nora and Heather shook hands with her and they sat down in a compact office next to busy consultation rooms. The meeting could only be brief, but it always seemed worthwhile to have a face-to-face meeting before relying on emails and phone calls.

"So, tell us a bit more about your charity, could you Steph?" asked Nora, the Parkinson's specialist nurse. "How long has it been going and what sort of things do you do?"

Steph was always pleased to have the chance to promote SSS and hoped that word of mouth would work its magic – and perhaps a mention on the hospital website.

"There was a local benefactor called Edward Devonish. You've probably heard of him. He was a farmer, known as Ted by all the older inhabitants in Appley Green, and he came from wealthy landowning stock ..." she paused, realising there was no time for detail. She could remember him as a charming man, who eventually plucked her from relative obscurity. It was all in the Diary; she must look up those pages ... He used to come in now and then to do a few lengths in the swimming pool at the sports and leisure centre, *House of Fitness*, where she was the manager – a lifetime ago, it seemed. He always had time to chat. At a packed village meeting – it was something to do with Gypsies – he had taken her to one side and invited her to The Manor so he could explain to her something of his long-term vision. "You, Stephanie," he said, "would be perfect for the job. If I died tomorrow I know I would be leaving it in safe hands. Because you understand." She promised she would. Little did he know, a few years later a drunk driver would slam into the nearside of his Mercedes.

Steph blinked and collected her thoughts. "Anyway, divorced and living alone, he died suddenly two years ago. Tragic. Great sadness in the village." *And great sorrow for me*, she wanted to add, but thought it best to keep aloof from the grief she had felt at his loss. "Sometimes it seems it's always the best people who go before their time, doesn't it?"

Nora and Heather nodded politely but Steph could see she had overstepped the mark. Be professional, she told herself sharply.

She continued, "His only child, daughter Natalie, had always made it clear she had no wish to be involved in farming, even at arms' length. His total estate, once sold off realised a tidy few million. Now, he bequeathed a portion of this to a charity and for that he set out some rules. It should be used to set an example of a charity giving special support to senior citizens who need it. For example," and she handed over a small brochure that set out the SSS mission, "more than personal care, medical attention, financial guidance. Not just housework either, necessary though that is, but on top of that, for those elderly whose families were too distant or too busy, they should be given *time* and *attention*." Steph stressed the key words, just as Ted used to. She would never let that man down.

Nora nodded, as she scanned the leaflet. "Certainly what people with Parkinson's need. Everything slows down and not everyone appreciates that."

A mental picture of Jackson filled the screen inside her head. "Ted knew that so many isolated old people need someone who can listen and respond; treat them with respect as an individual; without being in a rush, think what that particular person really needs based on the lives they have led."

"Aren't there charities and agencies who already do this? They have volunteers and even paid support workers who visit, don't they? Befriending services?" asked Heather, looking at her watch not quite discreetly enough.

"There are, and they do an excellent job, but there aren't always enough to go round. Carers are inevitably pressed for time by agency schedules. Time costs money. Often there's little continuity so carer and client really don't bond – don't have *time* to bond. Nobody's fault, just a fact of life. And volunteers come and go. Few people can afford to give of their time for nothing these days, however much they'd like to. Edward Devonish saw it as important that consistent, visiting friends should be rewarded and … well, have training to be professional so they could also offer information and support. He said it must be self-funding after five years and set an example so other branches will set up in other areas – without his initial financial backing obviously."

"So a lot hangs on the success of this pilot then?"

Yes, she thought, all eyes are on me in the village. "Exactly. It's my job to ensure that *Special Support for Seniors* has a future." Her commitment had extended to giving up a well-paid job but they did not need to know that either. There was so much more to it than that.

Nora raised her eyebrows and threw her a sympathetic smile. "To set an example? Wow, no pressure then! What a challenge Steph! To be self-sufficient sounds demanding, to say the least." Steph really liked Nora; she was excellent at her job and people respected her for both her expertise and kindness.

"Yep. But Ted Devonish had the foresight to see that if the charity could draw on his bequest indefinitely its staff would just see it as another paid job and be less motivated."

"So – you have to fundraise as well? I mean, as well as actually helping local clients in quite a direct way."

Steph nodded. "We need to recruit a dedicated publicist and fundraiser – obviously who can raise much more than they are paid. It's early days for that, though. First, we need to get the whole thing working."

"Who else works for SSS?"

"I report to a manager – whose role it is to secure other funding like lottery money, trusts and legacies, that sort of thing. And ..." she added, reluctantly, trying not to baulk at the words, "... manage me." The notion of being managed was too close to being bullied in Steph's eyes. Her mind flicked back subliminally to when she began keeping written records on how she was once 'managed' ... at a time when she was so desperate for work she dared not open her mouth to anyone about what her manager was doing ... Would she want Faith to read about that in the diary?

"What have you achieved so far then, Steph?"

A ripple of panic ran through her. What had she achieved? "Well, I ... I set up a 'Buddy Scheme', where a young person pairs with an older one, for example as lodgers or visitors who help with household maintenance and gardening; this is cheap but has had its quota of problems as you can imagine ...personality conflicts and so on ..." Nora smiled understandingly, while Heather raised her eyebrows in mock surprise. Steph sensed she was failing to engage with Heather. "I'm just embarking on a training scheme for older people who have never used a computer so they can use the Internet."

"What! You think computers can combat loneliness?" asked Nora, with a sceptical bordering on cynical note in her voice.

"It will put them in touch with other people. Yes, it'll help, at least. Not like with youngsters when you want them to get out and make friends. For some of the people I see – and you must come across them as well, even if not always in their homes - it is the last resort for them to make new friends of a sort."

"Mm, *virtual* friends," suggested Nora.

No, thought Steph, not some fantasy world; real human beings, but contactable online. Think how telephone and TV once changed lives. She held back.

After a pause, Nora went on, "It's certainly worth a try. Expensive though? And a bit risky? People taking advantage and all that." People 'take advantage', thought Steph bitterly, with or without the aid of the Internet, but she said nothing.

'Negative Heather', as Steph had already dubbed her, picked up the printed list of referrals Steph had brought with her and put it in her bag, as if preparing to go and bring the meeting to a close. "Good luck with that one, but you may be wasting your time. Those who have already latched onto computers will be OK, but most are completely resistant. Anyway I'm more in the business of getting people talking!" she added abruptly. "You'll appreciate that. It's my job."

She should have thought of that. Heather's role was to help people with speech problems. "Yes, of course, but ... it will be kept very short and simple. Twitter will be the main focus where the messages are confined to

21

just a few words. Other networking sites would probably be too much ... " Steph's voice faded. She was left feeling very unsure of how strong their support was for her venture.

On the way home she managed to park in the small car park behind St Matthews church and slipped into *Gift Goodies Galore*. She was sure to find some little extras for Faith in there, and could get a birthday card for Elsie, an anniversary card for Astrid and Arthur, a new pack of cards for Eric, a jar of Patrick's favourite tomato and onion chutney and ... well, while she was there, probably some little thing for Jackson.

4

"Did you pick up my third email this afternoon, babe?" Mia's voice disappeared along with the rest of her as she rushed upstairs and out of earshot.

There was little point in responding to her question and Justin saw no reason why he should make the effort to follow his wife in her tracks. It had been a long day, working as he did for Willem Hardrop Estate Agents with barely any houses on the market. He sat down and opened up his laptop at the table, theoretically one for 'dining', in the open-plan living area of their beautifully renovated cottage in Cowslip Lane, on the edge of Appley Green.

Yes, he had seen the third email, the one about them not sitting down and talking things through enough – especially about the holiday she had now booked in Sharm el Sheikh. Yes, he saw she had gone ahead without consulting him to get a good deal before it slipped out of their grasp. *Sorry.* Yes, he knew that she knew they should have discussed this before committing.

And no, he did not want to go. In fact the very idea of going to an expensive, hot place where he might feel culturally ill-at-ease with little to do – without Tracy – made him squirm with an odd mix of brain-numbing boredom and bile rising up inside him. For two weeks? It was just not going to happen.

It was easier to explain by email. How could he look Mia in the eye? He began composing all the reasons, without, of course, mentioning the real one. Once out of the shower, she would flit through her emails and may not even notice he had sent this one from downstairs, and not this afternoon while 'at work'.

Justin found half a bottle of Pinot Grigio in the fridge. Insipid gnat's pee to his taste; he rummaged in the wine-rack until he found a full-blooded claret. Glancing through the fridge he wondered if it was his turn to cook tonight. If so, he would offer omelette, which Mia would decline as too dull and then rustle up something infinitely more delicious, albeit lamentably low in calories. He smirked as he returned to his emails, but looking now at the fifth email of the afternoon from Mia, his smile dropped, *Don't forget it's your turn tonight. Pick up a chicken dish or hey, Moussaka? Salad for me. Whatever. You choose darling. Just make sure you do! Nothing in fridge and I'm off to choir tonight* ☺ *xxx*

Shit. It would be pushing it to try another email and claim, despite obvious evidence to the contrary, he sent it two hours ago … Mia then appeared in a towelling robe, with a turban upon her head, looking statuesque. Always the catwalk model, no matter what she was wearing.

"I didn't get anything," he confessed without looking up from the screen. Honesty on trivial matters came easily to him.

"What?"

"Food."

"Justin!"

"Sorry."

"No use being sorry. Is it?" She looked at her bare wrist. "What time is it?"

"Twelve past seven."

"I'll get something with the girls after choir."

So – what am I supposed to do? Never mind, looking on the much brighter side, there might be time to nip out and meet Tracy – they could grab a bite somewhere. Proper food.

"I have apologised. Just – completely crazy afternoon. You know." He shrugged with an air of hopelessness.

"No probs," she replied amicably over her shoulder as she went off, presumably to get ready for choir.

She had neither checked her emails nor made time to discuss Sharm el Sheikh. It was hardly his fault. She would have to cancel it and stand the loss. Mrs Rich-knickers could afford it.

"What are you having?" he asked Tracy, at the low-life dive of a pub that had two advantages of being located between their domestic zones and providing robust food. Also its ambience was dark, another reason they often resorted to it, with discreet nooks where couples could fumble and fondle if they were so inclined.

Having pored over a menu, she put it down on the table. "Not really hungry, to be perfectly honest," she replied. "Just hungry to see you." She had this way of crinkling her eyes, and leaning forward, squashing her breasts so they plumped up in the cleavage. He felt stirrings. Not many girls would be so ready.

"Well I am gagging for a slab of red meat," he murmured, with a cheeky twitch of the eyebrows. "With chips .."

"You coming back to mine tonight?" she asked, doing that leaning forward thing again and reaching out for his arm. He felt weak.

He shook his head. "Early start tomorrow morning – flying to Edinburgh. A .. conference."

The smile left her face. "Why don't you just move in with me? All these trips – would be easier closer to London, probably. Train only takes fifteen minutes, Paddington to Heathrow ... I mean, in the rush hour it can take half an hour just to get to the motorway from Appley Green, or the nearest station ... Doesn't it? Justin?"

She had it so worked out! Panic. It was bound to happen. *The next stage.*

"I'll think about it ..." This could be decision time brewing, but not tonight. Having been, until a few moments ago, in a state of considerable sexual arousal, he was in no mood to dump Tracy just yet.

"Shame we couldn't be together tonight – I have some news."

"Yeah?"

"The best kind. We're going to have a baby." Her face was wreathed in smiles – he thought that was the expression.

The blissful look on Tracy's glowing face brought it home to Justin like a bucket of melting ice being poured over his head, that she was a million miles ahead of him in this special relationship, one that was built upon deception. Unlike the more conventional web or tissue of lies, transparent and flimsy, his would stand in line supporting each other, holding hands, locking fingers until finally coalescing into an apparently valid scenario he believed was solid and real.

But now, in a flash, he saw it revealed as the paltry, sordid affair it was, although he would be the first to acknowledge that Tracy was sweet, giving and gorgeous who deserved much better since losing her former boyfriend, a 'fine young man', to the war in Iraq.

Tracy was waiting for a response. Tiny muscles quivered in his cheeks as he tilted his head and smiled back. "Aw, babe – I mean, well, wow!" He swallowed hard, feeling the blood drain from his brain. "A baby?" Had she stopped taking the pill without telling him? *His baby?*

"Knew you'd be thrilled." She giggled. "You must come and meet my parents and the rest of my tribe now." Jeez, her mother and stepfather live in Spain, father and stepmother somewhere near Durham, he knew that. But so what? All academic now, as they say. Plausible idea in theory, but there was absolutely no question of him meeting them. No way, no, no way. "So if you move in, just for the time being, then we can decide when and where to settle down. Obviously we'll need something way bigger for a family … a garden …" She was gabbling, excitedly. Of course, he was to her a boyfriend, her partner even, with whom she had been having joyful sex for around a year. This was the next step and she was the normal one. What was he supposed to say, or even more critically, do, now?

"Of course I'll have to give up work …" she added, lightly. "Look after myself a bit. I don't want to lose this one …"

Whoa! More information than he needed just at that moment. He thought he might pass out. His mobile buzzed and he glanced at it. A text from Mia: *Where r u? Choir off – have pizza. We can talk about hols. NOW* ☺ *xxxx*

5

With her old Diary tucked under her arm, Steph took her daughter a cup of tea. Faith sat up in bed, pushing her tousled hair back out of her eyes.

"Happy Birthday!"

"I've been awake for ages."

They both knew what was coming. Strange, they could probably both recite the words verbatim without even a glance at the page, but no, that would be just embarrassing. Faith had grown to understand the reason behind this birthday custom and even accepted without any sarcasm what Steph could see now was rather sentimental prose, harking back to a time when she, then barely more than a teenager, read a lot of romantic fiction.

Steph read, "*Everything about Faith's birth was perfect, once it was over that is. The memory of a long labour faded with amazing speed, calm euphoria soon replacing the agony. I looked down with great pride at the still moist newborn wrapped in the hospital baby-blanket, cradled in my arms, little eyes just opening like those of a kitten, trying to focus, trying to return my adoring gaze. I was twenty years old and this was the single best moment of my life – so far.*

Lucas gently smoothed stray strands of hair from my forehead, which he kissed with great tenderness. His caress was magical. He remarked that he couldn't have done what I'd just done and we both chuckled at the absurdity of this comment.

"I mean … I'm just so happy, Stephie," he said. I could see relief in his face, tears in his cornflower blue eyes, a startlingly beautiful accessory to his coal-black hair. He was, at that moment studying me rather than this amazing new life we had created together, clearly a work of perfection. He had this way of making me feel loved, precious and whole.

"Here, have a hold. She's yours too, you know," I said to him, sitting up cautiously, feeling sore below.

"Don't I know it," said Lucas. "She has my Auntie Rosemary's nose."

I know nothing about his aunt, or indeed her nose, and really do not care. There was something about the shapely Cupid's bow mouth that was like my Mum's, but I realised that at this stage you could probably see anything you wanted if you stared long enough.

I looked up at Lucas, loving him so much and, as if that were not enough, now we had a small being, that oh-so-precious amalgam, half him and half me. Would she inherit Lucas's lustrous black locks, I wondered, and his kindness? Or my long fingers, my habit of rushing at things? I really was quite ridiculously happy. I reached for his arm, needing to touch him, and he squeezed my hand tightly in both of his.

"So – did we agree?" I said. "Faith?"

"Definitely. She just looks like a Faith already."

I smiled as he took his baby daughter awkwardly, standing at first quite still, his knees hugging the edge of the bed, clearly fearful of dropping her. Then as he looked down at Faith, taking ownership, I watched him quite naturally begin to gently sway from side to side, as if some instinct had kicked in, some way to comfort. I was so lucky. What a perfect Dad he would be …"

There followed, in keeping with tradition, a minute of sniffing and sad reflection.

"Mum …?"

Steph knew what was coming.

"I really do want to know more about my Dad. I mean I know he was a musician and that you loved him, and what happened to him … well, in the end, but not much more on the bit in between, or after. Please?"

"I shall need to check it over first. Give me some time. I'm not promising. I think when you're eighteen will be better," she said, pausing to kiss the top of Faith's head as she stood up to go, "when you know what you're going to do with your own life."

After breakfast, Barnaby, Steph's eleven-year-old son, gave Faith a clay hedgehog he had made at school, and an hour of his time when he would be her 'butler'. He was a commendably thrifty child, not mean, but careful with his pocket-money. She then opened up a few cards and packages, realising she had the iPhone she had dreamed of as well as a beautiful topaz necklace and red leather bag from her mother.

"We can't afford all this," she said responsibly, genuinely astonished at the array of quality goodies.

Steph tapped her nose. "I've been saving. Don't worry." She avoided mentioning that she had not bought any new clothes for herself for over a year. It was of no importance.

On Saturday Faith went out with friends to *House of Fitness*, where Steph had kept in touch with the now manager, Maggie. Even after so many years since Steph worked there, Maggie remembered her and promised to give the teenagers some special treatment. It had all gone exceedingly well. They did massage and nails now, apparently. On Sunday, to prevent domestic mutiny, she sat down with Barnaby, to discuss *his* birthday, which would come up in the autumn … It was a balancing act, being a single parent, proving she did not favour one over the other.

Once both Faith and Barnaby were asleep, she pulled out the Diary and began to read. It was a while since she had dipped into its pages and she knew it would probably give her nightmares, but the quiet of the night seemed to be the only opportunity open to her.

'I'm falling into a bit of a sloppy routine in the cosy maternity wing of Appley Green Cottage Hospital, but it's a real luxury being able to devote almost every minute of the three days here to just baby and me, padding about in slippers and dressing-gown. I'm making friends, some new mothers and older women who already have one or two kids, who seem to know all the stuff. I'm listening up to everything: 'If it cries, feed it', says Una in the next bed. Maybe she just wants a quiet life. 'Let her yell for a bit, show her who's boss' is recommended by Arabella, who appeared to be a highly organised mother of four. A bit harsh though. Feeding times are really free and easy, 'different from in my day' says Mum. Breast-feeding is going well, the nurses give good advice and all in all I feel pretty chilled and cool. A proper Earth mother!

I want to share my special homecoming moment with Mum and Dad but have no idea how long I might need a hand, or might want them to stay, or they would want to stay. Lucas is doing everything he can, I know that, but is the first to admit he knows nothing about infant babies.

Shame Lucas can't collect Faith and me himself, but he's already committed to oversee some of his pupils at a mock music exam. Of course, he's desperately sorry about it.'

There was nothing so far that Faith could not read, just a day to day journal, and she might find it interesting since it is personal to her, thought Steph.

Faith has just had her last feed of the evening. It was just Mum, without Dad, who fetched us back to the flat.'

She could describe to Faith in more detail the two-bedroom flat they rented, on the north east side of Appley Green. It was the ground floor of a small, red-bricked Victorian family house and she had often pointed out the road as they drove nearby.

' *"We'll stay as long as you need us. Or, if you want us to go, then we will," Mum said tactfully, as she drove the short distance, speaking on behalf of Dad, I guess. I feel equally open-minded and easy-going, just so long as I have Lucas by my side as soon as possible.*

When I walked through the door, baby things seemed to have invaded. In our little hallway is the buggy, an enormous contraption ready to stroll. Standing tall next to it there's a box containing a highchair, with several packs of nappies stacked up under the coat pegs. The bay window-seats were festooned with pink balloons, cards and presents, some that she had received in hospital and others that had arrived that day. I somehow knew Lucas had put all this together before work. It had his touch. But Mum had set the table ready for lunch and there were good cooking smells wafting through from the kitchen.

She'd gone to a lot of trouble and I gave her a hug and a kiss to say thanks, handing Faith over to her as soon as we came in, because I know that's what she really wanted.

"Baby girl just beautiful. Aah!" said Mum, holding Faith up to the natural light to admire her grandchild properly, rather as if she were checking shoes for a perfect colour match with an outfit. Course, my parents had me, their only child, late in life and I'm lucky they're now retired with time to spare. Mum was over the moon when she heard I was pregnant – so young. Quite surprising really!

I asked where Dad was, looking around, expecting to see him with open arms, camera at the ready. But Mum seemed to barely hear me.

"She has a look of my mother, you know, something about the mouth?" My question then registered. "Oh, your Dad has probably just popped out to get a newspaper from the Post Office."

"Really?" How could he have timed things so badly? I thought that a bit odd.

Mum frowned at me. "He'll be back soon. For sure, he can't have gone far. He's expecting us after all.""

Although everything was pretty much as it should be, Steph remembered how reality punched a few holes in that soft romantic cocoon. Though casting a cheery light, the early summer sunshine served to show up dust on the TV screen and smears on the window-panes.

'Dad has gone. Space, or rather lack of it, is a bit of an issue here, and he spotted this in a matter of hours. After our evening meal cooked by Mum (roast shoulder of pork with apple sauce), he announced, "I feel a bit of a spare part to be honest. I'm just taking up precious room. Think I'll head off back home tonight. I can be there in half an hour, at this time of the evening." His plan is to come and pick up Mum when needed.

I didn't expect this of Dad - of all people! But he seemed to have made up his mind. (Probably over-reacting, but I feel a bit upset about this, but maybe it's what they warned of, in the hospital, 'baby-blues'.)

Steph could remember how she didn't want her father to go, or for him to want to leave them. There was a special bond between them that went back to when she was as young as she could remember, perhaps three or four years old. She would watch him for hours, utterly enthralled and entranced, as he worked on a painting. He stuck to his conventional style, what critics would dismiss as 'chocolate box', never destined for greatness, but their honest simplicity seemed fantastical to a little girl. Then she was allowed to hold his paintbrushes in her chubby little hands, solemnly assisting like a nurse at the side of a surgeon, handing him the appropriate tool. She learned to anticipate when he would need a flat one, a round or a fine one. A few years on she would mix his paints, blending colours, and make comments on progress, and before long she had her own little easel …

Since opting for retirement in his late fifties from managing a garden centre, her father always liked to be active and useful. She later accepted his role was limited in this domestic setting.

'So when he said this, I had to give myself a little shake and try to see things through his eyes. He probably wants to get back to his golf and herbaceous borders and his painting. Maybe he really has had enough. His sudden decision to disappear back home seems strange, because he did say he was planning to do a little painting of Faith as a newborn, but I can understand a small flat filled with all things baby could be stifling for a man his age.'

Steph closed the diary. It was too painful to think about her father. What she had read so far had nothing to do with what happened years later, but Faith was bound to ask questions about the grandfather she could remember. She was not sure she could handle that; forgetting was the easier option and probably kinder both to herself and to her father.

6

As Justin accompanied Tracy to her bus-stop, Sharm el Sheikh suddenly rose up sunny and golden, yielding itself as an exceedingly attractive option, or rather opt-out. A heaven-sent, blue-sky escape route, buying him time to sort out his life. How could he ever have imagined he would be short of amusement in a fortnight's paradise of pure, honest hedonism with Mia, his 'model' wife?

He felt he had cut short their evening and Tracy needed mollification before they parted company.

"Sorry babe. A report I need to finish tonight and then up at Gawd knows when for the flight to Edinburgh in the morning," he said, looking straight into her blue eyes with a credulously sincere what-can-you-do look.

Tracy shrugged good-naturedly. "It's OK. Pretty mad, though isn't it, us having separate flats? Especially now," she added, with an irrepressible giggle. "I'd come to yours, but …"

"Honestly, Adrian doesn't get any better," cut in Justin quickly, referring to his imaginary, unsanitary flat-mate with bi-polar disorder. "I wouldn't risk my worst enemy staying in that flat. Trouble is, he trusts me. Needs me really. Poor sod."

Tracy pulled her bag firmly onto her shoulder as she saw her bus approaching and leaned into him. "You're such a good person. I … do love you, you know," she whispered close up to his ear, a wisp of blonde hair tickling his cheek.

This altruistic touch had always helped him score extra points with Tracy. It was one of the most difficult lies to relinquish. To do that he would need to fabricate an elaborate set of further untruths to negate the initial one whilst not thereby making his living space suddenly acceptable for Tracy to share.

He planted a firm kiss on her soft welcoming lips as she slipped from his grasp. "I'll call you," he said.

He rushed in to find Mia in the kitchen about to tip his half of an enormous pizza into the pedal-bin labelled 'Food Waste'. He held back by the door a few seconds.

"Hey!" he cried out, successfully failing to grab her arm in time. "That's my pizza! I need that!"

She shrugged.

"Tsk. Such a waste. I'm starving as well," he lied, feeling full to the gills. Had his mother or sister been left with edible food they would have stored it in the fridge or freezer, but the concept of thrift was totally outside Mia's zone. Not that it bothered him in any way; it was simply an observation.

She was not the whiny kind of wife to wail laments, *Where have you been? You could've let me know.* No, after all she was the one who had gone out, and then unexpectedly returned home. What he did when she was out was his own business but sometimes her lack of interest could be hurtful. He rather wished she could show an inkling of jealousy or curiosity, although not enough to extract the truth, of course. That would be a step way too far.

He had the perfect means to distract her tonight. Still feeling horny from being with Tracy, despite her bombshell dampening his ardour, he slipped a hand up Mia's T-shirt.

"Anyway, you *clever* girl, You've booked Sharm el Sheikh," he said, hoping she had not seen his earlier email listing reasons not to go, which he would later delete from her Inbox. "How *fantastic* is that? How cool? We should be celebrating! Yay!" With the flourish of a magician he produced a bottle of champagne.

They settled down cosily together to view their holiday destination on the Internet.

"Just two weeks and we'll be there," said Justin, with genuine enthusiasm.

7

The weekend was now behind them. As Steph dipped a teaspoon into a jar of runny honey, waves of nausea ran through her. She pushed away her bowl of porridge, feeling sick at the prospect of what she had promised to do today. It went against everything she was working towards.

There were a few other tasks she must work through first. Barnaby was off school with a sudden cold, an expensive inconvenience. It cost her the services of a childminder for part of the day, since fieldwork required her to be an absentee mother, once she had cleared the admin that she could do from home.

She must check with Nick that everything was organised for Friday next week.

Barnaby was curled up on the sofa looking pale with a radish-red-raw nose, sniffing loudly as he checked his mobile. Steph threw him a box of tissues.

"Little bear, could you please use those and try and stop making those horrendous sounds?"

"I'm ill."

"It's a cold." A bit harsh, she knew, but she could not afford to molly-coddle or encourage the notion that being away from school was an easy ride.

An email from Nick pinged onto the screen confirming arrangements and technical provision for the training session in the village hall: *We have 4 trainers coming so some 'one-to-one' is possible. We usually find that soon the students will be able to help each other so this should be enough. 6 used computers available to be re-homed; just let me know how many additional set-ups you need on the evening. Always keen to please our customers. With best regards Nick Sharmack, Technical Marketing Executive, Simulac*

Excellent. Not state-of-the art equipment, in fact probably obsolete, but beggars could not be choosers. Arrangements coming together lifted her spirits a little. She had some definite takers and felt hopeful. In reality of course it was Jackson she was most concerned about and it would be a challenge to get him there. Closing down her laptop and sorting out her briefcase ready to leave the house, she still felt queasy at what was to come.

The doorbell rang, signalling the arrival of Sheena, a tall, elegant woman with the most beautiful facial bone structure, who literally lived down the lane but was originally from Kenya. She looked absurdly young considering her own four children had flown the nest. Sheena had been helping Steph out since Barnaby was a baby, but he now regarded the term 'childminder' as barely a step up from 'babysitter' and withdrew into a shell of resentment whenever she was mentioned or appeared. Steph let her in.

"Hi Sheena! Thanks for coming at such short notice. How's you?"

"I'm really good thank you, Steph. Still missing my last 'baby' though – she's settled in at Oxford now."

"You and Tod must be so proud of your brood. Now you can do something for yourself, though, eh?"

Sheena gave a weak nod. "S'pose. Not sure what I am if I'm not a Mum, though." She laughed.

Steph gave a little frown. As ever, there was no time to chat to Sheena about her purpose in life, much as she would love to … They had been through so much together and there were times when Steph and her two children would have been sunk without her true friendship.

"Oh, I know you'll think of something," she said, squeezing her arm.

She reached out to ruffle her son's hair as she passed by the sofa and he tried to grab her hand. "I'll text you when I know what time I'll be home, Barney bear. OK?" He was now plugged in to some music and suddenly deaf. She waved at him. "Do you have some schoolwork to do? Don't just waste the day, now will you?"

"But I'm ill," he protested, his hearing miraculously restored.

"Not *that* ill."

"What's to eat, Mum?" he called out as she opened the door to leave.

If he was curious about food, he was clearly well enough for school tomorrow. Steph closed the door. Sheena would sort him out.

She often wished she had parents to help. Many of her friends, also mothers, had the benefit of a husband or partner, *plus* the support of two sets of grandparents. Admittedly, not all were round the corner, but most had family backup who would lend a helping hand now and then.

It was sad to think how much they would have loved to see Faith and Barnaby grow up. And as for Lucas … Well, it was no good bleating on, she knew that.

She knew Jackson would be sitting waiting for her, ready for collection, clean-shaven and dapper, his silver hair neatly combed, an old but bespoke suit brushed speckless. This was such an important step for him.

A social worker had provided convincing reasons, on medical, nursing and financial grounds, that a privately run residential home would be the sensible, and indeed safe, option. He would receive the care he needed, have company and regular meals. He could bring some personal possessions to put in his own room – to make it 'just like home'. Better now, to get settled in, than wait for an emergency later and then end up being rushed to some other nursing home not of his choosing, or even hospital, without any say in the matter.

She imagined the persuasive arguments that may have been presented. Of course, it all made extremely good practical sense and he had graciously agreed to take a look and get a place on the waiting list. He would be horrified at causing the overstretched health system any bother. His selfless attitude was always touching.

She approached this building, bordered by muted clumps of lily of the valley in the shadows of overgrown rhododendron and azalea bushes with their shocking-pink short-lived floral clusters. It seemed like a wicked betrayal to even be taking him there.

It took a full five minutes to get Jackson from her car to the entrance of Owlsbarn Care Home, parked as she was in a Visitor space a mere ten metres from the door. Two metres per minute, she thought wryly, as his brogue shoes steadily crunched the gravel.

Steph knew better than to offer to fetch him one of the somewhat archaic wheelchairs nestling in the ivy-covered outer porch. Though he would have disputed the cause, she could tell it was stress making him freeze after five short shuffling paces.

"Relax," she whispered, patting his shoulder reassuringly, then offering him an arm to lean on should he need it.

He was counting in a whisper, trying to get a mental rhythm going to trigger a step forward. He laughed. Oh bless you, dear man, thought Steph! Most would be frustrated, angry and bitter. "I-i-idiot legs!" he stuttered, swiping a leg gustily with the long stick he used to help propel himself along. It was neither a conventional nor an orthopaedic walking stick, but similar to a shepherd's crook without the hook. "More stylish," he had once softly pointed out to Steph, eyes twinkling. It was certainly different.

Finally they arrived at the heavy oak door of the old wing of the Home and Steph announced their arrival into the security system on the wall. Once the door clicked opened for them, Jackson stepped in as nimble as you like across the threshold, its line giving him the point of reference he needed and enabling him to move forward. Having been greeted by a nursing assistant, they were ushered through to a woman whose badge claimed her identity as Deputy Care Manager, Lilian Frobisher, FRSN. Showing round prospective new residents was apparently worthy of senior staff time.

Now they were going to the main sitting-room, explained Lilian, as they passed along a hallway decorated with floral arrangements and landscapes worthy of a stately home. With Jackson shuffling along bravely, they went through a security door into a spacious lounge area, light and airy, various short warren-like corridors leading in and out and off from each corner to further locked, barred and bolted doors. Designed, it seemed to Steph, to both bewilder and block. Soft furnishings were a mix of greens and autumnal shades, with carpeting that could hide a kilo of Liquorice Allsorts. Armchairs lining the fresh buttermilk walls were by and large winged and upright, all made to support backs and necks. Some had waterproof-looking covers and an odour hung in the air that left no doubt as to their function, all masked by a heady mix of tea-rose perfume, pine disinfectant, mingled with cooking smells, coffee and lavender furniture polish. This assault on the nose probably went unnoticed by those accustomed to it. Huge plasma screens were on in two corners, loud day-time TV pouring out to dim eyes and poor ears connected to unreceptive brains housed by unconcerned people. The fact is, were it not for the TV, the silence would have been unbearably oppressive, broken occasionally by a solitary wail or some incomprehensible string of expletives. Steph knew that this was a Home registered to take dementia patients and was deemed suitable for those with advanced Parkinson's.

"We have many day-time activities," said Lilian, voice cheerful, expression bright, as she naturally and caringly guided a lost-looking frail woman wearing one slipper and no teeth, to a vacant seat, simultaneously hailing a care assistant from across the room. Steph wholeheartedly admired the people who worked in such institutions – despite bad stories in the media from time to time. It was something that required a depth of patience and dedication she knew she could never find in herself; she remembered feeling this enormous debt of gratitude when visiting her own mother in similar surroundings a few years back …

"… dominoes, board games and playing cards according to ability. Trivial Pursuit! We even have ball games!" Lilian went on, with a short laugh, inviting some response of incredulity. "I know. You may be surprised, but yes we do. Dancing. Oh yes. And singing. Music is a great joy and comfort. You like music Mr Jackson? Yes? Listening to music? Yes?" She nodded on his behalf and seemed encouraged by his meltingly sweet smile.

"Residents always do. And people come in to perform and entertain, as well as regular visits from the hairdresser, physiotherapist and chiropodist. There's even a lady who brings in her dog for those who like to stroke him – he's called Dave. A Labrador. Very reliable."

Lilian excused herself for a moment as she stepped aside to speak to a staff member in hushed tones.

But on the whole, thought Steph, looking around, the residents sit still, caged and acquiescent, serviced in some way from time to time. They sit quietly, most of them, and look around vacantly now and then. It was a state of affairs to which blame was not attached; just a fact of life.

With a tea-trolley heading towards them, Jackson was suddenly asked to step back. It was an abrupt interruption and she saw how fast anxiety flooded his face, sweeping away the smile he tried so hard to keep pinned-on from within the static Parkinson's face. He had been politely listening to Lilian, with immense concentration, hearing-aid probably full-on, thinking heaven knows what, then out of the blue he was asked to "please move".

"Come along now," said the lady in charge of the trolley, cheerfully, seeing no sign of any attempt to get out of her way. "There's a love. Just a wee bit more room …"

Steph put up her hand, as if controlling traffic. "Sorry! Just give us a minute, if you would, please," she said. "People with Parkinson's need time. OK?" Turning to Jackson, she whispered in his ear, "One, two, left, right, go!" and he neatly stepped back two short paces. Any onlooker might reasonably question why he had been so deliberately stubborn and slow to shift himself.

Lilian returned to them, by which time the trolley had moved on and Jackson appeared to be calmly awaiting the next leg of the tour. They were taken on to see a few

44

bedrooms, the dining hall and then outside to the grounds, pretty much deserted apart from a young man tending the lawns. Steph heard some shouts coming from inside an open window and then a cry of what sounded like distress, a little like something out of a gothic novel, thought Steph, fleetingly. There was distinct anger in the other, louder voice. There was no knowing what it was all about and Lilian steered them away round the corner to admire the rather questionable view across a wood reminiscent of a barrier of thorns surrounding the fairytale castle where lay Sleeping Beauty. She could see from the way Jackson had turned his head towards the sounds that even he had heard it too.

She drove Jackson back home, unable to speak, unable to ask the simple questions. *What did you think? Would you be happy there?* And he sat silently with eyes closed as if taking a welcome snooze, showing no sign of complaint or horror or fear of what they had seen. Words were unnecessary.

8

Reluctantly, Steph forced herself to leave Jackson alone for a day or so. She had other people to visit, new clients to see for their initial assessment, and such first visits always took even longer than subsequent calls. It was partly the record keeping or what Greg would call 'damned paperwork'. Keeping a paper trail was necessary, however, even though it gobbled up that all-important, precious time. At least they both agreed on that. Moreover, she needed evidence of her determined efforts to realise Ted Devonish's dream that no elderly person should be forgotten.

"Staff appraisal due next month. Did I say?" Greg asked her recently on the phone. She wondered what expression he had on his face when he said this. Was it dead straight or were there twitches of humour playing around his features? She had seen him once or twice before in a relaxed, mellow mood, when his whole demeanour changed. He was capable of smiling. His brown eyes, so dark they were almost black, would somehow spring to life; it was like sunlight peering round the side of a dark cloud, bathing the world at its feet with unexpected life-giving warmth.

She remembered once they had lunch in a pub somewhere; he drove her there, a few miles away near his house, somewhere beyond Farnham. It was a while ago, just when they had both taken on their brand new roles.

She had felt that her commitment to the SSS mission was stronger, more personal, than his. With Greg there was always the businesslike caution, the sober weighing up, with due consideration given to all possible hazards and pitfalls. She sighed, just thinking about it. Maybe it was the age difference; he was retired, he must be quite old, although she had to admit his tall, upright stance and broad shoulders seemed far removed from that age bracket. He still had his teeth and a good head of hair!

She had closed her eyes, counting to ten. There were only the two of them. An appraisal? Surely this was unnecessary.

"No Greg. I don't recall you mentioning," she replied politely, feeling now white-hot with resentment at the way he treated her as a subordinate. Then she thought of something that might just surprise him. "Would that be the 360° type of appraisal?"

"Hmm … what's that then?"

"Where all employees appraise each other. It was used where I last worked, to great effect. It prevents one person's opinion being too dominant. Much fairer."

"But there's just the two us, so …"

"Exactly."

"Doesn't make much sense, does it really?"

"We can appraise each other," she responded eagerly.

"Well, I'll look into it …" His voice faded, clearly hiding his ignorance about something he had never heard of.

Their little chat was a reminder that she was being judged by measurable results and must deliver good ones for the SSS pilot to work. Statistics would include the number of new clients and referrals to specialist agencies; length of time spent with each client and then more qualitative records of how the time was spent. This less tangible aspect was what the late Ted Devonish who truly 'owned' the project, had been really concerned about, but was the most difficult to 'prove'.

Nobody in the world could want her to achieve, and the venture to have successful outcomes, more than she did herself. She believed in it with every fibre of her being and could not afford to screw up in any way; she must keep Greg sweet because – well, he actually had the authority to sack her, she cautioned herself. That this would be a disastrous and ignominious end to her world, was an understatement. Ted Devonish's solicitor and executor were the Trustees and, as such, not only held the actual purse strings at this stage but would accept Greg's recommendations. They respected his judgement.

She could not deny her headstrong nature but she was determined not to abandon her computer project. In the bigger picture this was equally, if not more, important. Already she could imagine people latching onto it, starting to have fun. She knew Jackson would be so much happier at home, in touch with old friends and, more importantly, in daily contact with his family overseas. His life would be enriched. Transformed.

It was a last resort, after trying so many other ideas to cast some vivid and vibrant colour into his monochrome life.

Following a hectic day of visits and meetings, she logged on to Twitter and, after browsing an article on how too much online activity may affect the brain, imagined she was Jackson. Right: Describe myself. What would he say? *Retired architect, once famous! Loves good conversation and photography. Cannot cook but loves to eat.* Or, perhaps *Stuck at home with stubborn legs. Make me laugh and I'll follow you.*

It would be interesting to see what thumbnail biography he would come up with; for sure, something infinitely more curious and clever than she could create. She could take a digital photograph of him, or perhaps some icon that would conceal his years and decrepitude. He could avoid advertising the age and disability thing entirely and just be a normal lively person online. But would he want to do that? It will be fascinating, she thought, to see how open and honest he chooses to be.

She did a search on 'architecture' to see if anyone came up – people with a passion for architecture, perhaps. A page flashed up full of exciting mentions – a beautiful stadium in Capetown, something else in French – *Ah! belle architecture*, with a link to a stunning photograph of an ancient juxtaposed with a modern building. Her gaze travelled down the screen, opening up more links. There was so much here she wanted to grab her laptop and rush round to Jackson to show him right now, to push it under his nose and say, "Hey, look at this, Jackson! See! It's so easy – you can do this. And look here's other ways, other things. You can join this, talk to these, find out about …" He would love it. *Love* it. She just knew he would. Her heart was racing.

There were so many easy-to-use devices on the market now. But he had never seen a computer of any kind, let alone switched one on. He was not of the computer aided design system generation, may never have even heard of CAD, for he retired young – when he was around fifty, nearly forty years ago! Never even used a typewriter; his secretary had typed letters for him on an Olivetti, using carbon papers and Tippex. Very proficient she was too, according to Jackson's misty-eyed recollections, with her 80 words per minute certificate.

So engrossed was she in thinking about Jackson's past and reinvented future life, that she jumped when Faith's voice broke in on her thoughts like someone shaking her out of a dream.

"Dinner? Mum – are we eating this evening or doing some kind of sponsored Starvathon?" Her daughter was peering over her shoulder. "Hey! Who've you found on Twitter? You better not say anything about me. I'll kill you."

Steph chuckled. "Don't worry. I'm just imagining what my dear old Jackson would do if he were ..."

"Excuse me! 'Your dear old Jackson'? He's yours? Dear? Yet 'old'? What is going on?"

Faith knew little about her clients. Steph respected the need for confidentiality and rarely said anything about them to anyone. But somehow the opportunity to speak about Jackson was too hard to resist.

"He is a dear old man – one of the clients I visit."

"Oh yeah? And does he have 'special needs'?" teased Faith.

Now Steph felt anger rise up; cross with her daughter, protective of Jackson. "Faith. Stop that right now. Not funny."

"Oh come on. Only joking. By the way thanks again for the iPhone, Mum."

"Sometimes ... your humour is in bad taste. Just think of others now and then, instead of trivialising everything."

A brief but drawn-out silence hung in the air. Steph did not often get riled with Faith; she was probably far too easy-going as mothers go, loving her children so much she could not be cross with them often or for very long. Also she felt an unspoken need to compensate for them having no father to love or correct them.

"Sorr-eee," said Faith, in a little girl voice. "What's he like, then?"

"Well, he lives alone. I think his wife died a long time ago, not sure how many years. His three adult children, several grandchildren and great grandchildren – some of those are nearly teenagers by now I think, Barnaby's sort of age – live abroad."

"You mean he hasn't seen them grow up?"

"No. That's right."

"That's sad. I mean really – not 'sad' – you know …" Faith stuttered. Steph could not help but smile at her daughter's new wariness of being facetious. Then just as suddenly, her eyes filled with tears. Turning in her seat a little to put her arm round Faith, she nodded, but was, ridiculously, unable to speak. Why did Jackson affect her like this? "So where are they? His family?"

After a pause, she replied, casually, "Oh … er… really spread about. Aberdeen, Melbourne, Capetown."

"Wow! And he never sees them?"

"Not often – maybe once a year. Not quite so far away for his daughter in the far-beyonds of Scotland."

"Can't he go visit them, somehow? Or, is he just past it? I … I mean, you know, not up to the travelling, long flights and stuff?"

"He could never do it. I think he did a couple of times a few years back, but he can barely walk and needs a lot of rest. He has Parkinson's and bad arthritis." His complex bundle of medical and family issues was an extreme combination; no wonder it upset her …

"Doddery then. Is he, you know, ga-ga, or …?"

"Faith! Remind me to let you have a list of correct terms – no, he does not have senile dementia. And his mind is alive and well."

"What did he do?"

51

"Architect. He designed those red-brick civic buildings in Bloomstock, some Bank skyscrapers in Hong Kong, offices in London, Singapore – very *avant-garde* in their day – and loads of housing projects, not just upmarket but social housing too. He was – still is in his heart – a great philanthropist. A good person."

"Wow! What does he do now? Is he *very* old?"

"He's coming up to ninety. He gets through the day."

"What does that mean?"

"First thing in the morning, he takes his medication. A carer comes round to help get him out of bed, washed, dressed and so on, then breakfast. He tries to make telephone calls, read a little or watch TV, listen to the radio, but everything is an effort. His hearing is not that good either. Lunch arrives and then he usually has a rest. His voice is very weak too."

"And you are his 'friend'?"

"I hope so. But … I want to get him using the computer."

"Oh, yeah! You mean, he doesn't use a computer? He could afford some serious gear!"

"Faith, he's never even seen a computer. He wouldn't know that the screen linked to the keyboard, or what a mouse or cursor was."

"You're kidding me! Wow! I'd like to meet this Jackson. To find out about architecture. You know I want a career in design, but it needs to be something useful. I want to design things people can use."

"Well, architecture would fit the bill."

"Exactly. That's what I've been thinking. Guess it must've all changed since he was one though. But I'd like to ask him about it."

Steph turned to face Faith. "Would you? Really?" She would derive such pleasure from bringing together these separate elements, currently two of the most important people in her life. But she suspected that marrying personal and work life would be a breach of the rules. She would have to check.

"Maybe. I'll look into it." She sighed as she could hear herself sounding like cautious Greg; an uncomfortable moment, to say the least. "I didn't know you'd considered architecture as a career …"

Reflecting on this conversation, she opened the freezer to find some pasties or a savoury flan she could quickly heat, and asked Faith to fetch Barnaby from upstairs so they could both help prepare a basic salad. It was oddly disturbing. Maybe it would not be fair to take her daughter along to meet Jackson. Faith might be a painful reminder of his own grandchildren, or even great grandchildren, he scarcely knew. Supposing Jackson really took to her and then she became bored? And what if she became attached to him – as a surrogate grandfather? He was after all, a delightful and charismatic person, despite all his problems. Faith and Barnaby had no grandparents. No father, no grandparents – though Faith could remember her maternal grandfather, from fleeting visits … They would both be only too ready to latch onto the idea of adopting Jackson. She could see now that if Faith began talking about Jackson, Barnaby would want to get in on the act. It could get somewhat out of control. She must give this proper consideration, recognising that at times, some caution was necessary. Greg would be proud of her.

9

There are two village halls in Appley Green. One is a purpose-built block that Jackson would doubtless have dubbed as an architectural tragedy. Known more widely as the 'Community Hall', it was built in the 1960s, set in a sea of gravel, with a small car park at the rear and, despite its soul-less appearance, was booked up back-to-back with all manner of meetings, classes and workshops. The other, close by, is centuries old, stone-built, in fact once a small church that closed due to lack of use, and surrounded by gravestones. Called Saviour's Hall it was, this evening, anachronistically, transformed into a computer classroom. At one end, looked over by an arched stained glass window depicting a richly coloured *mélange* of shepherds and angels, there was a trestle table, covered in a red gingham tablecloth, and bearing a liberal buffet of home-made cakes and pastries. Some of the villagers – mostly middle-aged and female, Steph observed – would make a social occasion out of anything and could not bear to be totally excluded. This cheerful catering squad, backbone of the village, had made it clear they would willingly serve teas and coffees during a break, but had absolutely no wish to otherwise take part.

She looked down the list of people who had dropped in beforehand to sign up, biting her lip. She did not recognise many names as SSS clients, which was a little worrying. Although the brunt of the expense was covered by Simulac goodwill and marketing budget, SSS was, after all, paying for her time to organise this.

If Greg could see the way things were going so far, he would throw a blue fit, but Steph suppressed this image.

First to arrive were Babs and Tony, a couple she knew with a gemstone shop in the village. She did not regard them as close friends, more well loved local characters she would bump into in the bakers or the Post Office. He, with his grey beard, shoulder-length hair and John Lennon-style round glasses, and she, with her sharp Mary Quant hairstyle and op-art dresses, were a time-warp partnership of the sixties or seventies. Maybe fashion had come full circle; they seemed to pass in the village arty set as retro trendsetters.

"Good evening," said Steph, handing them a name card and plastic badge-holder and showing them where to register their presence. "As you see, you're the first. Well done for that. The young man over there in the black T-shirt, will show you where to sit and so forth. What's your interest in this then?"

They looked at each other sheepishly. Steph suppressed a smile, thinking how sweet and quirky it is when a married couple have been together so long they mirror each other's mannerisms. Would she and Lucas have grown to be like that, she wondered?

"Well, we never got round to using computers, really," confessed Babs, "and most of our friends do, so we feel a bit left out, to be honest."

"Quite a bit of catching up to do," added Tony, stroking his beard, raising his eyebrows, nodding and frowning simultaneously. Fascinated, Steph stopped herself from commenting that he must be good at multi-tasking and would probably take to social networking like a fish to a pond.

"I'm sure you'll catch on and catch up very quickly," Steph assured them. "It's going to be fun."

"We also have family who keep telling us our shop would benefit from having a website and that those laggards who are resistant to the Internet are left out."

"Well, I am afraid your family are right!" laughed Steph.

Their smiles faded, fear clouding their eyes and she silently cautioned herself to be more sensitive, less bullish. "Don't worry. We'll soon sort you out. Really glad to see you here."

Babs and Tony moved on to be greeted by Nick from Simulac and seated at two of the best flat-screen 'workstations', but Steph could see they insisted on sharing the same one.

She had arranged for one of her friends to pick up Jackson and was looking forward to him being there more than anything. She felt optimistic that Babs' and Tony's business motives could inspire others.

Then a lady dressed in tweed, cashmere and pearls, who Steph guessed was in her late sixties, marched in and made a beeline for Steph. "Good evening, I'm Gloria Whittaker. Are you the organiser?" She gave a firm, brisk handshake as she read Steph's name-badge.

"Yes. I'm Steph. I work for Special Support for Seniors and hope to get a few people along, such as yourself, to learn about computers, so they ..."

"Ha! Yes, indeed. I'm a bit of an old hand though," replied Gloria, quickly. "Been using computers for years, my dear. One of the original programmers, I was. Fortran, Cobol, Lisp, Algol, all the well known ones. Mainframes then, though, mostly. Computers as big as a house! No, wondered if I could be of help at all. Very happy to be of service. Used to do a spot of training too, in my day."

"Fantastic! How lovely of you …"

"Right! I'll just mingle and see what people are up to then, shall I? Help out where I can." She was gone, without a name badge or having signed up. Oh-oh, fire regulations. What would Greg say? Well, what indeed would he do if he stepped in to see what was going on here anyway?

Next arrived Joshua and his friend Sam, whom Steph had conscripted as they watched her put up the notice two weeks ago. She was amazed they had remembered.

"Hiya! You're here. How fantastic!" Soon there were eleven people seated at desks, with Nick and colleagues rotating between them. The various expressions of concentration were classic. Steph wanted to chuckle at the frowns; teeth biting lower lips, tongue protruding from an O-shaped mouth; a crooked, fixed smile that wasn't actually a smile at all, and eyes squinting as if this somehow helped their owner to see … Reading glasses were put on, taken off, put on again …

A recently widowed lady in her eighties with whom she had spent a couple of hours last week, coaxing her to attend, arrived complete with her walking aid. This is what makes this project special, Steph told herself, as she welcomed her. No way would this elderly villager have ever got to a class at the Technical College in Bloomstock. So often with Appley Green being split between different councils, one would provide the venue and the other a special bus service but the two things often did not work as a seamless operation. Moreover, she would need the encouragement in the first place, the moral support.

Some mates of Joshua and Sam, as they claimed to be, sloped in looking rather suspicious. Steph guessed they were older than Joshua. Both clearly curious to know what was going on, they were quick to pick up the Simulac leaflets from the table by the door. Steph got them to sign in and suggested they may be able to help, indicating that they should see Nick. More people arrived of all ages, sizes and complexions, and Steph counted up that just four of them were SSS clients. This represented about twenty per cent of the registered total and she was extremely pleased. She must make sure she saw all of them to see what progress they were making …

But, where was Jackson? Her friend from yoga classes she used to go to, flighty Tricia, who was giving him a lift, had not turned up yet. Steph checked her mobile. Yes, there was a text message – she had not heard it arrive through the buzz and hubbub. *J sprained ankle needs to rest up no good this time says next 1 will be there he keeps saying sorry bless tricia xx*

As her heart plummeted into her shoes, Steph vaguely thought she must show Tricia how to punctuate. This was a blow. A real, big, bitter disappointment that made tears rush to her eyes. She had to slip outside for a moment to pull herself together, which had the opposite effect of relaxing the tension she felt into hot tears that rolled down her cheeks.

'This was all for you, Jackson, and you're not bloody well here!" she whispered, crossly, to a rather startled tabby that happened to be passing by.

10

Faith kept asking, "Where's the Diary?" "Can I read it today?" "Why *not?*" becoming more and more resentful and inquisitive as time passed. Steph took to shifting it around to various hidey-holes, distracting her daughter, postponing the big unveiling.

Steph woke early on Saturday morning. All was quiet and she reached for the Diary hidden under a pile of stuff in her bedside drawer.

'Mum has gone home now. Faith is 1 week old and it was time to be just the three of us. Faith is asleep in the crib next to my side of the bed, just making small snuffling noises after her last feed of the day.

Lucas has cancelled some of his private lessons at home, just for a couple of weeks, thinking it might disturb the baby. He is so thoughtful. New term starts soon and he'll be back with classes at school. I said to him that Faith will just have to acquire a musical ear from an early age   Tomorrow will write about when Lucas and I first met, as didn't keep a diary then. Too tired now. Expect to be awake in about four hours!'

'Lucas has taken her out in the buggy for the first time on his own – to give me some me-time.

He was different from the other fitness fanatics who regularly came into the gym (House of Fitness, where I was general manager). He wasn't obsessed or competitive, which somehow blokes could be, even on fitness machines. Neither was he vain like some idiots who check their own body mass index on a daily basis. Some of the men were into waxing and fake tan, treatments they think make them attractive to girls. Huh! No, he was far away from that kind of narcissistic rubbish.

I'll never forget the first time he came in. He had with him four lads, in their early teens I'd say. He said he was a music teacher, (he explained later that he is what is called a peripatetic, moving around various schools and with students coming to his flat for lessons). Piano, keyboard, guitar – wow! I just gazed in awe at his amazingly unruly head of black curls. When our eyes met, I had that strange feeling as if my insides were melting, even though we had barely exchanged a few words. I remember wondering fleetingly if he was of Italian blood, though he was much taller than the average Latin.

"These young men have won a prize in a music competition," he explained. I noticed how the boys stood tall as he said this. Proud. The prize was to be trial sessions in the gym and he asked how much this would cost.

I had to pull myself together and make sure my business head was firmly screwed on, drawing on stuff my Dad had taught me. Coolly, I asked him if they were sponsored in any way.

He said not.

"Is it being funded by the school?" I was thinking maybe I could get the local paper in. Photograph, little piece on links in the community, other teachers, parents ...

"Oh no," he said. "This is my treat. These are ... " and he gave her a meaningful look, "... deserving lads. They work hard at their music and I thought it'd be good for them to have a chance to do something ... different."

Wow again! I looked at his honest face, and another mode of thinking slipped into place. "Why don't we let this be our treat ..."

The boys appeared somehow down at heel and not the fittest specimens. Two of them looked pasty and puny, as if not getting enough to eat, while the other two were close to obese.

"Yeah? It's meant to be a special prize – I was happy enough to foot the bill, but …"

"No. I insist," I said, reaching below the desk for some vouchers. "There you go."

He came back a couple of days later, after giving the boys a chance to look at the leaflets and think about what they wanted to do at the gym, to make the most fun out of their vouchers. I watched them dart about from one thing to another like toddlers, the treadmill, the weights, the rowing machine, some with more glee and agility than others, but I found myself observing the young teacher with flashing, intelligent eyes the colour of the sea on a cloudless day. Was he Celtic? He was watchful, encouraging, caring … I felt a warmth deep within that I acknowledged to be a powerful attraction. I did not even know his name.

As they came out of the changing rooms, all of them with wet hair from the shower, I caught him by the elbow.

"Hey! How was it? Did you have a good time?"

The boys' chorus of replies left me in no doubt. Clearly, I thought, my mind racing, they would want to come again!

Then I said, "I was wondering if you could do me a favour … er … sorry, I don't know your name. I'm Steph."

He shook my hand and gave me a smile that had a tingling effect on me! "Hi – I'm Lucas. I'm in your debt, so … fire away! What can I do for you?"

I felt my cheeks burn, even though his question was innocent, I could tell.

"These boys play instruments?"

Lucas nodded. "Guitar. Keyboard. Drums. They do a lot of work together."

An idea clicked into place. "Fantastic!" I said. "I wondered if we could get them along – I mean could they do something? I could get the local newspaper here – a bit of good publicity."

He raised his soot-black eyebrows as if the idea of seeking publicity was a bit alien to him, but his initial surprise mellowed almost at once.

"Be delighted. I'll check it out with the school and their parents and let you know. It would be good for these guys."

I handed him a House of Fitness card, feeling my heartbeat notch up as if I had just done fifteen minutes on the step machine. Thump, thump, thump! I could hear it!

Pretty soon those boys were excluded from some of his visits to the gym. His interest shifted towards me! Soon we were dating, unable to get enough of each other and very much in love. 'A whirlwind romance,' Mum described it to family friends.'

Steph bit her trembling lip, unable to read any further. For sure, Faith would love to read some of the steamy bits that followed, that would probably now make her cry - and blush, which very fact made her realise it would be wrong to share it. It was too personal, and Faith was too young. The Diary went under the mattress and Steph, as if awaking from a pleasant, but disturbing dream, realised she must get up and get on with her day.

Saturday, although crammed full, was usually a day to be relished. She loved cheering and whooping loudly for Barnaby and his team in a home match, football or cricket, come rain or shine, compensating for not having time to support him in away games. She took flasks of soup and packs of pies and rolls; and chatted to other parents. It was also a time, without fail, when she imagined Lucas at her side, their arms linked, or unashamedly wrapped around each other, watching their boy. She always remembered that time she first met him …Why was life so unjust? If anyone should be here, yelling at his son to 'get in there!' it should be him.

She and Faith would go to the local farmers' market or do the supermarket shop together. Once household chores were out of the way, Steph tried to set aside a little me-time for pure relaxation, in short supply during the working week, perhaps a foamy bath, scented candles, some nostalgic Duran Duran or Madonna. One day, she thought, it would be good to call up some friends for a girls' night *out*.

In the six years since her divorce from Richard, she had grown used to fulfilling an abundantly full parental role. On Sundays she made sure the three of them did something together, maybe cook a meal with everyone doing a course, or gardening, despite groans and protests from both of them.

'Some of my friends could *see* me *doing* this. Do you *want* me to be bullied, Mum?' Barnaby would yell and moan, as she persuaded him to weed the borders.

'I do have *homework* to do, you know,' was Faith's oft-used objection.

Steph stayed strong. They might play a board game, or watch a DVD, challenging though it was to choose a film that could possibly satisfy a mother of two who secretly yearned for a bit of romance; a teenage girl who had big plans, no boyfriend as yet and memories of parental disharmony that Steph once feared might leave her scarred for life; and a boy still to reach puberty, without a father, who thought he knew most things he would ever need to know in life.

But this weekend a part of her was frustrated by not being able to visit Jackson to see how he was. She tried to rationalise. He did not actually need her fussing over him; his twice-daily carers would ensure his ankle had medical attention if necessary. It could look strange if she started visiting clients at the weekend, so she must be patient and hold off until Monday. Checking her worksheet for appointments lined up for next week, she could see his next visit was fixed for Thursday. The plan was swift, slotting into place straight away in her head. She must re-arrange. Elsie could swap her Monday visit at 10 am for his. She could at least do this by phone, even if it was a Saturday. Glancing through her week's timetable the word *Appraisal* jumped out. It hit her between the eyes. *Tuesday 11 am*. She must do a little preparation for this on Monday, after she had seen Jackson.

On Sunday evening, they had just cleared up the kitchen.

"I'm going upstairs," said Barnaby. This meant he was going on his Xbox or Playstation.

"Thanks for your help, Barney bear. Bed by nine. Come and say goodnight before you go." He had been a good lad, even mopping the floor, not something many of his friends probably did, and certainly something that would remain their secret. By involving them in such tasks she created and felt a strong bond with her children. The radio would play music, they would chat, joke and tease each other. Steph wanted so much for her family – the three of them – to stay intact, for nothing to spoil what they had. Never again would she lean on a man for support.

"How's coursework going then?" she asked Faith.

Faith shrugged, never very forthcoming on progress and Steph knew better than to push. Her results were consistently good and maybe, at home, she needed a break from studying, not nagging reminders that there was more studying, essays to write, exams to sit, an endless stream of hurdles to be conquered.

"Fine." Then, after a pause, she added, "Can I meet this Jackson then? Did you think some more about that?"

All the doubts and reservations Steph had felt before resurfaced. She pictured Jackson sitting at home alone as she last saw him, reflecting on their *recce* of the nursing home. "I did. Yes I did think about it. I ..." She stalled for a moment. "I'm seeing him tomorrow – he's sprained his ankle apparently, so ..."

"So he'd probably be all the more glad of a friendly visit! It just sucks when you can't walk."

Steph thought back to when Faith had done this very thing on a ski-ing holiday – the only family holiday they had with Richard, when Barnaby was so young he had to spend most of the time in the resort's crèche. Faith had to stay behind with him, icebags strapped to her leg; the kind of tragedy that stays forever in a child's memory.

Her daughter was asking for something that could be life changing. He might inspire her to do something she'd already identified as a possible career. How could she refuse?

"What time are you seeing him?"

"Ten o'clock. A fairly quick visit ..."

"I could come – as part of home-study time – and then skip along to double History afterwards."

"I feel I should warn him."

"I'd be a nice surprise. I'd've *thought*. Huh!"

"Yes, sweet-pea, but sometimes the elderly don't like surprises. And you never know with a Parkinsons' person how they're going to be. The condition is very variable. It wouldn't be fair."

"Well, I could just slip in and say hello and then if he seems out of sorts I'll scoot. How's that?"

Steph was amazed how much energy Faith was putting into her case.

"I really want you to come, but ..." She was beginning to sound pathetic, even to her own ears.

65

"Anyway, you could just phone him and ask. Now, *couldn't* you?" Faith narrowed her eyes, folded her arms, looking unusually hostile, almost menacing, something Steph had not seen in her since she was a toddler.

Steph was quietly weighing it up.

"You don't want me to come. That's the plain truth. Do you? You think I'm just a *child* who'll let you down." Now she was patently playing the 'make Mum feel guilty' card and it was working. She was still holding a grudge about the Diary, thought Steph.

Steph put an arm round her and gave her a squeeze. "Of course I do. OK.'

What harm could it do? Now she was the one being unreasonably cautious.

11

Faith's jaw dropped when she saw *The Hideaway* with its geometry of split-level storeys and enormous windows that overlooked a vast tangle of garden. Her gaze seemed able to cut through the veil of purplish-green vegetation; dense wisteria draping the walls with variegated ivy winding its way searchingly through it, sweet scented lilac bushes and clumps of hazy lavender competing for attention by the front porch. Minimalist it was no longer.

"Wow! It's amazing!" exclaimed Faith, as she stepped out of the car. Then as if speaking to herself, she muttered, "Twentieth century modernist style. Never seen anything like this before – even in pictures."

"Is it? Modernist, whatever? I've seen photos – and I'm sure Jackson will show you if you ask him – of the house as it was newly built. It was brilliant white, quite starkly bare, apart from a few red-brick features. Bearing in mind the location, very daring in its day, apparently."

"Or evidently."

His morning carer responded to the doorbell and ushered them in. The young woman who spoke broken English with an East European accent, said she must go and please could they make sure the door was locked when they leave.

Jackson was sitting in a straight-backed leather armchair in his study with a leg resting up on a footstool. It always touched Steph that he would go to the trouble – or insist that his carer should bother – of dressing as if he were about to go out for a nice lunch somewhere. Not business-like, but smart-country-casual Prince of Wales check, with neat little touches, rather flamboyant, like the corner of a scarlet silk handkerchief peeping from his top pocket, matching his socks.

His grey eyes opened wide when he saw Faith.

"Well, well," he said, his voice a little husky. "This must be your daughter, Stephanie. Or could it be sister?" He winked at Faith, who had already given the room a scan, taking in the rows of books on buildings and photography that lined the walls. "Forgive me for not getting up. Just one more day to keep one foot off the ground, or put my foot up, so I've been instructed."

"That's really good news," responded Steph, cheerfully. "You look very comfortable."

"Hello Mr Jeffrys. How did you know?" said Faith, then turning to Steph. "Did …?"

"No, I didn't say you were coming. I guess there's a likeness," replied Steph.

Faith pulled a face as if she were swallowing a spoonful of vinegar. "Euw! Really?" and Steph scowled at her.

"Others can always see that kind of thing more than you can yourself. Anyway, Jackson, this is Faith. Yes, my daughter, who has decided she may want to be an architect and so …"

"Ah-ha! Wonderful. So it's Faith! Were your sisters not able to come?"

Steph felt the blood drain from her face. Was this dementia? Was this the first sign? Was he getting confused with his great-grandchildren? What …?

Faith grinned. "Nah. They're *hope*less and very un*charitable*." Jackson was returning her daughter's smile.

68

His eyes were twinkling. Steph could almost hear the penny drop inside her head with a clang.

After a merry half an hour that left both Faith and Jackson wanting more, Steph suggested that Faith leave them now to get back to school, as she had to speak to Jackson about an important matter that could not wait.

Faith stood up obligingly. She looked at her watch. "Sure, it's a twenty minute walk so … yep, fine."

"It was a delight to meet you Faith," said Jackson, holding out his trembling hand. "Please avail yourself of my library whenever you wish. It pleases me enormously that someone can use my collection of books – even though they are antiquated, like me."

"Well, it's their oldness that is their … attraction," said Faith, choosing her words with care and sounding suddenly very wise to her mother's ears. "I'd like to come again. If that's OK with you."

Steph saw a look on Jackson's face that she could not remember seeing before. It was as if he had come alive, as if he had just drunk of some magic elixir that replaced pain with unalloyed joy. A single tear crept from the corner of his right eye and he raised a trembling fist to wipe it away.

"OK? OK? More than OK! Please, please. Yes, of course, we can talk some more. Stay longer next time, if you can."

As they waved to each other and Faith left the room, Steph's heart was pounding. She knew he had received a letter from Social Services recommending that he would benefit from the safety and care offered by Owlsbarn. She had been sent a copy. Now she felt like the bad fairy.

"Shall I make us a cup of coffee first?"

"Yes please. That would be nice. Could you pass me my pills too, my dear? I think … er … I don't know her

69

name … the carer this morning, she's new. Not seen her before. She managed to put the pills just out of my reach."

She passed him the small box. "When are you getting the patches? It'll be so much simpler for you."

"Yes, indeed. For one of the drugs at least. Soon, the nurse said very soon. It'll make life a little easier."

"And should control your symptoms better shouldn't it?" she asked, wanting to be optimistic.

He nodded with a shrug.

"I was sorry not to see you at Saviour's Hall."

Jackson looked at her blankly. "The what? What was that then, my dear?"

"Oh, these computer classes I'm trying to get going …"

"Hah! Thought for a minute you were out to have me 'saved'!"

"I was really hoping you could've been there. I think you would've enjoyed it."

"Mm. I'm so sorry. It was the evening of my downfall, was it not?"

"Oh yes. I mean, I quite understand. It was out of the question for you to be there, but a shame you missed it. Next time? Tricia, my friend who was going to give you lift, said you'd try it next time?"

"If you say so. Of course. Fingers crossed and a prevailing wind." He did not look excited or even interested and Steph could not help but recall the very different expression on his face when Faith and he were saying their goodbyes. She felt hollow with disappointment.

"Let me just make that coffee, then."

As she waited in the kitchen the couple of minutes it took for the kettle to boil, she re-read the letter from

Social Services. They meant well, she thought, as she warmed the coffee pot; it was logical, helpful, even sympathetic in tone, but they did not really know Jackson or what a death-knell it would be for him to be removed to Owlsbarn. To be looked after in a well-appointed residential or nursing home might be right for others, but not for him.

She poured the coffee and sat down opposite Jackson. "You've had a chance to read the letter?"

Jackson forced a resigned smile. "I read it." His hand was shaking badly as he reached for his cup and she stood up in case he needed help. Once his fingers had hold of it the tremor was stilled. "What do you think Stephanie?"

He was turning it back on her. She could not be the one to make a decision, or even offer an opinion. If she advised him against the Home, and he subsequently lost his footing on the stairs or scalded himself at home, accusing fingers would be pointed. She would be interfering, contradicting Social Services assessment and she, or SSS, could be sued. All this flashed before her. Such an incident would also cause irrevocable damage to the charity.

"I think ... you should consider the offer very carefully, but also look at other ideas. Perhaps." She sounded tentative but had actually been exploring ideas for weeks. "Other options ... but I'm not trying to sway you one way or the other. You do understand that, don't you Jackson?"

"Whatever happens will be my decision. Mine. Yes. I understand that, absolutely. I am still *compos mentis* – I think! But the decision needs to be an informed one. I can listen to other options, if you could but think of a few. I did wonder about getting someone to live in here full-time."

Steph nodded. "Definitely a possibility, but costly."

"Maybe no more expensive than a Home. I don't know. But it would offer other … other advantages." He paused for a moment to get his breath; speech was such an effort. "Might suit me better, anyway. Don't you think?" It seemed he was a step ahead of her, however, so switched on for his age. "Perhaps you could make a few discreet enquiries for me."

"Of course. I won't mention your name, there's no need for that. Also, I could look at the possibility of you moving, but into a single storey place, well, a bungalow. Upmarket sheltered housing if you like, with a warden always there and alarm systems all over the place."

Jackson shifted in his seat awkwardly and frowned. "No need for all that. You could try and find me a bungalow, nice and airy with clean lines, but not a stuffy complex full of *old* people. No, no. That would be just – too much! No better than the delightful Owlsbarn!" He laughed huskily. "Oh, and … if you see a reputable estate agent, Stephanie my dear, would you be kind enough to arrange a valuation on *The Hideaway*?" He paused with a sigh; Steph wanted to hug him but knew this would be unprofessional, inappropriate. "This place is full of empty rooms now and … and a garden that needs a lot of money spent on it with a regular gardener to maintain it … and I'd have to sell up to pay for Owlsbarn anyway," then adding almost under his breath, "God forbid."

Steph admired his ability to speak so calmly about leaving his home, designed by himself, to which he must have a powerful, emotional attachment. Selling it did not seem the issue, but using the money to pour into a Home clearly was. She did not want to argue with him, but felt

72

she could see better than him that one day, or one night, when he falls, unable to raise the alarm he may regret not having warden-style accommodation. Parkinson's was a progressive condition; it would get worse. There again, he had thought it through because his idea was to have a carer living-in. But would they, could they possibly, be there at all times?

"I think a small place, eh? Still be mine then. Something to leave to my grandchildren. With a rota of two or more live-in nurses? Cost a fortune, true enough, but should make a pretty penny from this old ruin, I should reckon. Often have letters from agents." His voice was growing weaker from all the talking, so soft she could only just hear him. "Bit of a museum piece – like me. Hah!"

"You seem to have it all worked out anyway, Jackson."

He closed his eyes briefly and smiled one of his soft endearing smiles. "My dear, I've had a lot of thinking time and years to prepare myself. But you know, it's so good to have someone I can confide in. How would I manage without you to listen and understand?"

Steph was not sure if she felt reassured or humoured.

12

By the time Steph made her way back home, children were turning out of school. The village was alive with people: youngsters chatting in groups; mothers with pushchairs, their toddlers on the swings in the play area; cyclists weaving where they could; and a few cars parked, whose drivers had dared to venture forth. It was a fair day and one or two loiterers had randomly strewn themselves on the Green, sucking ice lollies. Some older folk sat on the traditional hardwood seats, contentedly watching the world go by.

There had been no time to discuss the computer classes further with Jackson and she felt frustrated and dissatisfied. Playing in the back of her mind was the insistent idea of Jackson, excited as a child, dipping into websites, setting up his own blog, visiting art exhibitions online, downloading digital photographs, ordering new books, perhaps even selling some of his valuable, specialist tomes that he would never use again. Then came the ecstatic expression flooding his features, smoothing away frowns and wrinkles as if my magic, as the image of his grandchildren appeared on the screen and their voices spoke to him. *Hey Grandad, Good-day. What's the weather like where you are? We've just been having a barbie on the beach …* Next, his daughter in Aberdeen: *How are you today Dad? Isn't this just fabulous? Sorry to hear you're not able to get about too well just now – I'll be coming to London in a couple of weeks for a wee conference and plan to drop in on you.*

Long overdue, eh? Maybe I could stay for a week or two? Jackson would be replying and wondering how he ever managed to get by without this wonderful technology. A mobile phone would be no good for this; the tiny screen would be useless for Jackson's poor eyesight, she reasoned. Feeling contented but tired, he would email a few old chums he could reach now. Speaking on the phone for long was too much effort; as he said himself, 'it's perfect apart from the speaking and the listening …' But the idea of him being able to *see* his family, in real-time, in colour, on a wide screen, this was what really motivated her.

As she was about to turn right at a junction, the driver ahead of her halted, moved, hesitated and then decided not to move forward. Assuming the car would carry on, she almost drove into his backside.

"Right! Too much day-dreaming. Appraisal. Focus!" Her spirits fell into a deeply depressing place but she reasoned it was a necessary evil. A good appraisal would mean more 'empowerment' – the sort of word that Greg might use, but she might be then 'enabled'.

Greg worked from home on the outskirts of Farnham and this was where they decided to meet. Steph had not been there before but found it easily, following a map and his simple directions. The pretty route was familiar, through heath broken up with the blue pools of Frensham Ponds fed by streams coming from Churt. Man had created what some might call a bit of a wasteland. Acid sandy soil proved to be infertile and unproductive for pioneering Neolithic farmers who, after stripping the land of its native woodland, moved to richer pastures. Spindly silver birches triumphed as survivors where sturdier trees like oak, beech and hornbeam failed with their need to sink deep roots. Rush-grass and bog-cotton could look bleak on a rainy day though, she knew that; but Steph loved the wilderness she was used to; the golden gorse and purple heather of summer, the all-pervasive bracken that would change its hue from springtime acid green to the copper tones of autumn.

She remembered days gone by, walking in this spot. She and Lucas used to borrow a neighbour's dog, a lovely Gordon Setter with a dark shiny coat and feathers the colour of a horse chestnut ... this mental image then connected with the next 'episode' in her Diary. How would she bear to read it? Even after so many years, she still longed for Lucas. Her mother would have said, 'Better to have loved and lost, than never to have loved at all.' True perhaps, but then the sweeter the love, the more painful the loss - and the memory of it.

Her journey ended in an unmarked road and finally a rutted track where she had to crawl along at under five miles an hour. Greg's front garden was a stunning shock of colour, with its cottage borders: tall, swaying hollyhocks, clumps of flame-orange montbretia, a lichen-encrusted trough overflowing with violet-blue Canterbury bells. Buddleia bushes were alive with tortoiseshell butterflies fluttering over their pink and white blooms. There was a bed laid out with cultivated heathers, rich mauves, maroon and pink, with a holly bush in the centre. She never had Greg down as a gardener, but clearly he was a supremo! As she walked under a wooden arch on her approach to the front door, the air was filled with the warm scent of honeysuckle climbing thickly over it. It was a riot of colour and profusion that would make anyone feel good to be alive; it swept Steph back to her childhood.

The house was a solid, traditional, country property full of character, with many rooms. She could imagine it would be an estate agent's delight to even describe it, let alone have the privilege of selling it. Greg ushered her through a large lounge with dark beams and an inglenook. She imagined it with a log fire crackling away, lighting up the cosy space at one end, and her mind's eye fleetingly introduced some warmer colours, cushions, light curtains and a few glowing side-lamps. The interior could be so much better. She reproached herself instantly for the sexist observation that it 'lacked a woman's touch'.

They walked through, with Greg leading the way. "You found it easily then?" he asked.

"No problem at all. Thank you."

"Good, good."

"What a charming house!"

"I'm glad you like it."

There was a welcoming aroma of coffee, a pot of which was already set out with plain, but stylish, white mugs, biscuits, a bottle of mineral water and two glasses on a large oak table in the dining room. A neat pile of documents was placed on the far side. It was organised just as if it were a business meeting room in a conference hotel, thought Steph. They sat down either side of the table, facing each other.

Once settled, Greg began without further preamble, "I looked into this 360° appraisal and understand in principle," said Greg. "The reality is, however, that for the two of us it makes no sense. How can you appraise me?" He gave a short laugh. "It would just be from your point of view."

Steph tried not to scowl. "Well, only from my perspective of course, but that's what it's all about."

"I could see it working maybe if we were a team of several, which we may be in good time," he said, dismissively, opening a notebook, with ballpoint poised. "You'll have the chance to give your input, anyway, Steph."

Steph wanted to point out that his appraisal of her would also be just from *his* point of view, but she decided to keep quiet. She must keep him sweet, not rock the boat in any way. She had a feeling of some disquiet in the pit of her stomach that he would somehow catch her out. Maybe it was guilt making her nervous. She had not, after all, been entirely honest with him, pursuing a project she knew would not win his approval.

"Right," he went on, while pouring coffee. "I've already noted down the Main Purpose of the Job. I'm just basing this appraisal system on a form I've used before, but I'll get it typed up," he explained.

Typed up? Who in this day and age, gets things 'typed up'? thought Steph, exasperated by the idea, but she made no comment, just looking at Greg over the rim of her coffee cup.

"I'll read that out: 'To support isolated elderly people by giving them regular time and special attention tailored to each individual. The hallmarks of this support must be friendship and respect, over and above the practical and medical care they might otherwise receive. To refer to other agencies where necessary for this specialised help.'"

"That's taken verbatim from Ted Devonish's plan. So I can hardly disagree," said Steph. "Nor do I, nor should I have any reason to contest it!"

Greg gave her a quizzical, rather bemused, look over the top of his glasses and Steph took some steadying deep breaths. A handsome black cat wandered in and sat next to Steph's feet, imploring her for attention with its faint mewing

"The next thing is 'Overall Performance'. Now for me to complete this, I do need your input. Tell me in your own words what you feel you have achieved so far?"

Nothing could have been clearer. An open question, giving her the opportunity to state exactly what she had 'achieved so far'. This was a Performance Appraisal and Objective Scheme and he was virtually allowing her to assess herself! It was unexpected, she was silenced, unable to find the words. Of course, he had not been monitoring her activities closely and she assumed that was down to his overall inefficiency, or lack of interest, or remoteness – his Gregness. But the fact was he did not have a clue what she had been doing.

"I … er … well, you see my monthly reports." Had he read them?

"Yes, but I would still like to hear the background, how you feel and what you have actually achieved. It's important to be able to move forward and set out our objectives for the coming year." He had not yet used the terms 'results-driven' or 'evidence-based', Steph vaguely noted …

This was important! The next year depended on what she said now. Her brain slipped up several modes, from sluggish to frantic.

"My reports show the number of clients and how this is growing. I have been effective in publicising SSS in a positive light and attracting referrals. I have …" – if she had known, she would have made a list – "… established good relationships with outside agencies. I've tried out a number of projects – and carried out pilots." She swallowed hard, cleared her throat, and went to reach for one of the glasses. The fact was yesterday she was too distracted to prepare for this. She should have anticipated. Idiot.

Are you all right? Would you like some water?" He was being nice, she noted, suspiciously. He poured some and passed her the glass.

"I'm OK, but thanks." She could feel the colour rising in her cheeks. The sleek cat had started rubbing against her legs and, though she wanted to let it jump onto her lap, she had to push it away.

"Your projects, then."

She took a couple of sips of water. "Yes. There was the buddy scheme – matching younger people as lodgers to older people who had spare rooms and needed help with household tasks."

"What were your conclusions?"

Actually this was documented in a monthly report. Had he read it? She did not like to quiz him, as if doubting his word.

"It was fraught and doomed." She saw him raise his eyebrows as he sat back in his chair. How could she have said that? So negative, and putting herself down. She took a deep breath. "Well, it was … very disappointing – as I explained in my February report last year." Yes, she had detailed how the clients had unrealistic expectations of having their entire house painted; whilst the youngsters imagined that keeping their own room reasonably tidy was a big enough sacrifice and certainly paid for their keep. One or two matches had worked really well, but the management time to ensure safety of all concerned, and liabilities cover, made it financially unviable.

"Do you think it could work with clearer guidelines …? I believe some such schemes have worked in other parts of the country." Oh! Ouch! That was below the belt. Was it true? "Maybe we could examine those successful projects – see if we can learn something ... Mm?"

She expected him to work in the term 'best practise' which, to be fair, would have been very apt, but no, he seemed to be having a jargon-free day today.

Thus the next half hour passed by, reasonably well. Steph managed to spin out her earlier projects and she felt her body relax. The cat was now on her lap, purring.

Then Greg leaned forward. "Your recent reports have shown a *decline* in activity, Stephanie."

This was a sudden body blow.

His cold facial expression and tone of voice were stern and uncompromising. The very direct look, almost a stare, made her heart thump hard. For a moment she was literally stunned, her thoughts scrambled.

After a long pause, she replied cautiously, "I've been focusing more on the home visits. I feel that is the core of what I should be doing, the real Purpose of the Job."

"But the overall time spent on those, and the number of visits, has reduced. If you have domestic commitments ... I mean, you must tell me if there are other demands on your time that are making the job difficult for you. I do understand – but it's important I know."

She couldn't think how to justify the hours she had spent with Jackson and his problems. "I have another project that I've not told you about. It's taken up some time."

He sat back again and folded his arms.

"I'm trying to get some computer classes going."

"What? For old folks? And do you have any takers?" He now seemed to be writing rather fast.

"Yes, quite a few."

"Sounds expensive."

"No, it's all on a shoestring, actually."

"How many?"

"Numbers are growing."

"And the purpose of this particular project?"

"Oh ... well, to offer an opportunity to learn how to do word processing."

She could feel her heart pumping hard again and her palms go moist.

"And presumably supply the means? The computers?"

"Oh, of course. These are people who have never in their lives used a computer ...er ..." her voice trailed off, realising she was talking to one of them.

"To write letters? What else?"

Steph racked her brain. Diaries? Reports? CVs? Memoirs? Novels? Travelogues? Minutes of meetings?

"Labelling family photographs."

"Nice."

"Notes for the doctor, their carers, that kind of thing."

"Yes."

"Shopping lists, to do lists, reminders ... it's endless." Her mouth had gone dry and she cleared her throat.

"Things they've always managed to do perfectly well by other means?" Greg waved his pen in the air.

But *you* are having your notes 'typed up', she wanted to retort. She took another sip of water. "Who types up your notes by the way?" she asked, making a point but also thinking perhaps she could please him by offering to do it, though how fiercely that would irritate her, she had not yet fully assessed.

"Oh, I get an agency to do it."

Steph felt furious, heat rising in her cheeks. A temp? He was *paying* for a 'temp'. How dare he use SSS funds to cover for his deficiencies!

"You would be most welcome to attend our classes," she offered, exploding with anger inside, but keeping outwardly calm, knowing full well that he would never in a million years accept such an invitation. He would be as keen on that as a vegan would be on a trip to observe the workings of an abattoir.

13

She took Faith and Barnaby to the cinema that evening to see *The King's Speech*. It was time they did something together and rarely did they go out in the middle of a school week. It felt good that even Barnaby was happy to focus on something other than thrillers and animations. In fact he was quite fascinated by the whole stammering thing, trying to perfect his own versions of possible speech defects on the way home, such that Steph had to dampen his enthusiasm.

The following morning, it was barely light and, after waking far too early with an ill-conceived soup of Greg, hollyhocks, computers and Colin Firth swirling around in her head, Steph tossed and turned. Her eyelids fluttered open, and aware she was not going to retrieve the sleep she badly needed, she sat up and pulled the Diary out of her briefcase next to the bed.

'I never felt like this before about a boy. His face was always in my mind. Constantly. He was (and still is) like a drug that floods me with warmth and happiness. I just hoped he would come back to the gym soon. Every day I was looking out for him. If he didn't ask me out or make a move soon, I'd be on my knees begging! I haven't told anyone about him, not about how I feel. Dad was helping me today sort out next year's budget and I realised he'd been speaking about five minutes and I didn't have the faintest clue what he'd said! Which made me feel bad, as Dad gave me so much of his time ...'

Steph paused in her reading. Memories of her father too – this was tough.

'Anyway, I couldn't help but imagine. I wanted his lips on mine – oh my God, yes. I wanted his hands to be all over me, to touch, to stroke – I imagined him giving me a massage! I would rip his clothes off. I can picture him naked, coming towards me ... Oh, this is bad. Really. At night – I would kiss my own arm, and touch myself, just imagining it was him. He's bound to have a girlfriend already. He could be married!'

'Saw Lucas in the gym working out on the weights. He is perfectly formed, even through his Lycra I can tell! (Especially through his Lycra) What is so wonderful is that he is such a beautiful person – kind, caring – that's what attracted me to him first, although if he had squinty eyes and a double-chin, maybe his sunny nature would not have hit me in the same way. Then – the most amazing thing happened! He came over to me to say that his group of lads could come to play at the gym; and THEN, as a thank you, he said, "Would you have time for a drink after work? What time do you finish?" I suddenly lost the ability to think or speak. Yes, yes, yes!! Now! Let's go!! Hey I'm the boss here!'

'I suggested a little pub in Elstead, where no-one would know me (probably). He seemed happy with that. It meant we had a good twenty minute drive (more time to spend close to him). I remember watching him, as we chatted, noticing the black hairs on his arms (which I found sexy like some women might go for a hairy chest), the strong profile and shapely mouth that I wanted so much to reach out and touch. He was a musician – creative, sensitive, but a bit wild, bound to be. He was perfect.

We spent two hours in that pub, just having one drink each and a bite to eat. I could tell by his eyes that he wanted me too. His gaze seemed to caress my face as he spoke, moving around it, and when our eyes met, it was as if magnetic forces were at work! Once we came out and got into his car, we both knew what would happen. No, not sex, he was not that brash, not on a first date. But, oh boy, did we snog each others' faces off.'

Steph pulled a face at her juvenile language. She was so young then – only eighteen. When she carried on reading the more anatomical descriptions of their passion, she knew she would have to whip some pages out if Faith did ever have access to her diary. Faith was now only two years younger than she was then! This was horrifying. She read about how they decided, at such a young age, to move into a flat together. Then she found:

'Oh my God. This is scary, this is awful! This is just wonderful, fabulous and I am so, so happy! I am pregnant. Lucas and I are going to have a BABY!!'

Faith would live her life differently, she felt sure. She could hear the unmistakable sound of Barnaby's footsteps on the stairs, and Faith running a shower – clearly it was time to get out of bed. Stirring up the past, stepping out of the present, was like psychotherapy, she imagined. She was not sure if it made her feel weak or strong - and her life offered enough emotional conundrums in the here and now. But, all things considered, it was addictive – she wanted to plunge herself again in all that turmoil as soon as she could find a convenient moment.

As she scrolled through her emails after breakfast, her neighbour, Lettie came round, bearing an enormous bouquet.

Lettie, about her age, was a free-lance multi-faceted artist originally from Wales whose husband used to work in the City but after being made redundant a couple of years ago, he was now managing a farm-shop just a few miles out of Appley Green. Steph was impressed at such a career sea-change.

"Oh my God! What's this?" said Steph, laughing.

"Delivered yesterday evening when you were out," said Lettie, almost hidden.

Steph nearly fell over. "For *me*?"

Lettie was effervescing with curiosity as to the possible donor and occasion.

"A birthday is it then?" she asked. She was a lively mixture of warm-hearted, nosy, outspoken and, working alone most days, always ripe for a chat.

Steph shook her head, searching amongst the blooms for a gift card with one hand as she took the flowers off Lettie with the other.

Lettie went on. "Wedding anni …? Oh no, oops, silly me. If opening your mouth and putting your foot in it was an Olympic event, I'd be going for gold!" She smacked her own head. Steph laughed, feeling she ought to get to know her better, but had not so far found the time in the six weeks since Lettie and Angwyn moved in. It was something she must definitely do – soon.

Just fleetingly Steph wondered if this was Richard, her children's former stepfather, playing some kind of sick joke. No, quite right Lettie, not wedding anniversary, but it was around six years ago this month they divorced. Maybe he thought she would be celebrating! For the first year or so, encounters were brief but necessary to give him access to Faith and Barnaby. He would arrive, unsmilingly, and lead them away, dutifully, for some 'treat' or other, but according to her faithful children, these outings did not work. It was not something they looked forward to beforehand or talked about afterwards. The visits soon fizzled out, contact now reduced to cards at Christmas and birthdays – but not always; clearly they sometimes quite simply slipped his mind. They were not, after all, blood-related.

She had absolutely no wish for any kind of reconciliation or romantic gesture. After the acrimonious time they had spent together he would be insane to imagine they could possibly salvage anything positive from their brief sham of a marriage. He was still with Julia now anyway, she assumed, and their two children; that was the last she had heard.

"I haven't the faintest who they're from," said Steph, as Lettie appeared to have taken root to her hall floor. "Anyway," she said, gently moving towards the front door, knowing she should be more neighbourly but anxious to return to get ready for her working day, "thanks for keeping them safe for me and bringing them round."

"Well, somebody's got the hots for you, Steph!" Lettie grinned mischievously. "In my humble opinion. *That* is a bloody serious posy!" Her broad singsong Welsh accent always made Stephanie smile.

Genuinely puzzled, Steph closed the door only to be bombarded with questions from her two offspring, questions she could barely endure, let alone answer. No name was given, although clearly they were intended for her. *Just to brighten your week, Steph* the card read. She shivered. It seemed a little creepy. Or was it a charming gesture? Perhaps all would become a little clearer and this anonymous donor would reveal his or her identity. She hoped so, because receiving such a lavish gift from some person unknown, made her feel slightly stalked, not gladdening her heart but rather leaving her flaky and not a little nervous.

As she worked alone on the Internet, Steph tried to chase from her mind the significant bouquet of lilies, roses, gladioli, freesias and other flowers she could not easily name. Imposing in her small living-room, the display stood, tall and proud, in a bucket draped round with a bright yellow check tablecloth. She could not find a vase large enough. She tried to both ignore this floral presence, and push aside old memories, as she searched for estate agents and property for sale in the area. Closest to Jackson's house was Willem Hardrop and she pinpointed an individual there called Justin.

She did a quick search and scan of property they had for sale, using quite broad criteria but specifying bungalow. Nothing came up. Well, the best thing would be to drop by the actual Agents in Appley Green and perhaps look up Justin. There was a photo of him. He looked approachable – and very good-looking, as it happened. She would try to win him over. She would ask him if he could let her know the instant something suitable for Jackson arose in the marketplace, so she could get in there smartly. With so little property available, it was necessary to be bullish and grab things before they went. Few people buying, but even fewer selling, which made no sense but was how it seemed to be.

Wary of how sneaky Twitter and addictive Google could effortlessly remove large chunks of time from a working day, she slipped into them for research purposes only. A deft search on 'Appley Green' and nearby villages and hamlets would winkle out any local 'Tweeters'. Monique from the market town of Bloomstock came up, with plans to start up a Zumba class in Appley Green; there was a recruitment agency; and the local Estate Agents, Willem Hardrop and, oh yes, that rather fit bloke she had spotted on their website. Yes, it was definitely him, Justin. His dark Celtic looks reminded her of Lucas. Did he have the same scintillating blue eyes, she wondered? Was he her 'type'? Ever inquisitive, and hopeful, she clicked on his Twitter name to see his Profile page. He might be Tweeting with people she knew in Appley Green! Realising this was all slightly ridiculous – just as she had heard a comedian point out the absurd thrill of seeing your own house, and possibly car, on Google Earth, when you could just do it the old-fashioned way. Admittedly standing outside to take a peek at your own house was not quite the same as an aerial shot, but nonetheless …. This was so typical! She looked at her watch.

For some reason, she could hear Greg's voice inside her head, 'Thief of time,' almost as if he were breathing down the back of her neck, watching her every move. Time-wasting, she knew that, but it confirmed her certain knowledge that playing around online like this would be perfect for people who had too many empty hours; folks stuck at home alone with nowhere to go and no one to talk to. She noticed that Justin was Tweeting with young Joshua, Liz Burns' son, who comes to her computer class. Justin or Joshua must have found each other the same way, by searching geographically, surmising they wouldn't have much else in common, with the age gap and so on. She continued to flick through various Twitter profiles, local Council events; a charity fundraiser on the village green, before exerting the degree of willpower needed to close down.

Today she had five client visits, one of them a brand new referral from Nora, and that alone would take at least two hours.

She decided she would gain more on the hunt for Jackson's bungalow by doing things, on this occasion, the traditional way. She would go and see that Justin with the trustworthy smile and bedroom eyes to discuss the matter, face to face. She would even walk; it was only fifteen minutes away if she strode out. She would ask to be put on their mailing list after making sure, face-to-face, that they had a clear understanding of Jackson's problems. She would arrange for them to do a valuation of *The Hideaway* too – that should get them fired up and motivated to find him the perfect home.

On her way she passed by *The Gemshop*, glancing at their display of polished paperweights, chunky rings and bookends. Babs and Tony spotted her and waved. It would be rude not to pop in, just briefly. She pushed the creaky shop-door and a bell rang.

Tony came forward, clasped her hand and shook it warmly. "We've found a professional website designer to do it for us. Now we understand a bit better, thanks to your class. Can't thank you enough."

Babs came to his side to endorse his enthusiasm. "This will really bring in the business, Steph," she said. "A fresh new start for us."

Certainly the shop itself was a shrine to nostalgia. It was flanked on the left by the understated frontage of a minimalist, bijou art gallery that displayed small works by local artists and sculptors; and to the right, the plate-glass frontage of *Hair and Now*. *The Gemshop* reminded her of the dark front parlour of her elderly Great Great Aunt Violet who died years ago. As a child she would wander round it, slightly in awe, touching, feeling with her fingertips the dusty Victorian collection of china dogs, cats, cows and hand bells. The clutter, the musty smell. It transported her back.

"Your online shop will bring in completely new customers – from around the world, then, do you think?" asked Steph, although even as she expressed her optimism, was wondering about the carriage costs of lumps of stone relative to their value. Maybe mail order would not be such a bright idea.

"This designer girl says it will. We hope it brings us up to date anyway."

"Well good luck, you two," said Steph, making her way out, realising how her day was disappearing. "Coming to the next class?"

"You bet," they replied in unison.

In Willem Hardrop's window, there were a few local properties displayed, but a large number were Lettings, and many others had a Sold sticker across them. Discounting these, there were few houses, cottages, flats or bungalows currently on the market.

She went in and looked around for Justin, but he did not appear to be there. An affable woman in her fifties, with a chiffon scarf of sweet-pea colours swirling around her neck, came up to her with a winning smile.

"Good morning. How can I help you? Do take a seat," she offered, in what her mother would have called a posh voice.

Joshua was sitting at his computer in his bedroom doing homework. He knew his Mum would be in soon to check what he had done, so there was no escaping it. It was a history essay that needed to be done properly for a special project.

The landline phone rang downstairs and he could hear his mother take the call. From the tone of voice he could tell she would be nattering to her friend for a good while, so he switched over to Twitter.

Not many of his real friends were on Twitter but since the class he had found a few people from around the village. Joshua heard sounds from behind. A rustle, a distant, tinny voice. Oh no. He swivelled round to see his Mum standing framed like a portent of doom in the doorway of his bedroom, with the portable handset clamped to her ear, and frowns on her forehead like sand ridges left by the tide going out.

"I can see what you're doing, Josh," she hissed. "Bye for now Jenny, call you back," she said, calmly, into the phone before switching it off.

Joshua could only think, thank you oh Guardian of the Universe, that she had not caught him out playing that Simulac game Justin had recommended. She would go into orbit.

"It's since you went to that class. Isn't it?"

Joshua shrugged then sat up very straight, even tilting his head thoughtfully. "Mmm. Maybe. I'm trying to help the old people. It's for a good cause, Steph says, and she thinks Sam and I are doing a great job. That's what she told us." He gave her his best innocent look.

"And what about your essay, Josh?"

"I am doing it. Just had a little break."

"Mm. I'm going to have a word with Steph. Your teacher says you're not putting in the effort you used to and you're sleepy in class. Not good enough Josh."

Greg's open criticism had knocked her back, despite the good things in life, like Babs' and Tony's enthusiasm for their website (all down to her class, they said); and the way Faith and Jackson were getting on so well. Receiving a gift of flowers, however, made her feel anything but loved or admired. Without knowing who sent them, how could such a surprise gift make her happy? She could only think it was her very ex-husband, Richard, and his motives for doing this were unfathomable.

Feeling low, she sat watching TV, not really taking in what was on. If anyone had quizzed her she was not sure she could even say what the programme was or what time it started. Her brain was shooting out all over the place. Reading her Diary would not be a good way to calm down and, in any case, Faith was still up and about.

Now she had told Greg about her classes, he would want regular updates. After all, along with the extra visits to Jackson, which for some reason she had not mentioned, they were taking up time and he had been quick to spot that. The only way forward was to make absolutely certain, with belt and braces firmly fastened, that her class was successful. It must succeed enough to overcome all Greg's resistance to the Internet, and his masculine pride that would never induce him to admit he was wrong. Men seemed to present her with nothing but problems.

A tear ran down her cheek and she sniffed. Faith was in the kitchen making herself a bedtime hot drink. She didn't want to be caught snivelling and rushed to the bathroom to blot her eyes, collect her thoughts and stamp out this unwanted emotion. Tears were a bit too frequent just lately … She would be strong. She would do this thing. She must.

She now needed to constantly juggle her normal visits, which by their very nature and purpose, should not be rushed, and all things related to the 'computer club'. Tomorrow she was going to fit in a visit to Gloria, the fearsome woman who strode into the class with her undeniable offers of help. Now that was another positive. She really must take stock and get a sensible perspective on things. Gloria could be an invaluable ally, a solid role model for others of a certain age.

14

Gloria lived in one of the grander houses of the village, about a mile out from the Green. It was set in grounds typical of the land around Appley Green; the usual furzy heath, feathery green bracken, spinneys of silver birch, overlooked by tall, dark Scots pine trees. Here and there would be a substantial house with a prosperous, often military history, and Gloria's was one of them. *Jay's Nest*, it was called, accessed by a winding driveway lined with rhododendrons

She ushered Steph through to what she called the drawing-room, which had a large bay window, high ceilings, ornate coving and curlicues. They sat facing each other, but comfortably at an oblique angle, in capacious chintzy armchairs. Bone china cups were placed on lace runners that protected the mahogany occasional tables. It had a rather colonial air about it.

Gloria did not need much prompting from Steph to talk about her past career. She was certainly a redoubtable force, especially for a woman of her era. Some women of even her mother's generation were reasonably content to be wives and mothers and Gloria was older, so she was pretty exceptional. A mover and a shaker.

She was also happy to tell Steph that her husband had been a Colonel in the British army; previous generations of men in the family having spent their lives in the Indian Army or Indian Civil Service, making large fortunes in overseas trading enterprises. Steph assumed, from this history, which Gloria spilled out in some detail, and from this fine house, adorned with ancestral portraits, that her impressive career was never triggered by a shortage of cash.

'My mother was something highly secretive during the war – to do with codes and so forth. Anyway, mustn't bore you to death with all of that."

Steph playfully toyed with the notion that Jackson might hit it off with this energetic, highly intelligent and really rather aristocratic woman. How wonderful if he could find a kindred spirit to share his fundamental but thwarted love of life in his last years. But, she feared, that busy Gloria might not have the patience to provide the supportive companionship Jackson needed. She did not come across as a particularly warm person, despite her strengths.

"And do you have children? Grandchildren?" asked Steph, noting a lack of framed photographs that almost always adorned sideboards and shelves in the more typical houses she visited.

Gloria's lips became pursed and tight. "Hm. I have a son. My only child," was the curt response as she rose to pick up the coffee pot. "More coffee? When is your next session? Do you have a date fixed? I left your class in something of a rush and failed to ask. My fault entirely."

"It's the same day each week."

Gloria consulted her diary and confirmed she could be there.

"I have a couple of friends from a society I belong to who would like to come," she said. "They're older than me, certainly over seventy-five – not sure exactly."

"This is the age range I am trying to reach. Even older," said Steph. "Excellent, please do encourage them. It's for those who can't get out much, or who may not be able to for much longer, to start appreciating the Internet." She was thinking of Jackson as she spoke, no-one else.

"Well, I'm right behind you there. Absolutely, m'dear."

"Are you into social networking then, Gloria, and doing things online?"

"Of course, of course. Keeps me in touch with what's going on in the world, and old friends – those who use a computer or some other device. Anything I can do, just say the word."

Lovely woman, willing to give her time for nothing. She would enjoy the involvement and being seen as something of an expert by her peers. Yes, a good meeting, thought Steph, as she got back into her car. It was afterwards, as she was driving on to her client, Elsie, who lived in a cottage overlooking the village Green, that she mentally rewound to the look on Gloria's face when she had asked her about children.

So Gloria had a son. He might be thirty years old, even in his forties, but she did not want to talk about him and there were no pictures to show she was in any way the proud parent. No graduation or young man in the armed forces, no wedding, no grandchild. Not even a family holiday photo. Steph's natural curiosity left her feeling intrigued and wanting to know more.

Despite the fact that this visit had taken up more time than she could afford, the meeting had pepped her up and filled her with new energy. But this mystery was something she knew she must somehow extract from Gloria one way or another, or she would die wondering! He was not dead - not referred to in the past tense - but perhaps he was very ill, something terminal, or disabled ... No, there would be some pity for this, surely. Maybe he was in prison and she was ashamed of him. But this did not quite tie up with the frozen look of almost hatred that gripped her face. This was unnatural. What could a son have done to make his mother despise him so much? Clearly something so despicable she could not bring herself to speak about it, or possibly even think of it. This was not healthy, Steph could not help but think.

If you had issues, she thought, feeling unusually philosophical, surely it was better to be able to talk about them.

In bed that night, she felt uplifted – and, paradoxically, more grounded. The visit to Gloria was a distraction, admittedly, but it was good to have the support of such a strong, inspiring woman, who was worth the time.

It gave her the courage needed to pull out the Diary and read on, skipping past the well-worn page she shared with Faith each year.

Lucas and I never really talk about the idea of a wedding day, even though we have a baby. If he proposed, I would say yes! Tonight Lucas said something about how out of his four best mates from school days, three of them married, "too young, frankly" he said, and two of the three have split up! Already! Divorced! Perhaps that's what has put him off.

Of course Mum is always dropping huge hints, saying things like, "Young people don't seem to do things in the right order these days …" sighing heavily and adding something tactful, like 'but I'm sure they know what they're doing. It's all different now."

I suppose it doesn't make that much difference.'

'I keep having runaway thoughts. I imagine myself as Mrs Lucas Richardson. Yes, secretly, it would make my life entirely perfect for Faith to have Lucas's surname. But no, I am NOT

going to be the one to suggest it. I can imagine the wedding reception at the Hunters' Lodge Hotel, the kind of place girls dream of. I can see it all - a day with friends and relatives, not showy, but a special day to show the world our true love, our commitment. But, there, Lucas and I are so much in love, there is no chance of either of us ever being unfaithful, or splitting up. The very idea is — unthinkable.'

'Life has become a bit of a merry-go-round. Not much time for keeping up with this diary!'

'Faith is six months old today. I love being a full-time mother, but it can be hard for Lucas, funnily enough. He's always so full of energy and enthusiasm, keeping up with teaching (and gigs) as well as being a fantastic Dad, but no more, I tell myself, than countless other parents must be doing up and down the country. He was determined not to miss too much of Faith's early development, like last week seeing her sit up unaided — so sweet. He takes a good share of household tasks, because he knows when I return to work everything will be fifty-fifty. A dual-income is even more important now; we really do need mine (because I can still earn more than him). He is really hopeful of a career with his music — aside from teaching. An A&R scout for a record label came to one his band's gigs last week, and seemed to really like what he heard. But in case this doesn't work, we've agreed that I return to work and somehow we'll manage between us. I went to see the local nursery in Appley Green today. I've heard good things about it from lots of working Mums in the village.'

'I had to write this straight away, hoping it might make me feel better. Just now I handed Faith over, into the arms of a smiling young nursery assistant called Sharon. I gave her a folder full of lists, with instructions and bags of Faith's favourite things. I just feel torn apart. Guilty. How can I betray the trust of my little,

100

adorable bundle of life who, in her innocence, looks to me and Lucas for everything? It was only for a couple of hours this time, but I know what lies ahead.'

'It will quickly build up to a full working day; my job can't be done part-time. I feel jealous that Sharon may be the person to see Faith's first steps, when it should be me and Lucas.'

'It's nearly three years since I was lucky enough to get the job of managing House of Fitness, a small, privately owned gym in Appley Green with a handful of members; now it's expanded into a strong, blossoming establishment. We have a swimming pool, sauna and Jacuzzi as well as all the fitness stuff. Ricky Runcliff, the owner, lives abroad and allows me to more or less get on with it.

I couldn't have done it without Dad lending his commercial expertise he gained the hard way building up the garden centre. He's constantly giving me good tips, but gently, like: "Do your research. Give people what they really want but don't be afraid to tell them what they need!" He willingly gives me his time for nothing to help me make a real success of the business. He lets me take the credit so how can I possibly complain?! In a way this should bother me, to have a parent always with the ready advice, but I love my Dad so much, it somehow doesn't. My friends think I'm a bit odd, but I know he'll back off once I'm good and ready.

Ricky returned from his other ventures in Spain to fill in for me during my maternity leave. He said, "I can't find anyone who could fill your shoes for a few months. Easiest thing is for me to do it myself. So long as I can count on you coming back? Yes? You will?"

When I was six months pregnant, his offer was a no-brainer, impossible to refuse. So I agreed, feeling blessed to have such a rewarding career and an appreciative boss. Lucas says I am the 'victim of my own success' - managing it is now such a full-on job.

Lucas is the eternal optimist! Keeps saying how together we can do it – bring up Faith as good parents with us both working full-time. He is my rock and he rocks! Yeah!'

'Ted Devonish came into the gym today. It's a bit like having royalty drop by, with everyone feeling they should salute or curtsy! He usually has Natalie with him, as he did today, and is so patient with her, teaching her to swim in the shallow pool, first breaststroke, then the crawl. He's quite old to have such a young daughter, but he's a really cool Dad! She's a feisty little girl, though, so I kept an eye on her for him today while he completed the routine forty lengths he always does with military-style dedication.

For a while now gossip about Ted and his wife has been rife. She left him for another man. How could she?! So, the very gracious Mrs Devonish can scarcely hold her head up in the village now. I'm still reserving judgement on this. There's probably no sure way of knowing what goes on inside a marriage. Maybe his wife has good reasons, although it is a challenge to imagine what they could be, for Ted's a really nice man. Because I helped him out today he invited me to go to our in-house café with them.

*"It's special for my daughter and me to be together," he confided. Ted Devonish confiding in **me**! Imagine! "This is a good place for us to have a bit of each other's company. Neutral territory, y'know." I just nodded and smiled. "As you get older," he went on, pensively, "you need family."*

I feel sorry for him because Natalie lives with her mother now and this was keeping him apart from her most of the time, just as she was growing up.

His eyes then filled up with tears and I sensed that, for all his land and wealth and aristocratic pedigree, he was at heart a lonely man.'

It felt very strange indeed to recall those days, sixteen years ago, getting to know Ted Devonish. He sought her company out many times after that, but when she sat and listened to his woes in the café, as she did many a time, she had no idea what it would lead to.

Greg sat on one of the rather broken down wooden seats that were shaded by an old oak tree on the Green. He gazed around the village. It was the kind of place that made you feel good to be alive. There was no main road with rumbling traffic cutting through it, an aspect that made it outstanding amongst English villages. Film crews had put it to good use and he could see why. It had a way of sweeping you back in time, despite the TV aerials. Soon they would probably be consigned to history.

He had noticed a more imposing bench overlooking the pond that was, he observed, dedicated to Ted Devonish's father, local landowner who had also been a great benefactor to the parish, particularly in the years after the Second World War. There was a small brass plaque. They were a family of some prestige with an illustrious local history. He was worried about the SSS project Ted had bequeathed. He somehow felt all eyes of this community were secretly upon Steph and him to succeed on Ted's behalf; especially notorieties in the Parish Council and suchlike authorities.

He wanted to absorb more of a feel for the village: its atmosphere, the people, what made it work as a community. The population must be large enough to sustain good local amenities, but were the villagers extended families, or mostly people from outside now? Was it a dormitory village, or buzzing with life? He lived over twenty miles away and did not understand its demographics intimately.

His prime role was to secure funding and oversee Stephanie, who really was running the show at the community coalface, but he needed to know more because whatever made the Appley Green heart beat impacted hugely on what strategy SSS should be pursuing.

Were the elderly people here devoid of family backup? Had Ted seen something in the senior population of Appley Green that made them especially in need of extra support? What about youngsters in the village and the disaffected unemployed? Well, although he died before his time, he was getting on in years; so he felt an affinity with the elderly of the parish. That made sense, and Greg suspected his charity was founded on the centuries-old, strong, Devonish family connection with Appley Green, not because the locality was particularly different from the rest of the country. But Ted Devonish wanted this pilot to be the flagship that could lead an entire fleet sailing into the four corners of the British Isles. He smiled at his own imperfect imagery, but, anyway, that was what made it so important. Yes, it must succeed and set an example.

His thoughts turned to Steph. Maybe he had done something very regrettable. The bouquet was perhaps a gesture that might confuse and cause trouble, but he had felt sorry for her. Keeping a professional detachment was not easy when he could see she worked bloody hard, struggling to be all things to all people, with little income. He admired her tenacity. He knew what she earned, but she said to him at the outset that with two children who meant everything to her, she would not throw herself into a high-flying career that might keep her away from them. She had lost their father; she would take steps to ensure she never lost the affection of her children. She wanted them close. Steph had once told him all this in an unguarded moment over lunch, and he had seen a sadness behind the determined look in her eyes. This job though, she had told him, would give her enormous satisfaction. It would, she tried to explain, 'make her feel alive and worthwhile. It was something to strive for.'

He stretched out his legs and locked his hands together behind his head, looking up into the sky. They must work on this together more. They were joint pioneers. He must involve himself more closely. For one thing, he should overcome his own aversion to computers.

A breeze stirred the leaves of some nearby silver birches, making them shimmer in the fading afternoon light and he sensed it would rain. He wished he had his camera; the lighting would have made for a stunning photograph. A heavy cumulo-nimbus was overhead, rolling towards where he sat. He decided to stroll around the village and take a look at what went on here. Churches, the library and village-hall notice boards usually were good indicators. Oh, and the people. Yes, most of all, the inhabitants.

He thought back to when he used to run a construction firm, when he had a team of people under him to fulfil varying roles. Each of them had *their* own team and so on. Much of his work was dealing with people – clients, employees, financiers. His secretary took care of his diary, arranging meetings, typing up contracts and so on. When the industry took a nose-dive, it seemed a good time, though he was not yet fifty, to get out and be useful to the community. His wife had died and they were a childless couple. He had been prudent with money all his life, so could afford to opt out into semi-retirement. SSS was just what he needed, or so he thought.

Wandering pensively down the small parade of shops that branched off from the Green, he was about to take shelter in a café when the square tower of the Parish Church came into view as being within easy reach.

He stopped a young woman pushing a buggy along. "Excuse me. Is the village hall close by the church?"

"No, it isn't actually," she replied. "You need to go over the other side of the Green, just before the primary school … there's two actually, quite close to each other."

He tapped his head. "Oh, I know. Yes. I saw the school sign earlier. Thanks so much."

By now it was raining hard. He would leave it to another day. Yes, he would be back, he decided, diving for cover into the *Tea Shoppe* for a cuppa and a slice of their excellent looking carrot cake.

15

The number expected at the next class – now unofficially but openly referred to as the 'Computer Social Club', because people were really beginning to catch on to this – was so large that Nick from Simulac had to bring in a couple more computers, and many were having to share now, like it or not. It had become a social occasion too.

This was the third session, the second one having passed off without incident, still without Jackson but with many other new recruits. Now, popularity had taken a leap as word spread. Snowballed! Steph was secretly delighted. Maybe she could do some kind of customer satisfaction survey to convince Greg that this was proving to be a success. Measured results. He'd like that; and she would enjoy watching his face as she presented them to him.

"We been Tweeting to one another," said one elderly student, another at his side. She knew both these two already had computers at home, untouched until now. "Daft really, but a bit o' fun. I found Richard from the TV. You know the one. I'm following 'im anyhow though I don't doubt he ain't followin' me. It's a laugh, innit?" They trundled off together, both wobbly on their pins but somehow supporting each other like two sides of a swaying triangle. People were finding new friends. How could she get statistics to reflect that?

Then Jackson walked slowly through the door clutching his long stick with his usual grit and determination, head held high, and Steph felt a surge of relief, a fizz of happiness. She saw Tricia's back retreating into the entrance lobby. He would have declined any further offers of help.

She rushed across from where she had been standing chatting, to greet him.

"Jackson, I'm glad you made it! How are you?"

"Yes, here I am, fully medicated," he replied, looking quite pleased with himself. Tucking the long walking stick under one arm, his trembling hand reached to pull back his jacket sleeve cuff. He checked the time. "I should be good to go for an hour or so." He laughed at himself. "Then I may turn into a pumpkin."

How much could he learn in a mere hour? Not much but enough, she hoped, to excite his imagination so he would want to come again. She must make this evening's precious hour an enjoyable experience. Whatever he did now would probably shape things to come. She would make it relevant to him as a person. She would sit down with him and show him some of those websites and articles she found earlier, things relating to architecture, building and the world of design. Then she would show him the basis of email and describe a little how Skype could work for him. He would be so amazed and so pleased that she had opened up these possibilities for him. Training on the keyboard and mouse would come later.

Yes, indeed, his eyes lit up as Google helped her find Frank Lloyd Wright's work; the Bank of China building in Singapore; Edwin Lutyens and the Hayward Gallery; various Art Deco buildings from around the world; questions bubbled up like milk boiling over in a saucepan, unstoppable. Steph could tell his eyes and brain were

108

working faster than he could speak and others might have trouble making out what he was saying.

She opened up Outlook Express.

"But how … how do you choose the person you want to send a message to?" he asked, his voice rasping slightly. "What if you …" and he paused to take a breath, "What if you want to change something you've typed into this confounded machine?" Steph patiently showed him the principles of deleting a letter, word, document or email. "And how do you make a letter of the alphabet into a capital? Suppose I wanted to have it on a piece of paper, instead of the screen, in order to simply post it?"

This was the way he would find out, but some of his queries reminded Steph of how far he had to go, how much there was to learn when you knew nothing. Others there had at least used a typewriter. She could see a frown deepening as he tried with great persistence to make the mouse double-click. She had not asked him to, not even thinking they would get to that stage, but he had watched her and wanted to try. His earnest wish to imitate was almost childlike.

By the end of the hour he was truly fascinated and motivated to learn, so Steph felt a vital part of her mission was almost done. He did not need to struggle with this old technology; she would persuade him to get himself a touch-screen tablet computer. And the rest would follow, wouldn't it? Regular tuition, practice and help. But already, even on this first evening, the first of many as she fervently hoped, he was showing obvious signs of impatience and frustration.

He sighed. "You see, Stephanie, I am afraid the fingers will not do as they are being told to by my old head. It's the old story."

He looked crestfallen. She had raised up his interest and his hopes but he seemed to have fallen at the first hurdle.

"Don't worry about that," she reassured him, kindly, "there are easier ways to do this."

Should she give up? No, she thought, not even giving this option a second thought. He would get there, with time and with help. She would not let him give up. Forget the mouse; he would be fine ...

She looked around. Her gaze embraced a roomful of happy browsing people, Gloria helping Babs and Tony surfing for other gemstone shops. They were evidently very excited that they could find none quite like their own.

What on earth would Greg say if he saw this room right now, she wondered? No matter how much apparent enthusiasm and interest on the faces of these people, he would still be worried about the hidden dangers. He would call everything to an abrupt halt; and she would probably lose her job. He would whip the rug out from under her feet, but no way would she take that lying down.

A few days after this class, as Steph and Faith cleared up after the evening meal, Faith began talking about her last visit to Jackson. She had started making her own arrangements, dropping in to see him at a fixed time without Steph.

"I borrowed these books," she said. "Look, Mum, there's a photograph of him and his wife and their children. It's a whole section on his life and career."

Steph wiped her hands dry and took the open book, hard-backed and square, from her daughter. She stared at the tall young man, handsome enough to be a film star, with an arm round the shoulders of his equally gorgeous wife. She noted his broad shoulders, filled out chest, the muscular arms and a facial expression that spoke of humour and energy, a man just sparkling with pride. Standing in front of the parents was Estebel, his daughter in Scotland, Dirk, the son now in Australia and Samson, living in South Africa. There was a few inches difference in height of the three small children.

"So in the background is the house. His house," remarked Steph, gazing wide-eyed at the page. The caption read *Jackson Jeffreys with his wife, Alison, and children in the garden of his own award-winning home The Hideaway July 1951*.

"Yes, the one he still lives in. Awesome isn't it?"

She thought of the memories the building and garden must hold for Jackson, from the time it was built to now. Nothing could bring all that back, not even a computer.

"I promised I'd take the books back tomorrow, but thought you'd like to see this before it goes."

"It's lovely. I've only seen small photos of him, when he was younger. More formal. Nothing like … that."

"It's kind of sad, though, isn't it, I mean, growing old and people dying. And his family now – he never sees them, Mum. I mean, that's just wrong. I can't imagine us ever being like that. Can you?"

Steph felt her bottom lip tremble and her eyes fill up. *Exactly,* she wanted to say. She put her arm round Faith and kissed the hair on the top of her head, wondering how her daughter would react when, one day, she realised more of the truth about her own grandfather.

Steph tried to give herself a break. She was to attend a conference in London that was 'relevant to her role'. Entitled 'Options for Care of the Elderly', it did seem undeniably relevant. Greg had sent her the brochure with a letter suggesting she might 'benefit from attending. It would be useful to us both if you could be there. I would have gone too but have a diary clash.' She felt faintly aggrieved that she apparently needed training, but thought she had better give it a try, fall in line. A lifetime ago it seemed, she used to tell her staff at the leisure centre that there was always something new to learn; a course was often good for personal and professional development.

Moreover, there would be a spare hour; maybe she could do some very early Christmas shopping while she was there.

Even on the train she found herself unable to detach herself entirely from her mission. When an elderly woman boarded the carriage, or an old chap sat quietly reading the Sports pages, she would wonder about their circumstances. Did they live alone? How did they manage and were they in good health? It was lovely to see fit and happy retired couples enjoying themselves too, out for the day perhaps, to have fun in London. It helped restore a sense of balance to see senior people perfectly able to travel and go about their business. Sometimes her work presented a distorted, rather bleak, view of the ageing population.

She came away from the conference, her head buzzing with ideas. Greg had been right on this occasion and she did not mind admitting it. The entire day had been stimulating. It was really useful to talk to people from various agencies and organisations in the coffee and lunch breaks. No time for the shopping-spree but she did not mind that. She had no money to spend on impulse-buys anyway. Much better to be cautious, make a considered choice, look for the special offers and best deals – online, of course! How could Greg *not* use the Internet? She smiled a little wickedly, with memories of the last successful Computer Club session still fresh in her head. She would prove him so wrong!

Feeling sleepy on the train heading for home, she could scarcely avoid hearing the voice of a man sitting in front of her. Not yet the busy rush hour, it was quiet enough for her to hear him, but not so quiet that he could speak softly and make himself heard to whoever was on the other end of the line. He was talking clearly and loudly. She wished he would shut up, frankly. Then she realised that this was an agitated voice. She sensed gritted teeth, perhaps a clenched jaw.

"Look, sweet, it's just not possible for me to move in. You know, Adrian *needs* me and all that. I'm afraid, that if I left, he might … you know what I'm saying … do something *stupid.*"

So he's gay. Bi-sexual in fact. Fascinated, Steph listened – there was no law against it – her listening, or his being gay or bi-sexual. So, what the harm? Unless he was an actual bigamist. Now that *is* illegal …

"Tracy … hear me out now. Please don't cry. No. No. NO. Perhaps you could go and stay with your mother until it's born and then …" His voice trailed off and there was a long pause. "Well, no. I didn't mean that, but … you couldn't move in with me either because … yes, that's it. Well, maybe he *should* get help! Do you think I haven't tried?" Another pause. "I don't know where our future lies, to be honest, Tracy. I love you, you know that, but with me working abroad so much and … well, what sort of a father would I be? Can you imagine? I mean I'll provide – give you money, but I can't promise to …" It went very quiet. "No. Not possible. It'd be wrong to make promises I know I can't keep. As for marriage vows

113

... this was a mistake, Tracy, you getting pregnant and you need ... we need ... to face that. How did it happen anyway, for fuck's sake? No, I don't mean ... you know ...hmm ... mm ... mm .... Right, well, accidents were never part of my plan, to be perfectly honest with you. And I *have* always been honest with you. Haven't I? Look, have a think about what I've said. No! Please don't do that. And stop crying, for *Christ's sake*! Just *shut up. Bloody shut up!*'

He had now lost it and was hissing and spitting down the phone. Other people in the carriage had tuned in, a captive audience of which he was totally oblivious.

It went quiet for about twenty minutes. She could hear him exhaling loudly and clearing his throat from time to time. Maybe the fact he was surrounded had finally struck him. What an incredible dickhead – and a devious, lying bastard! Bi-sexual, with two women on the go! Good grief!

Her home stop was just five minutes away when his mobile rang. "Hi babe!" His voice was soft, velvety. Wow, thought Steph, that was a quick mood turnaround. But she sat up very straight as she heard him go on. "Yeah, I'll be home in about fifteen minutes. What's for dinner? Marvellous. Can't wait. Yep, meeting was bloody ace. They bought the whole deal. Suckers. I reckon we could be moving out to Marbella in about three weeks. Yep! Honest! I know ... be perfect for you too, babe, yeah? Keep up your tan and you can hop off for your shoots just as easy from there as from Heathrow. Better climate and give us a fresh start. Yep! Yep! I know. See you soon. I know you do. Champagne tonight."

This conversation had been in dulcet tones, tender and so full of hope. Sweet. But having heard the first little chat with Tracy, how cloying and false. What was he said to the first one just now? *I've always been honest with you, haven't I?* Steph felt so upset with this young man she wanted to kick him, thump him, confront him, *shout* at him – something. Her heart was actually racing with rage. The train pulled in to the station and he stood up to get off, lurching slightly, at the same time as she did. He turned, looking not embarrassed, but pre-occupied as if he were living in another world, totally unaware of people around him. He seemed to be in a trance. He lacked empathy, Steph decided. What were these people to him, strangers who had been drawn into his sordid domestic life by simply being in that train carriage? Nothing at all.

Yet in his carelessness he should have had the presence of mind to realise that someone from his home patch might also be on the train. Steph could barely believe how someone so young could be so dense, so witless. It's not as if he had dementia, for heaven's sake.

Then she saw his face. Indeed she made a point of it. She wanted to memorise it.

She drew in a short sharp breath and felt herself go pale. He was more suntanned than the photo on the website, but it was definitely that Justin, who had filled her with the sweet anguish of Lucas's memory.

Steph felt comfort in turning to the past, even though she knew she had such painful memories to face in those fading hand-written pages. But for now she was still in the part when she and Lucas were blissfully content and full of hope, when life was good. If people like Justin were part of her world now, to escape back to those times was like being hugged and held tight. She flicked through, seeking out the bit where Barnaby was born.

'It's ages since I wrote the Diary – but the reason for that is obvious. No time. But we'll soon have another baby (a boy!) and I'll have even less time! So I'm just scribbling a small update before putting out the light.

Hard to believe but Faith is due to start her second term at primary school in September!

"Mummy, I'm going to big school - again," she says proudly and often, as if this is somehow a surprise to her. She took to school easily; her normal day was usually spent away from home so for her the transition was straightforward. Many other young children from the nursery, her little world of friends, are there too.

Before she started school in the early summer, Faith was tying up the laces on her new shoes, determined to do this without help. I made sure she could dress herself and do as many things as possible on her own to give her maximum independence at an early age. I did not want any teachers saying this child, farmed out practically from birth, did not know how to hold a knife and fork, or pull up her own knickers.

I said to her, "Clever girl! Bet not many other girls and boys can do that when they're only four."

"But I'm almost five," she pointed out generously. She's such a love.'

'I'm into my seventh month. Mum helps me out a lot. What would I do without her? Today she arrives, all bustle and efficiency from the moment she steps in through the front door, along with Faith whom she often collects from school. Hot summery air swept in with her.

She always cheers me up and knows how I'm feeling. "It's tropical out there. Phew! You and your bump must be feeling it," she says. She breezes straight through to the kitchen. "Time you stopped working and put your feet up." Spot on, Mum!

I winked at Faith, took her little school bag and gave her a hug. I was reminded of how overwhelmed I felt at House of Fitness *today, the stuffiness in those areas where there was no air conditioning; so much so that I suddenly told Maggie, my PA, that I would take the afternoon off. Nature seemed to be telling me I should slump in a chair and 'put my feet up'.*

Dad wasn't there and I asked Mum where he was and she said he was 'having one of his off days' whatever that means. I didn't know he had days like that. Being retired I suppose, and part of getting older, maybe you get a bit fed-up. "Not too clever, as they say" added Mum.

Then she looked a bit down too, so I said to her I reckon he probably jumps up and runs round the golf course once she'd left, then makes sure he's sitting down with the crossword by the time she gets home! At least I made her laugh, but then, oh my! I wasn't ready for this.'

Steph put her head back, realising where this 'scene', vivid inside her head, was leading. Some of it would be good for Faith to read, for her to understand, but now she was not sure if she could read on herself. She took a deep breath.

'I noticed how her smile quickly faded, as if she was holding something back. Then she said, "Oh! He gave me this for you though." She kept talking as she disappeared into the hall, presumably to fetch something. "It's the little picture of Faith he started so long ago you probably thought he'd given up on it, but he used digital photographs to get the likeness so she didn't have to sit still. I think he knew that would never work!"'

Steph looked up at the picture on her bedroom wall that she looked at every single night and first thing each morning.

'It was a beautiful oil painting, really not that little, of Faith as a baby. Yes, it had certainly been a long time coming, but the delay made the surprise quite dramatic! It just rolled back time to those baby-years. (More of that to come shortly, nappies, broken sleep etc Oh, happy days!)'

Now Steph allowed her gaze to wander slowly around his mastery of colours and shading, the subtle glow of her cheeks, the detail right down to eyelashes and finicky bows on her dinky satin shoes. Faith, the baby, was all in pink wearing a frothy dress her parents had given her at birth for her to grow into and a soft, lacy cardigan knitted by her mother. Sitting sturdily, on a white heirloom shawl, crocheted by Steph's great-great-grandmother, she was giving a quizzical look at something out of shot, as if on the brink of moving to investigate something she had spotted.

'The painting has a sweet, old-fashioned quality and I love it so much it made me cry.'

It took Steph back to her fondly remembered childhood years of being her father's assistant at the easel; she knew how much work and love had gone into this.

'As if the care he had taken somehow needed to be justified, Mum said how Dad had missed me being a baby, with him being abroad most of the time. Sad he'd not been there at all to help Mum when she came home with her first, and as it turned out, only baby - me. I'd never thought about it before.

Then I turned back to Mum and frowned at what I noticed for the first time. She had bags and dark circles under her eyes and she looked pale; well, not exactly that, but more yellowish, as if she

118

*had jaundice. At this time of the year she was usually brown as a nut from gardening and trips to the coast. So I asked her if **she** was all right - I always assume my Mum is fighting fit.*

Then — and here's the thing — there was a long pause. She seemed to be deciding how to answer. 'I ... I'm sure it's nothing to worry about,' she said, at last, 'but I had a test and I've been asked to go back ...'

'What kind of test?' I asked, shocked that my essentially immortal mother could possibly be unwell. She was never ill, as far as I knew.

'Oh ... er ... blood test and a scan ... ultrasound. Look, let's not worry needlessly about something until we have to. Wait till I get the final results. No point. Is there?' She looked directly at me as if daring me to contradict, which I didn't.'

Steph closed the diary, deciding this was not good reading before sleep. It had swept her back to that time when she was eight weeks away from giving birth to Barnaby, with a week to go before she would, thankfully, cease working. Once again her boss, Ricky, was coming over from Spain. It had worked out well enough, nearly six years before, but this time Steph's assistant, Maggie, was going to be pretty much managing *House of Fitness*, overseen by Ricky.

When Faith was about nine months old, Lucas and she decided they would like another baby. It seemed sensible time-management to have two close together, maybe even three. She did not write up all the details in the diary but conception had taken longer than they'd foreseen. Making love became a bit clinical, its main aim being procreation. In fact, they even became concerned that they had an infertility problem so they were overjoyed when at last the pregnancy test proved positive, but with a five-year gap, they would have to pick up the routine of having a tiny baby all over again. She remembered worrying that Faith, not long after starting school, might be jealous of her Mum being at home with a baby taking up all her time and affection.

16

A few days after Faith returned the books to Jackson, she commented, "We had such a lovely time. Your Jackson and me."

"Oh?" Steph looked up from the report on Domiciliary Care she was reading and reached for the remote to mute the television.

"Yes. He's amazing."

Barnaby piped up from the other side of the living-room, where he was examining the contents of a puncture repair kit, "Who is this Jackson anyway?" The promised reward was to go outside to dunk the inner tube into a bucket of water and watch for bubbles, like spotting the sweep's brush pop out of the chimney-top; both fond childhood memories for Steph. "What makes him so great? You both seem a bit silly about him. If you ask me."

"Which we certainly didn't," retorted Faith.

Steph closed up the report and put it aside on the sofa. "Jackson is an old man I visit as part of my job. I try to help him – he has an illness called Parkinson's that stops him doing a lot of things and sometimes makes him shake or stop still."

Barnaby pulled a mildly sympathetic face. "Euw!"

"He's a bit more than one of your clients though Mum. I'd class him as a friend, really. Wouldn't you?" said Faith. "You must see him much more than your other people. He told me you go round about three times a week."

He told her … Really? He said so? Surely not as often as that … "I know what you mean. But I have to keep detached – not get too close. You know."

"How can you befriend and not get close? That does not make sense Mother."

"If I get too involved with one person, then others would suffer as a result. I have to spread myself quite thinly."

"But you're supposed to be taking time. I read your SSS leaflet and …"

"Yes. OK," snapped Steph, guessing that was how her daughter had picked up a word like 'befriend'. "You're right."

Faith was giving her a funny look. "Anyway, it was a sunny day and he'd got a caterer in to make us this fantastic 'spread' – that's what he called it - which we ate on his balcony overlooking his 'wilderness' – that's what he calls his garden. He does have problems with swallowing sometimes. Did you know? Anyway, it was so cool. I wish I had a Grandad like that, or even better a Dad …" She stopped as Steph put down her report, closed her eyes and held her breath for a few seconds.

"Sorry, sweet-pea. Life's not perfect, as you know."

"Mum. Sorry. I didn't mean … Can we get out the old photo-albums of Grandad – and Grandma? Where are they? I haven't seen them for … well, years."

Where indeed? Deep in thought, Steph put her report in her briefcase. She paused, deciding whether she could bear to look them out.

"I don't know. Tell me more about this lunch, then. It's more than he's ever done for me!"

"We-ell, maybe I'm more his true friend than you are. He told me about how exciting it is to see something you design actually being built, and," Faith gave a little chuckle, "how him and his wife Alison battled it out and stuff on the interior décor of *The Hideaway*...they had different ideas, you see ..."

Her sweet daughter was sticking knives in her stomach without even knowing it. Steph was jealous.

I must cut down the frequency of my visits to Jackson, Steph decided. Greg had noticed this statistically, alluding in his appraisal report to 'the considerable variation between the time and attention distributed between clients'. True some need more than others, she thought, but by and large, most averaged out; so my Jackson hours had probably peaked on some homespun graph he used to monitor my every move ... Now my daughter, and even my son, had spotted the attention I give Jackson. Am I being 'a bit silly about him', she wondered, Barnaby's observation echoing in her head?

She took stock of her work diary. She must prune her schedule, cut out a few visits, or maybe keep them unofficial, not mention them to anyone.

She was not sure what to do about Justin. Perhaps she should just keep her nose out of it. But that would feel wrong, very wrong. People apparently under his spell were suffering, or would suffer, if his nefarious goings-on were not stopped. The way he could tell lies and deceive was evident from being witness to just a couple of brief phone-calls. He might be an absolute control-freak. He could be a danger to society. She thought of previous newsworthy cases where people would say, 'Hindsight is a wonderful thing. If only we'd said something.' 'I always suspected he was a bit odd, but you don't like to interfere, do you?' 'If only we'd reported what we knew at the time.' What else might he be capable of? Rape? Paedophilia? Adrian, Tracy and the other woman he appeared to live with – they were all victims. The world is full of two-timing cheats but the smooth way he could slip from one persona to another in the blink of an eye was impressive – in a bad way. And some of what he said did not quite stack up – she wasn't sure about the Adrian, presumably his lover. She tried to think back to what Justin had actually said. It was easy to forget, confuse or misinterpret. Surely his girlfriend, Tracy, would not accept his having a gay relationship, yet he had referred to him as plain as plain when he spoke to her. No. Perhaps her overactive imagination had reached too far on that one. Adrian could be just a friend in need …

Before going to bed she had a look in the telephone directory, only to discover he was not in there, then at Justin's Twitter profile page to see if she could find mention of an Adrian. She noticed Justin and Joshua were Tweeting each other. They were probably doing Facebook too, but she did not check this. This was evidence enough; they must have found each other by some geographical search. This was worrying.

Steph slept badly that night. The following morning she awoke feeling anything but refreshed. When she had managed to slip into a broken sleep, her dreams were violent and disturbing, filled with images of her dead father, Faith, Justin, Jackson, Greg, other unknown people slipping and sliding in and out of rooms, clutching the air, laughing grotesquely.

Faith and Barnaby had left for school and she was about to leave the house, when the doorbell rang. Perhaps it was the postman with a book she had ordered online, too big to push through the letterbox.

She opened the door, dressed, ready to leave the house.

A woman stood there, not a friend or neighbour, but she looked familiar. She also looked like a person trying to suppress some kind of anger.

"I'm Joshua's mother Liz Burns." Of course, she taught at the school. "Have you a moment?" Her tone was clipped, her manner unfriendly.

"Please come in. Five minutes enough? I'm sorry but I need to be off to …"

"Yes. I'm on my way to school in any case. It's about these classes you're running. I've told Joshua that he's not to go any more." Her directness was quite intimidating.

"Oh! I believe Nick from Simulac issued some kind of consent form you signed?"

Liz looked at her blankly. "No, I never got one. I … I'll speak to Joshua about that."

"I'm so sorry, again. Obviously Nick didn't check it was returned." Steph was feeling fragile enough without this. "I thought he was doing that. Perhaps he thought I was. Oh Lord. Please sit down," she said, feeling dizzy. This was my fault, she thought. I am responsible overall.

"It's just taking up too much of his time. It's bad enough him playing so many games …"

"Oh I know, it's the same with my Barnaby. Some of them are fine, but others …"

"It's not just the kind of games. We make damn sure he only has appropriate ones! It's the time they're taking away from other things and he does not need encouragement to use social networking sites, believe me!"

"Point taken."

Liz stood up and made her way to the front door. Naturally, Steph trailed in her wake to see her out, lost in thought.

Should she tell Liz now that her son was Tweeting with Justin? She'd be furious. With a throbbing head her brain chased crisscrossing thoughts. Now was not a good time. If she fanned the flames of Liz's anger, her project and SSS might be finished, its reputation in tatters. It would be all round the school, then spread through the village like wildfire.

Steph watched Liz let herself out.

"I'd like to thank Joshua for his help – perhaps he could just drop in some time, when he's passing?" she called in desperation after Liz, but she was too far away to hear.

She could quietly advise Joshua to stay clear of Justin. Would he do this without mentioning it to his mother? She felt ashamed and guilty – corrected by a teacher, as well! A busy day ahead, she started up the car, her mind still racing.

"Should have been more *careful*," she muttered to herself, as she drove out of Appley Green. "Must put this right. Get Justin to stop Tweeting with Joshua."

She would confront Justin. That's what she'd do! After all, she had enough dirt to dish on him to be able to threaten him pretty effectively … She would at the very least find out why he was in touch with a boy of Joshua's age anyway. It was possible they just knew each other, simple as that. If it was just an innocent friendship then – fine! He would tell her that. Except that he was such a consummate liar she would never know whether to believe him …

Or, she thought, another idea clicking into place, I could first take advantage of the fact that Justin was, as yet, unaware of her existence. He was not at Willem Hardrop's when she called in; another agent had taken care of her. He had no idea of her presence on the train, for he was assuredly away in another world of his own. Maybe she should gather a little more evidence against him – his double-dealing, if not triple-dealing. She could find out a bit more about his gay partner, Adrian; she could follow Justin back to where he lives; find the poor girl, Tracy, whom he was going to clearly abandon, and the woman with whom he was allegedly going to emigrate to Spain, who was probably being used. If he were actually grooming young people as well on the Internet and was a possible danger to Joshua, then she would of course have to notify the police. But that was a massive allegation and she would need to have cast-iron backup to support it. Photographs, voice recordings …

If she ignored him, the consequences could be a lot worse. If she simply warned Liz, then it could be stirring up alarm … but if Justin turned out to be relatively harmless to young boys, where would that leave her? With gossip being what it is in a village, her reputation would be shredded.

She felt herself sinking into a place she did not want to be. Was she now about to embark on something very like blackmail? Or stalking? Or both? Worst of all this was going to gobble up time she did not have to spare. This was a massive, massive distraction from her work and from her key mission to bring Jackson in touch with his family, but it was not something she could just push under the proverbial carpet.

As she drew up outside the house for her first visit of the day, she heard herself give a little groan. Who could she turn to? She closed her eyes. There was no one.

17

Yet again, Steph's night had been disturbed. She had lain awake in the silence of the dark night, the sound of a waterfall in her ears, that turned into a pounding she realised was her own heartbeat. This cannot go on, she thought. After a fitful sleep, she awoke early and picked up the Diary. She had no time or opportunity to do this during the day and it was not good, she concluded, digging up traumatic stuff just before going to sleep.

I'm writing this from my old bedroom. Mum called this morning to say that she has inoperable cancer of the pancreas. Just like that! She sounded so matter of fact about it! "I won't be able to help so much now,"' she said. "I'm so sorry, love." She was apologising! This is terrible.

This is my second week on leave, still missing work, strangely enough; the people, the routine. Can 'put my feet up' quite a lot. Faith, now at 'big school', is easy to look after in comparison to the challenges at work - and a joy.

But now I am DIZZY with the shock of what Mum has told me. I can't quite believe it. I asked her all those questions like, "What can I do? What can I do for you? ... How are you feeling?"

Do you know what she said? "I need to take it a bit easy, they say."

I asked her what doctors actually said to her. Was she in pain?

But there was a silence down the phone. *"Don't ask. More of a nausea really and … Ask me no questions and I'll tell you no lies."* This is all she would say.

My God! How long? How long does she have? This is serious. Inoperable, she said. Can it be cured? I don't know how to ask these questions. Somehow they would not form properly from the words and fears that are crowding my panic-stricken head. And Mum doesn't seem to want to talk about it. All she was doing was apologising as if this were some mild inconvenience. Well, that's just not right.

I've dropped everything and come over to her. It's my turn to help my mother now. So here I am, with my Mum and Dad, back in my old bedroom. Lucas says he'll manage OK, though I don't quite know how, and I'll just have to flit back and forth like a headless, egg bound, chicken.'

'No diary for a bit. Too awful. Would not make good reading. Now we have our beautiful baby boy – Barnaby. Lucas is talking about giving up some of his schools. He's still hopeful for a career in music alongside teaching, but it'll be a while before we know if this will make any money. This evening is Halloween. Outside groups of children dressed up in ghoulish Halloween costumes were roaming the village and knocking on doors. Anyway, we were sitting down during a precious peaceful interlude, with Faith and Barnaby both asleep when Lucas looked up from some paperwork he was doing.

"I should build up the home tuition. It fits in better with family life," he pointed out. *"I can be here to help out with Barnaby, pick up Faith from school and you can get over to your mother."*

The cancer is too advanced for radiotherapy or chemotherapy to do much good. Treatment makes her feel so ill, she pleaded for them to stop it.

I feel riddled with guilt that my nurturing mother, always at my side when necessary, ready and willing to do ironing, shopping, cooking, reading to Faith, whatever was needed ... Even with working odd shifts at a small shop that was open all hours, she always had time for us. Meanwhile, this dark ugly beast has been growing inside her and she didn't even notice herself that there was something wrong, until it was irrevocable. Too late, too late ...

Lucas said tonight that maybe we should think about moving into a bigger house as an investment, then he could take small classes, like groups of five or six, from home. I said that now was not a good time, with Mum and everything. He put his arms around me and said he was just thinking ahead. Our future.

I think he needs to keep his options open in case he needs to go back to the schools. "Don't burn your bridges, Lucas," I said calmly, trying not to start an argument. Soon, something will have to give.'

Lucas's house-move proposition, even as a long term idea, is no good. because the fact is I might have to give up my work at the gym and get a part-time job instead. Life is all too grindingly difficult! We should be enjoying life, our little girl and our new baby, not simply battling through just to survive, to exist. Life's too short! Mum is a painful reminder of that.'

Steph reflected that people everywhere go through these things all the time. Parents die, babies are born, work comes and goes, families move house. This was the stuff of life. She remembered how she would tell herself they were lucky to both have jobs and two healthy children and over again she would count their many blessings.

'.. but if I give up my job, Lucas will have to wave goodbye to his idea of increasing our mortgage ...'

130

She was brought back to reality by Barnaby striding into the bedroom, still in his boxers. "I'm going with Faith to see wonderman," he announced.

"Excuse me?" she said, hurriedly slipping the Diary under her pillow and getting out of bed.

"Your hero bloke! You know. Faith said I could go with her."

Steph's mouth fell open. "I don't think so!" She shook her head, surprised that her daughter would go ahead and fix something like that without telling her, or asking her permission in fact. "I'll speak to her about it …"

She tapped lightly on Faith's bedroom to warn her she was coming in. "You awake?" she pushed the door open.

Faith was dressed, brushing her black wavy hair - the complete opposite of her own straight, fair hair - in front of the full-length mirror. She turned to look at Steph with an easy-going smile; she was so beautiful, a female version of Lucas, Steph felt a lump in her throat. If only Lucas could be here with them now to see how his children had turned out …

"Hi!" said Faith. "You look awful."

"Hmm. Thanks. Faith – did you tell Barnaby he could go with you to see Jackson?"

"No-o. He kept going on about it and I said I'd ask you," said Faith pulling her hair up into a scrunchie. "He took it as a definite maybe. Think he feels left out."

She had half-guessed this might happen from the start. Steph sat down on Faith's bed. "This may be getting a bit too cosy, you know. I shouldn't be involving my family as closely as this with work."

"Oh, Mum. He's more than work. A blind man could see that!"

Steph looked up sharply. "What do you mean?"

"You like him, don't you? I mean, obviously he's way too old for you, but anyone can tell you find him … er … strangely attractive."

Steph was horrified. "Faith for heaven's sake. What on earth? He's nearly ninety years old! I don't *fancy* him if that's what you mean."

"Oh, OK. But you know … there's plenty of older men these days, actors, politicians, rock-stars – beats me how, can't see it myself, but they still seem to be able to pull …"

"Faith! Enough! I do assure you that you have *completely* got the wrong end of the stick. Please. Just forget this conversation. It's absolute rubbish and I don't have time to play about with daft notions like this. Now. Barnaby. The answer is no, you can't!"

Feeling so bad-tempered, she walked out of Faith's room to take a hot shower and count to twenty.

As she half-heartedly munched a slice of toast and marmalade, standing up in the kitchen, gazing out at some leaves dancing in the breeze on her lawn that needed mowing, Steph silently tried to formulate a plan. She must do something – fast – but she was not sure what.

"I'll go there by myself then," said Barnaby, as he closed the front-door behind him. Now he was cross, hurt and disappointed and was trying to exercise some kind of clumsy revenge. She had to believe that he would not do that. They were coming up to school holidays when she could not be forever checking up on his whereabouts. He would not actually take himself off to see Jackson on his own, would he? Of course not.

She passed by Willem Hardrop, then took a step back, feigning interest in the window display. Surreptitiously peering over and between the panels filled with property details, she could make out some heads inside. There were four desks, as far as she could remember. The chiffon-scarf woman, who had looked after her and noted details of the desired bungalow for Jackson, had sat at the front on the right. She did not appear to be there today. It was harder to see who was sitting at the desks further away in the back corners, but then someone stood up and walked towards the door. It was a man. Was it? Was it Justin? As he came close she could see that it was not.

The door opened and the man with brown hair, and a round face, who was not Justin and actually nothing like him, was saying to her, "I noticed you searching for something, and clearly not finding it." He threw her a charming smile, eyes flashing. "Can I help at all? That's what we're here for."

As he stood in the doorway, she peeked inside and – yes there he was on the left at the back. He was, as ever it seemed to Steph, on the phone.

She didn't really want to go in there, although Justin did not know who she was. Then a thought struck her! She should firm up an appointment for *The Hideaway* valuation, to make sure of a time to suit the agent, her and Jackson.

"Yes," she said. "Actually, there is something …"

She followed the agent through to his desk and explained the situation. He sat, checking his screen for a moment. She noticed that Justin had now walked out the door into the village.

"Ah, yes. A visit was made yesterday." He gave her the figure estimated in the current fluctuating mar always open to change, but they were optimistic that there were the beginnings of an upward trend … de-dah, de-dah …

"Oh! But I made it absolutely clear that I should be there too."

"Well, I don't know the details. Our agent Justin Rancher did it. Unfortunately he's …"

"Just gone out. Yes," she supplied, glancing at his name sign on the desk. "This is not on, Mr Hinton. I'm really not pleased about this. Mr Jeffreys is very frail, needs things carefully planned out, warning, you know? In fact, he is a very vulnerable old man."

Vulnerable. Yes. With that maniac Justin turning up and probably giving his place unwelcome close scrutiny and a highly inflated valuation to ensure the business, he would be physically, mentally and financially *vulnerable.*

Steph hastened away down the street feeling confused and overwhelmed, not knowing what to do next. Check on Jackson? Go to the school to see Liz? This could wait. Text Joshua? His mobile number was somewhere among the list of computer club members so they could be contacted in the event of a cancellation. It was important to check out Justin before she started raising alarm bells with Liz. She had been through all this before! Her head was swirling wildly with a plethora of information she was trying to sift through.

Something inside her head was re-sorting her priorities, ranking them into order of importance, as if of its own volition.

would get on with the today's scheduled visits as had happened; it would be wise to avoid ntion to any of this by recklessly abandoning ents for the day. Greg's eagle eyes would ns at a distance of a hundred metres.

Then there was the slight risk of Barnaby rocking up at *The Hideaway* unannounced – no, he wouldn't do that, would he? A boy of eleven *could* do it, easily, but surely would realise how furious she would be with him.

There was no reply from Jackson's number. It was a bit early for him. Maybe he was still in bed. But no, his carer would have been in by now. She could check with his carer's agency to see if he was OK. Her fingers flicked through the numbers on her mobile; she didn't have theirs. It was on her laptop and that was in the boot of her car. She walked at a brisk pace back to the car and found the number. It kept ringing and ringing until a recorded message kicked in at the agency.

If Jackson had been intimidated or harmed in any way … No, no, no, her imagination was getting over-excited. Justin was just doing his job, after all. He would be fine. But why had he gone ahead without her, when she *expressly* said she must be included in the appointment? But, she would have heard. Surely. SSS would have been notified. That was *her*. SSS. Main point of contact. But if the carer had found him distressed, or lying on the floor from having tried to open the front-door by himself, or … Would they have contacted her? *Would they?*

She collected her thoughts. Justin would be subtler than this. He was a con man! He would gain Jackson's confidence, insinuate himself into his life to somehow gain from the situation … But on his way out, he would be eyeing the valuables. Instinct told her that she must check out Jackson. She could skip one of her scheduled appointments; this would not cause a problem. The remaining vortex of troubles into which she felt herself tumbling would have to wait their turn.

At least Justin had not seen her and she knew he was based there today. He had left the Willem Hardrop 'shop'

– maybe he had gone for the day on appointments, or maybe he would come back to his desk. The ideal would be if he left the premises this evening; she could watch him from a little distance and follow him back home. She might then see where he lived – would this be his home with woman number two, or the flat he shared with Adrian? Or would he go off to see the other one, Tracy?

Trying to cope with the day's workload, her mind bouncing from one thing to another, Steph did a quick rethink on the Jackson-Barnaby issue. Her son was feeling excluded; he could be a stubborn child and would be awkward until he got his way. She could not just give in now, but perhaps there was a way round this where she could relent and save face.

On her way to her second scheduled home visit of the day, she passed close by the drive to *The Hideaway* flanked by huge rhododendron bushes. As her car approached she felt herself being tugged as if she were a pile of iron-filings in the near presence of a magnet. Checking the time on the dashboard clock, she veered off towards the house to see if Jackson was there. This went against her best advice of *never* turning up without warning, as he might have trouble getting to the door, panic and trip.

She rang the doorbell three times and paced around, heart pounding. Why oh why was everything going wrong, so very wrong? Everything she touched seemed to turn to dust. She pulled out her mobile from her jacket pocket, as perverse proof she was no longer thinking rationally, as if further proof were needed, for she realised she should have tried to call him again, after her first foiled attempts when he was probably still in bed or before his first dose of pills had taken effect … She put her hand to her forehead in disbelief, as her phone blanked. Empty battery! With so much to distract her, now she was neglecting the most mundane tasks, things she usually did automatically without a second thought. Plug in, recharge every other evening to be on the safe side ... but she hadn't.

She walked around the house to take a squint through the windows. She had to put her face up against the glass to peer into the ground-level study where Jackson would, on a normal day, be sitting in his solitary state, perhaps making a phone-call or reading. Blackmail a possibility, stalking a reality – now prowling! The back of his leather chair was at an oblique angle away from her view. The room seemed very quiet and empty. Dead. Then she glimpsed his arm, then his softly quivering hand on the arm of the chair. She breathed a sigh of relief. He had his hearing aid switched off and had not heard the doorbell, she supposed.

She did not know what she had been expecting, but he was safe in his chair, which meant the carer had been in and he was dressed, breakfasted, medicated. Business as usual.

Her reassurance was incomplete. She was still frustratingly in the dark as to what transpired during Justin's valuation visit, apart from the obvious fact that he would have traipsed around the house, up and down stairs, to measure and view and describe, with Jackson feebly left behind, unable to do a thing about it.

But she proceeded with her day's work and matters of apparently lesser importance that could be addressed with a *relatively* cool head. All things are relative, she decided.

"I just need to slip out to the shops – I'll be about an hour," she said casually to Faith and Barnaby. It was nearly five o'clock, when Willem Hardrop closed for the day. Guilt burned in her cheeks, as she thought of all the

137

times she had reprimanded them if she detected so much as a faint whiff of a lie. Honesty was always the best policy, of course it was. But, somehow this was different. If they were older, they would understand.

They barely looked up. It did make life easier now that Faith was old enough to 'babysit'; so difficult before when, every time she wanted to leave the house at a time when Barnaby was at home, she had to take him along. Food shopping was not his favourite thing.

She successfully pursued Justin, he in his silver convertible, she in her rather battered but inconspicuous dark blue hatchback. He had turned into Cowslip Lane, a narrow country road with overgrown verges, overhung with silver birches and beech trees that formed a green tunnel, barely more than a single track with passing places here and there. Then he braked and pulled off into a small gravel drive.

She slowed down, at this point feeling rather conspicuous. She still did not want him to see her, so drove on until she could turn around. So now she knew where he lived. Still unsure of what she would do with this information, she went on to Waitrose to justify her trip out.

Back at her laptop, with the small basket of provisions put away and a meal cooking on the hob, she called out to Barnaby, "Barney bear, come down here a minute could you!"

She could hear him coming downstairs, no doubt expecting a meal, "Where's dinner?" he asked, looking around.

"Won't be long! Mexican chilli beef with nachos – your favourite. Can't you smell it cooking? Mmm, delicious."

"I like tuna pasta bake now."

Steph knew he was being deliberately difficult and ignored this.

"Can you show me how to do this? It's gone all funny and I don't know how to undo it."

She pointed to the words on the screen, after 'accidentally' pressing the Insert button. "You see! Every time I type a letter it just replaces the one before. Completely mad!"

Barnaby smiled smugly. "You just need to press this – here, look."

"Oh! Easy when you know, isn't it? Thanks, clever-clogs. Hey, do you know, you might be able to help me out with Jackson. Perhaps next time I go, after schooltime, you could bring your laptop and show him how to do a few things. He would like that, I think. But just for one visit. Is it a deal?"

She felt fairly confident it would be enough to satisfy Barnaby's curiosity and make him feel included. Her son's idea of using the computer would not inspire Jackson particularly, but it would solve the problem of Barnaby feeling miffed. If she had thought Jackson would take to using a computer 'just like that', she might have organised something just for him without setting up the class. Much easier! But she knew Jackson too well. He would have felt he was being too much bother. He would be horrified at being singled out for special attention, which would take up hours of one-to-one home tuition that could never be justified for an individual client.

"Yeah! Thanks, Mum!" It was worth it to see the look of delight, perhaps triumph on his little face. He wasn't even attempting to be aloof and cool about it.

She did not like this feeling she had inside. She felt, yes, dishonest. Manipulative, even. It felt deeply uncomfortable, but she could see no other way to overcome her many current difficulties.

After she was sure both Faith and Barnaby were sleeping soundly and, despite feeling utterly drained, she opened up Twitter. Driven to find out as much as she could as soon as possible, she tried to find some evidence of communication between Justin and Adrian; and Justin and Joshua. As she was 'following' both of them she was able to at least catch snatches of any such chatter going on.

On the first couple, Justin and Adrian, after scrolling through endless Tweets, there seemed to be nothing. But of course if they were sometime-cohabiters, sexual partners, or even close friends, they would have scant need to use Twitter to communicate. That made sense.

Then she found something that made her sit up very straight and still, squinting at the screen.

Joshua Burns, nicknamed Gameking, was pretending to be a young adult, rather unconvincingly - in fact it would be transparently obvious to any other adult - and there was some arrangement, a meeting with Justin! Rats. She put her head in her hands. Her worst fears come true. Should she tell the police? How old was he? Fifteen? Younger? This did look very dodgy. Should she tell Liz? If she did, it would be seen as all her fault – that would be the end of the Computer Club, maybe of SSS, and she would have to disband her efforts to get Jackson using the Internet and reaching his family by email and Skype. All would be lost. It was twelve minutes past one. Her mind was swarming with possibilities as adrenaline notched up her heart rate, pulse and brain.

How had it come to this? As soon as possible, she must find Justin and confront him.

18

Certain her current state of mind would lead to even worse nightmares, and desperate to escape, Steph could not resist the temptation to retreat into the past, even though she knew it would not make easy reading. It was an undesirable choice, the proverbial rock and a hard place. Her past or the present, which was worse?

'Dad seems to have locked himself away in a world of his own, unable to cope. It's all too much for him. Spent most of today with Mum. Oh God! She's going downhill so fast I can't bear it, but at least she's getting the best possible care at the hospice. I try to make her comfortable, make her smile even, but what can you do when it gets to this stage?

When I stepped into the kitchen where Lucas was busy at the sink, he turned to look at me despairingly, knowing that there was little he could say or do to help. He had fed Barnaby with a bottle of expressed breast-milk and both baby and Faith were asleep upstairs. He's so brilliant. I know what a busy evening he must have had.

Our little flat seemed a haven of peace and comfort, yet I know Lucas had also fitted in a keyboard and a guitar lesson, regular fixtures on a Wednesday evening at four and five o'clock. He's like a cob swan, I often tell him, all serenity above the water, with his feet paddling away underneath, working to keep them afloat. Yet his hard work teaching pays what most would consider below a proper living wage. It's erratic too.'

Steph lay back in bed, somehow unable to let the Diary go. She held it tight to her chest, all the memories locked away in its pages. If she had known where all this was leading would she have done things differently?

He took me in his arms and held me, allowing me to sob for a while into his shoulder.

All this is destroying our sex life – what with me having felt like a beached whale and stressed over Mum. No spare energy. Now a small baby, so much hungrier and more demanding than Faith, is depriving us both of sleep. My lover must be feeling so frustrated, poor lamb.

Thank goodness I have Lucas, best partner in the world. Best friend. Lover, yes. Still sometimes wish I could say 'husband'. It would make Mum really happy to see me, her only daughter, actually married before ….

Not all Dads help out like he does. I love him so, so much.

It went through my mind - Could I suggest we get married for Mum's sake? No. It just sounds wrong. I can't use her in that way.

Gorgeous spicy smells were coming from the oven where a chicken birani was slow-cooking. He's perfect enough – partner or husband, what does it matter? Why am I even playing with such romantic ideas at a time like this? Perhaps part of me is trying to escape from the horrible reality coming up.

After eating some of the chicken and rice (which was meltingly soft to eat, as if Lucas had thoughtfully guessed I would barely have the energy to chew), he said, "Guess what's for pudding." He was trying to cheer me up, I know that and loved him the more for it, even if it was not really working.

I thought of Mum who struggles to force down a few sips of beef consommé.

It was my favourite, that chocolate pudding he does with rum in it.

Life goes on. Lucas knows that. One thing I know for sure is that he will never let me down.'

'At first I had to smile to see Lucas studying a budget spreadsheet on his laptop! with a full analysis of our incomings and outgoings. It struck me as very out of character. But he was stroking his stubbly chin and frowning, like he does when he's really concentrating.

"The two schools I gave up, the ones that are further away …" he began, thoughtfully, as if thinking aloud. "I … it was hasty. You were right. I realise that now but I can't get them back in a hurry so …" He raked his fingers which, I noticed were trembling, through his tousled black hair. "I'll have to find more home pupils, as I thought I would anyway …"

I suppose I've burnt my bridges on maternity rights. Yesterday I called Ricky to say I wouldn't be able to go back as full-time manager and he was straight with me. He said he can't hold it open for me or offer it as a job-share or anything like that. He was really sorry.

It's always been more than a full-time job; so he was right. It would be difficult to split in half and Maggie is more than ready for promotion. I am no longer indispensable! So I said I understood and hope to get something else when the time comes, when Barnaby is perhaps two or so, just part-time. Lucas was understanding and said **then** he would do all he could to retrieve his old work at local schools, and further afield if necessary.

But, oh boy, **now** he is saying he can't. He can't get the work back from his old schools – it's gone to another teacher.

He looked up from the screen and nodded, saying, "Our savings will keep us going for a few months … so we should be fine." He squeezed my arm, but I looked at his drawn face and could see real worry in his eyes.'

144

'Mum has gone. It took three days and nights for her to finally let go, as her organs softly and silently closed down. Nobody could say it was unexpected, but her last few months have flown by and the finality of losing her is still a huge shock. I feel ... scared I suppose. Mum has always been there, always my champion.'

'I wasn't prepared for the ache I feel, the terrible void left by losing my Mum. Dad is bereft and, usually one for hiding his feelings, rarely showing any kind of what he would regard as weakness, seems inconsolable. I cannot get him to open up. He says now he can't face attending the funeral, which I said he must do. Our conversation went something like this:

"Dad, I know it's hard ..."

"How can you know?"

"I've lost my mother. It's hard for me too."

"How will I manage without her? Thirty-nine years we've been together."'

'Dad faced the funeral bravely in the end, welcoming old friends and relatives, looking almost detached from reality, a bit of a 'cold fish' as Mum would have coined it. Suppressing his real feeling I suppose but it almost seemed as if he didn't care. I'm not sure which is worse, the wallowing self-pity or the stony face.'

'Dad comes over to see us from time to time. He tries to help, but often drops things or trips over a toy and then says he's sorry and 'always getting in the way'.

Today he said, "I'm not much use with babies. Your mother used to take care of all that side of things."'

Steph thought about that, wondering how much longer she could keep her eyes open to read, before sleep took over. Certainly when she was a small baby he was posted abroad with the army, until he was demobbed and came back to work at a newly opened garden centre and to pursue his love of painting. She was about three when he came to live at home permanently and, apparently awestruck at this relative stranger, this was when she took to watching him at work with oils on a canvas. It helped them, like nothing else, to get to know each other. As he painted, they would chat; a few years on, he would tell her all kinds of things about when he was a boy, how he met Molly, then even things that she realised much later her mother, Molly probably knew nothing about, like previous lost loves. As she grew, she supposed he got carried away, forgetting that his confidante was not really old enough to fully understand, or perhaps that was why he could talk so freely … her memory of their conversations was naturally vague, it was so long ago, but the spirit of the time they spent together would always be with her. He made her feel special and helpful, grown-up and important …. then later he passed on his experience of building up a business, leading a team of people. She owed a lot of her success at *House of Fitness* to him.

'I said to him, as I looked at his pitifully anxious face. "Of course you are, Dad. Barnaby loves you and so does Faith."

"Grandad, I love you when you play with me and bring me presents," said Faith, right on cue and looking exceptionally cute.'

'Months go by and money just gets tighter and tighter. Unpaid bills are mounting up and we are in debt. I shall have to find full-time work to get us out of this.

Lucas is adamant I shouldn't, reckons Faith and Barnaby will suffer. He seems unhappy even with the idea of part-time but reluctantly agrees that this may be necessary.'

She could not bear to read any more.

146

19

Greg had revisited Appley Green and taken another wander around. He noticed a village notice-board outside a hall that used to be St Saviour's church. He read the bit about its history. There appeared to be two hamlets, with one church apiece, grown together to form the village today; the Green appeared to be the lynchpin that held them together. There had been a church on this site since Norman times, but latterly the current building had fallen into disuse.

He glanced at another poster, immediately spotting the SSS logo. Was this the computer class Steph was organising? It must be. He was a little puzzled by the wording. Maybe he would look in on their next session; it might be a nice surprise for Steph. She had this way of ploughing on with things and not always asking him for the support which, he was beginning to acknowledge, she did actually deserve. She bore, quite uncomplainingly, an enormous weight of responsibility in her job.

I must get over my qualms about computers and be more supportive of her, he decided, as he crossed the greensward of the village Green. He once regularly used the Internet and email but had lost trust and was certain that the elderly were especially vulnerable. Two friends had suffered from identity theft from fraudsters with proven links to online activity and there was all the hype in the media, Wikileaks revelations, and so on. Every day he heard something in the news that would put him off.

Paedophiles on social networking sites! He had also suffered financially from the dotcom bubble bursting on the stock market a few years ago. Maybe he had over-reacted, but he just decided to steer clear; some people probably thought he had technology phobia!

It was a beautiful, warm, cloudless day with no sign of rain. After a bite to eat, he would explore some of the alleys and back lanes, really get a feel for the place, its history, its community. He had heard there was a small museum, mostly to do with military activity in the area, much of the surrounding heath being army-owned land used for training. Sometimes you could actually hear guns firing, so he had been told. A blessing in disguise, he supposed, that had thus far saved Appley Green from being swallowed up in suburban sprawl.

He picked up the local paper, a good way to get an instant flavour of events and opinions, then called at the bakery to purchase a taste of 'local fare' in the form of a beef baguette; the beef not produced nearby and a baguette hardly the most English of traditions in baking. However, they did a few prepared rolls and sandwiches around lunchtime and it felt good that the young woman serving seemed to remember him from the time before when he bought a granary loaf and some flapjacks. This was a day when he felt more retired than at work and yet, today somehow he felt guilty for not being fully and gainfully employed. He was far too young to be even semi-retired, he suddenly decided.

He returned to the same bench seat he sat on before, managing to secure it just after an elderly couple laden with shopping bags had risen to continue their walk perhaps back home. He could quietly observe the Appley Green world go by and browse through the local news.

An article on page 5 caught his eye. It was about Simulac and looked rather like an advertorial, one of those feature advertisements that purport to be an impartial bit of reporting but are in fact paid advertising. But no, this was genuine editorial. The local company was helping out people in Appley Green to become easy with computers and the Internet, especially the silver-surfers. Simulac was praised for its 'generous and commendable community spirit'. Then he frowned. Wasn't Simulac the company logo on the poster publicising Steph's class? She had told him the project was just for word-processing.

He felt troubled by this deception. Did Steph think he would not have listened to her arguments, to her reasons for doing this? She knew about his deep reservations and doubts. He folded the newspaper, frowning as he thought about this, feeling keenly disappointed that she had not given him the complete truth. Suddenly the day did not seem so golden. What else was she hiding from him?

20

Faith was meeting friends in Bloomstock and Barnaby had trooped off to the local playing-fields; so Steph knew she had a very rare hour or two alone at home in peace and quiet.

Today was my birthday. I was really taken aback when Lucas announced that we were going out. He'd arranged a babysitter and everything – even found a registered childminder, called Sheena. I was a bit unsure that we could afford to go out – anywhere. But Lucas was determined – and seemed very excited about something. His eyes were shining and he was singing as he chased me around the flat to help me get ready to go. He said he had a surprise.

I trusted him. Tonight was the first time we've even contemplated going out in the evening since Barnaby was born, or even since Mum died.

We sat at a table for two in a cosy nook of The Fox and Rabbit in Appley Green, basking in the flickering heat of a log-fire blazing in an inglenook that once provided local people with an oven for baking bread. Although nearly spring, evenings are still cool. It felt so romantic, I wondered why we hadn't done this before.

(For whoever might read this – grandchildren? In years gone by the inn was a staging-post for carriages and drovers who drew many highwaymen to their routes through the wild heath land. It's now a great favourite with local people. Just thought you'd like to know.)

Almost as soon as we were settled, Lucas came out with his short-lived secret he was clearly struggling to keep to himself.

150

He folded the menu and leaned towards me. "Good news!" he said.

Well, he's got a part-time teaching job that will fit in perfectly with everything else. The best possible birthday present! He explained that it was a post teaching Drama, just temporary. A teacher at Heathfields had to resign – totally unexpectedly. Health issues. Not good news for the teacher concerned but …

I didn't know he was qualified for this but when I asked him he looked quite insulted! Apparently he studied Drama as subsidiary at Music College. I never knew that. He said he loved it and, although he has no real professional experience, he's a fast learner.

And I've never seen a grown man bubble with enthusiasm before!'

'This job really did come along at the right time. Lucky, lucky, lucky. Will pull us out of a financial hole, anyway. Lucas scarcely gets more than four hours sleep at night fitting all the pieces of his life together!'

'I am a bit worried about Lucas. He's looking thin and a bit gaunt. He's throwing himself into theatricals like a man possessed. But this morning before he went off he reassured me, "Not just a stop-gap you know. This will be a way forward too, Stephie." Our future certainly does seem bright now. I had to laugh at him as he packed up a box with a bizarre mixture of props and tools: a bobble hat; vase; screwdriver; an old framed abstract picture we pushed out of the way under the bed once Faith's portrait painting took its place on the living-room wall; a table-lamp and a four-way block; a saucepan and Barnaby's teddy with the tartan trousers. He kept asking if he could borrow these things for a drama lesson. He said he wanted the kids "to act ex tempore, you know, improvise," he said. 'They're terrific when you let them off the lead, especially the ones who're hung up on poor reading skills."

151

He smacked a big kiss on my cheek. "I love this, you know," he said. "With a successful production in my portfolio I can scale up to an even better permanent teaching post. In tandem with music, it's a winner. Give up the piecemeal stuff – which is never going to make us rich, is it? Onwards and upwards!" He then enclosed me in his arms and gave me a long lingering kiss, sharing his optimism with me, reminding me that I am part of his passion for life. I could feel his passion for me too, pressing hard against my stomach. "I love you, but," he said, pulling back reluctantly and looking at me cheekily, "I guess, we'll have to wait until tonight."

He went off whistling and I feel so happy. Perhaps our troubles really are over.'

'The last diary entry was a while ago, but I've not written anything since because later that day, just after I'd given Barnaby some chicken and carrot purée and was about to undo my shirt to round off his lunch with a quick feed, came the phone call.

Lucas had been trying to fix some stage lighting on his own, they said, perched on a tall ladder which tipped.

Five days before his play for Easter, my darling Lucas fell to his death.'

Steph sat still for about an hour, staring at the bookshelves, yet seeing nothing. She had disappeared inside her own head, as hot tears ran freely down her cheeks. After all these years, she wondered how life could be so cruel, and it's not as if it stopped there.

Faith was working on their living room table, composing something on her laptop. Steph was sitting back in an armchair, fighting bad memories and sick with worry, but apparently considering her current work diary for the coming few days. It had some unusual entries marked in pencil she intended to erase once they were firmed up in her mind.

She looked up at her daughter who seemed lost in concentration; Faith would soon be working for her A' levels and was hell-bent on getting good grades, as she had for every other exam.

"What are you busy with? Working during the holidays?" asked Steph, curious.

"Oh, it's a story for a competition. But I'm thinking about what my teacher said last year about writing styles." Faith sighed. "I like English, but my teacher says sometimes that in my arguments 'I can't see the wood for the trees'. I'm never quite sure what he means. What do you think, Mum?"

Steph thought for a moment in the context of A level English. "Well, it's something to do with losing focus of the main theme. Letting too much detail obscure the obvious or what is really important."

"Yeah. Thought so," groaned Faith. "I go off all over the place away from the subject ... I know I do."

"Well, if it helps I did too, when I was at school, writing essays and stories."

"It only helps if you can tell me you got out of the habit. Otherwise I am just *doomed*!" she replied, with mock gravity.

They both laughed, but Steph stopped to think. In business reports she needed to be concise and all the facts had to be relevant.

"I think there's hope for you," she assured her daughter. "You've taken the most important step already."

"Which is?"

"Recognising the problem."

"Oh, stop being wise and make me a cup of hot chocolate," teased Faith, tapping away again.

"Cheeky."

Steph returned to her work schedule. She must somehow get through the school summer holiday with Barnaby still in one piece. It was always a juggling act, with him going off to friends' houses or the village youth club. There were her work appointments tomorrow involving three home visits and a meeting with the local branch of Age UK at someone's house, luckily close to where they lived. Her gaze focused on those other pencilled-in entries: *11.30 Justin at Willem Hardrop*; then in brackets she had written in *(Joshua/Liz)* – this would depend on the outcome of her meeting with Justin, which was ostensibly to discuss the valuation of *The Hideaway* he had done without her, but really to quiz him on what a lying villain he was.

She had already seen Jackson and asked him about Justin's visit and, to Steph at least, he seemed evasive.

"Yes, the young man from Willem Hardrop came along. Thank you for arranging this so quickly."

"My pleasure." Anxious for him to say more, she tried to keep calm, and waited for him to speak.

He cleared his throat and took a deep breath. Steph was used to this; it helped him to find the strength to speak at length. "Nice enough chap. Very helpful and I was happy with the estimate. They always err on the optimistic side, though, I realise that, but if they go too high there'll be no offers to buy, in which case he'll make no money at all. So, have to credit him with some common sense, don't you think, my dear?"

"But did you let him wander around the house?"

"Of course I did!"

"Weren't you worried?"

154

"It's his job. I had to let the man do his job, mm?"

"So you trusted him?"

Jackson gave her a quizzical look. "You know, sometimes, and forgive me for being personal, but sometimes my dear, you strike me as someone who has been seriously let down. By a man. Or men. Am I right, Stephanie?"

Yes, he seemed to be going off the subject, she felt, really not paying proper attention to the point at hand. She took his question to be a rhetorical one and laughed it off.

However, it seemed that he must have had some concerns. "Anyway," he said, leaning forward and patting her arm. "I had my CCTV on!"

She had no idea he had closed circuit television cameras installed in his house.

"You see, this house was 'state of the art' and as soon as this new technology became available, I had hidden cameras put in. They're all over the house."

She was flabbergasted. "So where are the screens?" She wondered if there were 'bugs' hidden in plant-pots too.

"Oh, in a section of a back bedroom, behind a partition."

"This all sounds very 007. Did you take a look at his activities, then? His movements around your house?" It must have been an ordeal to get up the stairs on his own, for his own bedroom was now on the ground floor. How many other things about his house, his life, had he not revealed to her?

"I did. He was quite proper and did nothing untoward as far as I could tell."

Steph still felt unconvinced. Maybe Justin was, at times, out of camera shot.

She was quite looking forward to further investigations now, to hear Justin's account of his visit to *The Hideaway*. Then she would slide the conversation into other areas.

Further on in her week, there was another Computer Club session, and she was due to meet with Greg. He had asked her out to lunch. How very odd, she thought.

Faith closed up her laptop. "I'll make myself a drink, then. Do you want one?"

Steph gave herself a little shake as if to wake herself up. "Oh, sweetheart, I'm sorry. I was actually going to do that, but …"

"I know. You're thinking about something else. It's how you are these days Mum. I'm kind of getting used to you only being half here even when we are in the same room, but is it likely to go on for much longer? I mean, is there something going on? Money? Man problems?" Faith pulled a face, as if embarrassed, yet genuinely wanting to find out what was troubling her mother, and Steph could see all this from the way she screwed up her face, just as she always had as a little girl when she was unsure of herself.

As Faith passed by on the way to the kitchen, Steph caught her hand to give it an affectionate squeeze, "I'm OK, but it feels really good to have someone ask me. I feel better already."

"Well, you're easily pleased. Now do you want a drink?"

"Thanks – yes I'll have a nice cup of tea. Thanks. There are some cinnamon and sultana buns in the cake tin …"

They sat down together and Faith, tucking her legs under her on the sofa, looked at her pensively, as if not quite satisfied with the answer her mother had provided.

Steph had often confided in her daughter, but only up to a point. It was easy to slide into a mode of chat more suited to a friend or sister; she had to remind herself how young Faith was, although she seemed wise beyond her years sometimes.

"It must be hard visiting old folks all the time. A bit depressing?" Faith said, rather like a counsellor trying to get a client to open up.

"No. Strangely I love my work. It's the most satisfying thing in the world. You know that without your efforts, they would be that much worse off."

"But some of them are hopeless cases, aren't they?"

"Oh Faith! I'd never say that. There's always something that can be done." Steph found herself unable to say too much. She could not confess her fears about Justin and Joshua, it was so far removed from her job description, although ... "At school, do you get guidance on using the Internet, I mean not how to use it, but ..."

Faith laughed. "Mostly we can tell the teachers how to do stuff!"

Steph frowned. "But do they warn you about what not to do – like meeting strangers and all that kind of thing?"

"Course they do."

"Good. I guess they assume parents put down some rules too, though. Protect with passwords and that kind of thing."

Faith shrugged and yawned. "Guess so. You think the old people need to have some warnings too? About meeting toy-boys and young girls that might lead them astray?" she asked with a cheeky grin.

Steph smiled, thoughtfully. "Well, actually, I am sure they could be quite vulnerable to other things –

fraudsters and conmen. Older people may be more trusting and they're often targeted by bad people. I don't know, but it does concern me." Was she leaning towards Greg's beliefs, she wondered?

"I forgot to tell you about when I saw Jackson last week."

"Well, you told me you'd been to see him."

"Yes, but I forgot to tell you he's coming in to the school to give a talk."

Steph felt herself blush with the surprise. She should be pleased. It was the kind of thing that SSS strove to encourage, participating in the community. Yet, hand on heart, she found the news deflating.

She feigned delight. "Oh, that sounds wonderful – is he happy about that?" Would he be up to it, she wondered, protectively?

"It was his idea! But I said I'd check it out with the school and I did. They're really keen. The teacher will collect him and take him home. I was able to explain to her about his problems – like he'll need a microphone and just be able to do about half an hour, sitting down."

"What is he going to talk about?"

"His career, I guess. Not sure exactly."

Steph did not like to ask if she could come along. Yet she felt somehow absurdly jealous that she was not part of the plan. Why had she not thought of this brilliant idea herself?

21

Steph was greeted by Justin himself at the Willem Hardrop Estate Agents' 'shop'. His firm handshake was a good one, as if he had had training for it; not too long, or limp, or intimate. Nonetheless, she felt herself recoil from his oily, salesman charm. How could she have ever seen a resemblance between Lucas and this snake?

"How are you today?" he asked brightly, indicating the chair as if she could not see it for herself. Maybe he was just trying to appear cool and courteous.

"I'm well thank you." She looked at his tidy desk. His mobile phone lay close to hand; the sight of it reminded her to switch hers off for the duration of this chat. She thought back to when she had heard him speaking on his and wished with all her heart she had never been on that train at that time. "Have you lived in Appley Green long?" she asked, making small talk but, reasonably enough, ascertaining his knowledge of the area.

"I began here about five years ago, but worked in Bloomstock before that. Moved as my wife had a house here. A vacancy came up and it seemed sensible and convenient to move. Lovely village, Appley Green."

His wife? She could sense he was used to bonding with people. He looked at her with an open, honest expression but disappointing mud-coloured eyes.

"Yes, lucky old us! I agree. An amazing mix of people live here."

He nodded. "Now – you have come about the valuation on *The Hideaway*." He slid across a folder to the centre of his desk and opened it up.

"Yes. I should've been at the house when you went there. Perhaps there was some misunderstanding about that?" Concealing the anger she felt inside, she could hardly credit her own acting abilities.

"So my colleague told me. I can only apologise for that. The original appointment we made with Mr Jeffrys was cancelled due to the breakdown of my car; the plan was originally to co-ordinate with you. Once my car was fixed I had to catch up on visits and was passing his drive. I thought I would try and re-arrange, but he came to the door and said I could do it there and then." He sounded so businesslike. Straight as a die!

She was unsure whether to believe his entirely plausible story. But what reason was there not to? She could double-check with Jackson later.

"Did you try calling him first?"

"Of course. I didn't have a mobile number for him so I left a message, as his answer-phone was on, to say I would be with him in five minutes. I did not assume he was actually out. I understood that he has Parkinson's and would need time to get to the door or even the phone. Is that right?"

He gave her a disarming smile.

"Yes, that is right."

"It was the best I could do in the circumstances. I thought it was fairly urgent to get the valuation done, and certainly from our point of view, if I am *honest*," Steph raised her eyebrows at this concept, "we would not want to give any prospective customer the opportunity to turn to a competitor. If Mr Jeffrys had been unhappy with me arriving on spec, he would not have been at the door to welcome me, I guess!"

His logic seemed flawless. They discussed the state of the market, the price quoted and estimated the probability of offers. He handed her the printed brochure.

"Did he ask you to prepare this already?" She flicked through it and noticed old photographs of it as a newly built house; Jackson must have loaned them to him to scan in.

"With digital print making it all so easy, we do it almost routinely, at this early stage in the process. For a property of this calibre, obviously we will have it produced in an even more glossy format."

"Is it actually up For Sale then?"

"Not yet, no. Mr Jeffrys said to wait a while. Something to do with his family coming to see him?"

"Oh. I see." *His family is coming to see him.* She filed this away in her brain.

She realised this was her one and only opportunity to find out about other matters and decided that, with his reasonable approach so far, she should grasp the nettle and go for it. She would just ask him straight and voice her concerns in plain English.

"Justin, do you mind if I ask you some questions?"

"Of course. Fire away. I can't promise all the right answers, but will do my best."

"No, no. It's about something else. A few weeks ago, I … I noticed you on Twitter. I saw that you arranged to meet a schoolboy called Joshua. I know him. He lives in Appley Green and I am concerned that he is pretending to be older than he is .."

"Oh sure, could that be Gameking? Wow, is he just a teenager? He fooled me, I must say."

She looked at him straight in the eye. "I was just curious to know why were you arranging to meet him. Knowing his real age, as I do. What's he up to? He's only fourteen."

"Oh God. Yes, I can see how that might look. We were going to swap games – just meet up on the Green one evening and maybe go for a pint or two … You see, I really thought he was an adult. Wow! I'm really glad you told me. Thanks for that. And no wonder he decided not to show up!"

"Will you unfollow him and block him so he cannot follow you?"

"Yes. I will." This was all going too well. "But I'll explain why to him first of all and warn him never to deceive people online …"

At this point Steph had to stop herself from jumping out of her chair. She lowered her voice to say, "Deceive? You would know about that, wouldn't you, Justin. Deception?" She had the presence of mind to speak quietly and appear calm, thus not attracting attention from others in the room.

He was caught in the full glare of her eyes, however, and sat back in his chair, clearly alarmed at the turn the conversation was taking. His face had turned the colour of a parsnip, Steph noticed.

"Excuse me?"

"Justin. I have been … mm … concerned since I overheard you. It wasn't deliberate, but there was no avoiding it. Do you recall a conversation, actually two conversations, you had on your mobile phone on the train from London, one evening about a month ago? Two women. One Tracy? Plans to live in Marbella?"

He closed his eyes and put his hands over his face. "Oh, ff … You heard all that?"

She nodded and he clammed up, guilt written all over him. Like a rabbit in the headlights, he froze for a minute before muttering,

"Look, I can and will explain, though it's ..." He paused and Steph guessed he was stopping himself from saying *none of your business*. "... complicated. Please hear me out. Not now. Certainly not here." He was so polite, no wonder he managed to pull the wool over women's eyes.

"Where would suit you? When?"

"Perhaps away from Appley Green ...?"

"Not too far. I'm working."

"Er ... there's a little park in Bloomstock near the council offices with some bench seats. How about lunchtime today? One o'clock?"

Steph had a client to fit in. It was already noon.

"I have a visit to make on the west side of Appley Green. Make it one-thirty?" It would be tight, but this was too important to wait.

He was as keen to talk as she was to listen, it seemed. No doubt he would try and lie his way through the whole thing.

As she left, she felt herself shaking. What had she done? What was she getting herself into? Hopefully, the Joshua situation was saved, without either him or his mother, Liz, needing to know that she was involved. And Jackson was safe. She breathed a huge sigh of relief on that one.

22

Despite all her present troubles, Steph had a burning need to remind herself of how she could have been so stupid, so reckless, so blind that she came to marry Richard. With all the benefits of hindsight it seemed now beyond belief. The Diary would help transport her back to how she fell into the trap. It was late and she should be asleep, but the lure of the diary was becoming irresistible.

Barnaby has learned to roll over and over like a little barrel. Soon be crawling, bless him!

Today Dad made an astonishing pronouncement, all things considered. He came over and was unusually fussy over Barnaby, having arrived with a bag full of presents: big soft building blocks, plastic animals and, rather oddly, some paints …

As she read this she remembered how odd this seemed. Barnaby was not quite ready for paints!! but of course these were long-term presents …

He played Snakes and Ladders with Faith and gave her some goodies too: a doll, a little sequinned bag, colouring pencils and some jelly babies. They were rather quaint things and he'd obviously chosen them himself.

Then he said it. "I've decided to go back home. To live, I mean." He spoke sadly, unable to look me in the eye. I felt as if I'd been punched in the stomach. Surely I'd misheard or misunderstood. By 'home' he means Somerset, where his older brother and younger

*sister live. I know he still has really old friends, from schooldays,
who lived near Taunton and many nieces and nephew, but even so
... How could he do this?'*

*'A part of me wants to be understanding, but I just cannot get
my head round this. We've always been so close. We need each
other, Dad and I, more than we've ever needed anyone before!
Surely. I thought today about what he had said.*

*"We can visit each other, can't we?" As he asked this
ridiculous question, he held my hand firmly in both his and studied
my face, looking, I suppose, for a reaction. Did he want me to beg
him to stay?*

*But I said, "Of course we can, Dad, but ..." There were so
many buts I hardly knew where to begin. His decision, which must
have involved much deliberation, weighing up the reasons for and
against, made me feel unloved, unwanted and unimportant, the very
opposite of how he had always made me feel all my life, for as long
as I can remember.*

*I lost my sweet, loving mother - just a few weeks ago - and, yes,
I appreciate he lost his wonderful wife. Then Lucas, Oh God, the
love of my life, the father of my two children, has just been suddenly
and unjustly wrenched from me - and my father, my very special
father, is now proposing to leave me to raise two children alone.*

I'm not sure I can ever forgive him.'

*'The first few months were the worst. Dark. Too awful to write
about at the time. Even now it hurts. Just keeping the flat ticking
over, caring for a baby, taking a child to school, what seemed like a
meaningless series of mechanical chores as I try to work out my grief.
Sometimes, still, my limbs feel heavy; I can't smile. I have to put on
a face, held head high, for the benefit of friends and neighbours, but
now the practical worries are kicking in. Unpaid bills are piling up
again.'*

Lucas, a paragon of most virtues, had never had much of a head for money, despite his poring over the occasional spreadsheet. Steph always knew they would never be wealthy unless his band had made it big-time, but this seemed nothing more than a dream. Music, and latterly drama, was his passion; teaching was his vocation in life and she would never have wished anything otherwise. He tried, but as a self-employed teacher, he never really thought things through on the long-term financial side until it was too late. There was no life insurance, no pension for the future, nothing to make his loss a little easier to bear in that sense.

'Good news I suppose. I've found a full-time job at a large, local authority Leisure Centre far beyond Bloomstock, I shall be a small cog in a much bigger wheel than House of Fitness. It involves managing a membership database and course bookings, which I could do standing on my head. Just hope that I can work my way up the ladder towards a management post.'

'I hate leaving Barnaby behind all day, every day, in the Appley Green nursery, but can see no alternative. Then there's Faith ... she's a tough little girl, but has taken to wetting her bed and having bad dreams since her Daddy knocked his head against the corner of a steel case and never came home from school. She never did see the play on the school stage that we had all been looking forward to so much. Instead she went to a funeral.'

'Been in this job a few weeks now. My line manager, Brodric McTavish, is an ignorant pig.

"Stats report on my desk tomorrow by 11," he said, as he walked by my desk this morning, clearly on the way out of the building and not apparently about to stop for a chat. Endowed with the charm and good looks of a salted slug, his clipped Scottish accent

with staccato notes reminds me of the prison warder in that really old sitcom *Porridge*.

At such short notice, this was not easy. I gather statistical data on a weekly basis and convert them into a monthly report which is submitted a week **after** the end of each month. Now he was requesting it, unreasonably, a day **before** the last day of the month. It's impossible. There's no time! God knows what will happen tomorrow.'

'At precisely eleven o'clock, with only incomplete figures to show him, I hung by his desk while he continued on a long phone call, ignoring my presence.

Eventually he came off the phone. "Why are you standing there?" he asked, abruptly, with an icy glare.

"The report you asked for?"

"And what report would that be?"

"The monthly figures."

"So. Where are they?"

"You will surely understand it cannot be complete – it's only the last day of the month today."

He bristled. I could see his jaw clench even through a layer of flab. "Just a few hours of the working month to go. No' a problem." He waved a dismissive hand in the air and went to pick up his phone to make another call. "Estimate. Adjust next month." He punched in a phone number and consulted his watch. "Let me have figures to date."

It's not as if I've been negligent in my work. His demands were out of order. Coolly I explained, "The last week's figures are not collated yet. I need a day to do that, at least."

He said nothing, but glared at me across his desk. Then, "And what am I supposed to tell the Directors?"

"If you'd given me enough warning .."

"I think it's your job, Steph, to keep on top of these things, to keep up to date."

"These figures have never been asked for before the end of the month ... before," I faltered, trying to find the energy to defend myself in a businesslike way. I'd had a bad night with Barnaby who is teething. Such a feeling of exhaustion and misery closed over me, I felt tears spring to my eyes. A display of emotion was not something my boss could relate to in any way and rather than risk it, I walked away.'

'I am determined not to let the bastard wear me down. He's a bad manager and I am stuck with him. That's life. But I am keeping records of what is escalating into bullying in the workplace. He takes pleasure in belittling me in front of colleagues, monitoring my every move and picking me up on the slightest error. I've got school and college reports to confirm I am normally a conscientious and efficient person so I know the problem is really his, not mine. It makes the workplace the stuff of nightmares, but I shall soldier on. What are his motives, I often wonder? Perhaps he is simply a control freak and has a downer on women in general.'

'Today I asked him straight, "Have I done something to annoy you?" I confronted him head-on, weary of the petty crossings out on an email I'd sent to staff about expenses claims. He had gone to the trouble of printing it out in order to desecrate it with red pen! Sad little man.

He laughed loudly. "Steph. It's no' within your power to annoy me."

I did not smile back. 'It seems that you take pleasure in criticising and ridiculing me." I tried to stare him out the way he does to me.

"Silly girrrl," he said witheringly as he calmly walked away. Vile man! The devil incarnate! I hate him so much I'd like to put arsenic in his coffee, were there some conveniently to hand. But, instead I just take deep breaths, count to twenty and vow to ignore *him. I do feel horribly trapped though, imprisoned in work I need to survive. I wonder if the sun will ever shine again.'*

Steph turned down the corners of her mouth as she read this, a bad taste in her mouth. No wonder …

'Today, there was a crisis on the reception desk. Both receptionists were off sick with a flu bug going round and I was asked to step in until they could get a temp from the agency.

An exceptionally striking man around the age of forty came to the desk, fresh from the changing-rooms, carrying a sports holdall. Wow! He had broad dependable shoulders, an easy-going smile and a way of walking that drew attention, especially from the females within reach. Not a swagger, exactly, but he seemed like someone at peace with the world and happy in his own skin.'

Yes, maybe she should not be so hard on herself …

23

Greg had tried twice to get Steph on her landline and three times on her mobile. She was obliged to submit her intended daily schedule, as part of the charity's Lone Worker Policy. She posted it to him every few days and phoned him if it changed for any reason. He did not always look at it, but the important thing was to know where she was, if necessary. There appeared to be a gap in the schedule and he had received no update from her. Perhaps she was having difficulties with it being school holidays. He understood her son was not yet a teenager; it must be difficult, but he felt frustrated by her elusiveness. Disappointed. She should have her mobile always with her and switched on during working hours, whether she was with a client or not. It was in the Guidelines, for her own safety as much as for the convenience of others.

In fact, it spelled this out in the said Guidelines; to be patently un-contactable would be taken as an 'EMERGENCY'. It would suggest an 'unusual situation', possibly one of 'personal danger': an accident, being held hostage, under threat, or theft of the phone. He must do something. If it were simply that she had failed to recharge her mobile he would be angry with her, for sure. He was planning it already.

Slamming his front door behind him, he set off for Appley Green. There was nothing for it, he would seek her out.

He drove to her little terraced house, not far from the secondary school on the west side of Appley Green. There was no one there, unless the son had had instructions not to answer the door to strangers. He put his hands in his pockets and trudged around, muttering to himself, wondering how to go about this.

It seemed sensible to try the neighbours. Many young people in Appley Green worked from home, he had discovered in the course of his investigations, and many others were retired; so it was far from a dormitory village or ghost town. Some inhabitants were employed in Bloomstock, Farnham and Guildford and others in the village itself. He was aware he did not know everything, far from it, but he was getting there. The picture was building up like a jigsaw.

Although within easy distance from London in theory, the car journeys to either motorway or nearby train stations were along such slow, narrow roads it deterred some from commuting to the City.

He waited for a few minutes after lifting the brass doorknocker on the small blue front door of the neighbouring house. These were originally alms' houses, so he noticed from a stone carving above a central archway.

He heard the barking of a small dog from within. At last an attractive woman opened the door; dark, glossy curls fell loosely to her shoulders.

"Good morning," he said. "I do apologise for bothering you. I was after your neighbour, Stephanie Perriman. Can't get her on her mobile. Any ideas?"

Lettie raised her eyebrows and shrugged. "Well, she's always out and about, see. She works in the community, like *out* in the community, if you get what I mean." Greg smiled and nodded, deciding to let this chatty Welsh woman carry on. "In fact, the charity she works for has some really strict rules about tracing her footsteps at all times. Like Big Brother, isn't it? She told me that. A right pain in the bum!"

Now it would be embarrassing for this nice person to know he was pretty much the charity personified.

"But she didn't happen to mention where she might be? I mean it was just on the off-chance."

"I'm sorry I can't help you really. You're welcome to wait in here, if you like."

Greg was rather taken aback by her trust. He was, after all, a stranger.

"That's kind but I'll have a prowl round the village. See if anyone there has seen her."

So, leaving his car behind, as is the Appley Green custom if at all possible, so he had gleaned from the one and only part-time Traffic Warden who randomly patrolled the village bearing threats of heavy penalties, he set off on foot. Passing by the *Bakery by the Green*, *Gemstones*, *Hair and Now*, the *Tea Shoppe*, a tiny art gallery called *Pieces of Eight*, a second hand bookshop, *Gift Goodies Galore*, a small Butcher's shop, the Post Office and Willem Hardrop Estate Agents, he decided to call in somewhere to see how close-knit this community really was. Maybe if she had passed by this morning, someone may have noticed and given a little wave. He sensed he was clutching at flimsy straws, but it would only take a couple of minutes.

He turned back to the gemstone shop, actually rather intrigued to take a look at what was inside. It looked impossibly old-fashioned, like stepping into a Dickens' novel, but there were two people inside who seemed to be just gazing out of the window with time on their hands.

A bell rang as he opened the door. The musty smell brought back distant memories of jumble sales in a scout hut. The man and rather retro-stylish woman came forward to greet him, putting him off browsing. They seemed over-enthusiastic to collar him for a sale.

"Excuse me, I haven't actually come in to buy anything. I'm so sorry" he said, with what he hoped was a winning smile. "I just wondered if you might be able to help me. I'm trying to find someone. Stephanie Perriman? Do you know her?"

Extreme concern filled their faces simultaneously. "Oh. I hope nothing has happened to her," said the woman with an interesting hairstyle. Why would something have happened to her, in their eyes, he wondered?

"You know Steph, then?"

"Of course we do!" they both replied together and laughed. "We go to her computer class, to learn more about the Internet and all that." Why, thought Greg, was Steph helping this couple? Outside her remit on every level, he would have thought.

He saw the man's smile quickly vanish. In fact, he was frowning now, squinting at him. "You're not the police are you?"

"No, no. Oh dear," said Greg, hurriedly.

"It's just she works a lot on her own, going into people's houses. I mean, there are risks attached."

"Yes, quite. I didn't mean to raise alarm bells. She works for me and I'm trying to track her down. Can't get her on her mobile, that's the thing. Although this is very unusual, which is why I *am* a little concerned."

"But she works for a charity – SSS. Special Support for Seniors. Everyone knows Steph," said the man.

"It is paid work ..." chipped in the woman, "Not voluntary ..."

"... but she puts in a lot of extra hours we reckon, don't we?"

"Oh yes, we've often said. Busiest woman in Appley Green, most probably."

"Really."

"I never knew she had a boss though," said the man, stroking his beard thoughtfully. Greg realised how much he was the back-office worker in SSS.

They were both now regarding him suspiciously. "No," confirmed the woman. "Neither did I."

"She never mentioned anyone else being involved. It was old Ted Devonish's mission really, wasn't it?" They were protecting her!

"Yes, absolutely right," said Greg. "And Steph and I are working ... er, together ... to fulfil his dream. Indeed, that is our joint mission. I was really wondering if you happened to see her pass by this morning. Just looking for clues to see where she might be."

They looked at each other, with folded arms, forming some kind of silent pact. He was touched by their loyalty to her, although it was not overly helpful. Clearly they were not going to believe him until they could check it out with Steph. He bid them 'good-day', still bemused by their connection with her, and left the shop. This little saunter was proving to be quite interesting. He was getting to know Stephanie so much better, without her being anywhere near. Although she might be. She could be watching him!

Next he decided to call in *Hair and Now*, as it occurred to him what better way to find out about a community than to have your hair cut and hobnob with the hairdresser. They were famous for chatting to their

174

customers about holidays, and where they were going out this evening, and suchlike. He would make an appointment.

"You don't actually need to make an appointment," said the very young girl at the desk, wearing a badge saying Adina, probably a trainee hairdresser doubling up as receptionist, he thought. Even Greg was struck by the beautifully sculpted cut of her sleek red hair, wondering if she had modelled the style on the Gemstone woman.

"Oh – I can just pop in then, like years ago at the Barber's?"

She smiled. "Exactly. For a quick man's haircut, I mean a man's quick haircut," she giggled, "we can fit that in *here* and *now!*" She threw out her arms in a theatrical gesture and it occurred to him how nice it must be to have a grown-up daughter to make you laugh.

"You enjoy saying that, don't you?"

"Well, it is what we are about. Unisex, but when you want it. Oops." She blushed. "Always putting my foot in it, me," adding in a whisper, "Don't tell anyone I said that. It came out wrong."

"Your secret is safe," he whispered back.

"So did you want it now, then?" She seemed oblivious this time and Greg struggled to keep a straight face.

He looked over her shoulder at the clock on the wall. "I don't actually have time, but I will definitely come in another time, or maybe even later on today. Can I ask you, Adina, do you happen to know Stephanie Perriman?"

"I know her daughter. Faith. And her little brother …"

"But would you know Faith's mother if you saw her?"

175

"Course I would. She visits my Gran. Wish my Mum was like her. She lets Faith go to *House of Fitness*. All right for some."

Greg thought he had better hurry things along. "You don't happen to have seen her go by this morning, do you?"

"Yeah. I did, actually. She looked fierce, with her head down, like this." Adina then hunched up her shoulders, stared down at the floor and strode around the salon, at which point her superior called out, "Adina what the very devil are you doin' over there?"

Greg replied across the shop, where a couple of ladies in various stages of cuts and highlights were watching in the mirrors and laughing at her antics. "I'm so sorry, this is all my fault." He quickly asked of Adina, "About what time did you see her?"

Adina pulled a face. "About half-past ten? Maybe later, half-eleven? Euw, I dunno really."

"Thanks – that's really helpful." He meant it although he realised it 'came out a bit wrong', tinged with sarcasm. He was really rather enjoying himself.

"See you later, then. Oh, just thought! I slipped out to get a bag of doughnuts to go with our mid-morning coffees, and I did see her out the corner of my eye. Funny that. I had no reason to remember, but now it just comes to mind – she went into that Estate Agents."

Greg sauntered down to the small parade of shops until he reached Willem Hardrop. He was curious. Was she looking to sell her house? Another of her secrets? He was beginning to really question how she filled her working day. Surely the service she provided with SSS did not extend to helping clients put their property on the market. No wonder she worked long hours.

He pushed the door open. Perhaps there was a way to find out.

A slim woman wearing a linen suit and chunky jewellery asked him if she could help.

"I was wondering if anyone here has seen my colleague? She is with SSS – Special Support for Seniors, called Stephanie Perriman." He handed her one of his own business cards; which he realised he should have done in *Gemstones*, although it might have deprived him of the useful chat he had there.

A young man, rather Mediterranean in looks, stood up from his desk, packing his things into a briefcase, preparing to leave it seemed and the woman went up to him. By really straining his ears, Greg could hear her saying quietly, "You saw that lady, didn't you – about *The Hideaway* valuation – the one who felt left out? Did you manage to calm her down, Justin? It's just that someone is asking for her."

An instant look of fear spread across this man's face and Greg was now both puzzled and worried. He quickly pinned on what Greg instantly recognised as the superficial smile of a poor salesman. Nothing in the eyes.

Justin came across confidently with arm outstretched to shake Greg's hand. His palm was moist, Greg noticed. "Yes, indeed. No problem at all. All sorted. What … I mean, is there some way I can help you, sir?"

"I was simply trying to find her!"

"Oh. Well, she said she had a visit to make somewhere on the Birchwood housing estate I think …"

Greg breathed a sigh of relief. "Oh, that's fine then, she's back on track, I guess."

"You have to keep an eye on her, like that?" asked Justin, genuinely interested.

24

Steph arrived at the home of Arthur and Astrid Kersham. She knew they were counting on her visit and there was no way she would let them down. They lived on the relatively new housing estate north east of the village centre, built in the 1970s rather controversially on fields that had been a pig farm. The five-bedroom house was of a mock-Tudor design and, with their middle-aged family long flown the nest, they were planning to downsize into sheltered accommodation.

She had brought with her a pile of brochures to show them.

Astrid, almost blind now, came to the door, keeping it ajar on a loose chain. There were numerous stickers on the leaded porch-window warning off doorstep traders.

"Who is it?" Astrid asked, from behind the door, having the good commonsense not to say "Is that you Steph?" while knowing full-well that it was her because, as ever, Steph had arrived on the dot. But any female stranger or high-pitched man could easily respond that he or she was indeed Steph and gain access with evil intent. Appley Green has one of the lowest crime rates in the country, but it was wise to be cautious. Her clients were advised to protect themselves in this way.

"It's Stephanie from SSS," replied Steph, brightly. "Hello Astrid!"

The door opened and she was warmly greeted and taken through a dark hallway scented with lavender to a sitting-room where Arthur sat at a table scattered with minute pieces of a model-making kit. Strains of what Steph thought was Dvorak's New World symphony were playing full volume, not because they were deaf but just because they liked it that way; it was one of her father's favourites and momentarily took her back to her childhood, as she would watch her father daub canvas. The association brought with it the smell of linseed oil he used to thin his paints. She should listen to classical music more often, she thought. Why didn't she? How would her children ever enjoy such music if they were never exposed to it? If Lucas had been around, they would have grown up as musicians. Astrid's fingers were running over a remote control to find the on-off switch.

While such thoughts were bubbling away, and with the music now silenced, she went up to Arthur and gave his shoulder a friendly squeeze. "Ah-ha, what's it this time Arthur?"

"Warhawk!" He showed her the box. "How are you then, Steph? Good to see you."

They sat and talked openly about how they had been since her last visit and their feelings about selling up. It was a big decision but, having weighed things up with Steph's help, had decided they could still live independently so long as they kept together.

"Not quite ready for a Home yet," said Arthur. "So long as we can be together. After all we've been married for sixty-one years. Not likely to get separated now, unless one of us pops our clogs, and we have no intention of doing that, have we my love?"

"Not today anyhow," replied Astrid with a wink. "Together we just about make one good person!" They always said this without fail, but Steph never tired of hearing it. Such a sweet couple, always in good spirits.

179

"Thank you for the anniversary card, Steph. There's not many that remember."

Arthur could no longer take more than a few steps and Astrid's eyes could make out very little other than light and shade. He could drive, with his Blue Badge for free disabled parking, however, and his eyesight was excellent for his age. They were a well-loved sight around Appley Green, with Astrid pushing his wheelchair, in and out of shops, under Arthur's guidance. "Left now, easy, straight for another couple of yards," while calling to passers-by, "Lovely day!" and continuing perhaps in the small supermarket, "Stop now, here's the cheese counter, well would you believe it, Ethel is buying aubergines …" They both pooh-poohed the idea of a motorised scooter or a wheelchair he might manage on his own. Where would that leave Astrid? And how lonely he would be. Steph knew the boundaries of what she might suggest to this particular pair of troopers.

"You two! You're such a team …"

She spent a good hour with them, quite happy for them to reminisce about their lives, making mental notes of how she could further assist. There was a small-scale development close to the shops and the village Green. It would be ideal. They had stated their first choice as a ground-floor retirement flat with a warden, and a small garden. Somehow, bravely working in tandem they managed to cultivate easy plants like heathers, hostas and peonies, with tubs of petunias, and a patch of lawn. Their existing garden always looked immaculate, though they confessed it was too time-consuming now. They would never admit that it was in any way tiring or hard work, nor would they employ help. Steph found them an inspirational couple. She was always thinking hard as she listened, now wondering about alternative

180

accommodation if there were no Appley Green places available: nearest shops that offer reliable delivery service of basic provisions; day centre that has lively activities; pub and church with good wheelchair access … never taking notes while they talked. She would entirely lose herself in her work.

Then she caught sight of their antique clock on the mantelpiece. It was a matter of principle, according to the commandments of Ted Devonish, never to appear rushed. Arthur was telling her about a particularly efficacious chilblain cream a chemist used to make up for him.

As he paused for breath, she said, "I am so sorry but I need to go. I have to be in Bloomstock to meet someone for lunch." She quickly but smoothly collected her bag and briefcase and rose from her seat. "How time flies!"

"Oh! Somewhere nice?" asked Astrid.

Steph wondered when they last went out to eat in a restaurant. It would not be an easy thing to do – but maybe with a bit of help …

She made little of it. "Just a picnic!" she replied, close to the truth.

"In Bloomstock?" exclaimed Astrid.

"Well, there is a very scenic patch of grass close by the council offices with a park bench! We can sit and admire the architecture." She knew the buildings had been designed by Jackson Jeffrys of this parish, but was not sure if they did.

They quickly agreed a date for the next visit and she left, rather more hurriedly than usual.

At least, she was not still married to Richard! What would her life have been like if she had stayed with him? She cast her mind back, as she drove along, to the last Diary 'episode' she read:

He began by asking for information, then I noticed he seemed distracted by my breasts. Well, he was a man. This is what men often do - let their imaginations go walkabout. I could overlook it.

"Haven't seen you here before. More's the pity, I would add," he commented, with a smooth smile. His accent was distinctly upper class, probably the product of an expensive education, I sensed. Possibly a blue-blooded pedigree. His manner has a kind of … I don't know, a bit like Ted Devonish I guess. (Haven't seen him for years …)

I explained about Mandy and Sue being off sick, that I work in the back office and stepped in to help out. It's strange I've not come across him before, but I don't know everyone in Bloomstock, unlike Appley Green where most people connect in some way when you've lived there a while …

Anyway, he said, "Well you certainly brighten up the desk! I'm Richard by the way."

Steph pulled a face when she read this. How could she fall for such a cringeworthy chat-up line?

He courteously held out a hand and I took it. Mmmm. Flesh on flesh. A warm, firm handshake, although have to say I felt no sexual attraction. Not like the electric tingle I felt when Lucas first caught me by the hand and asked if I was free to go out for a drink with him. That first time on a date alone, without a bunch of his protégées, even then it was clear I wanted him and he wanted me.

"I'm Steph," was all I actually said to this Richard. Flirting does not come easily to me. Since losing Lucas, I can never imagine taking any man as a lover, not even a tall, handsome male with a mop of blond hair and a flashy smile. The very idea makes me squirm – and yet, there is that essential part of life that is missing

182

and sometimes, if I'm honest, leaves me aching with a restless frustration.'

'I saw Richard again today – my birthday! In The Fox and Rabbit, (the Appley Green pub noted for its good food and friendly service!) A friend (Jo) persuaded me to get a babysitter and come out for some supper to celebrate as much as I could. I made sure we didn't take the table by the fire where Lucas and I had sat that evening exactly a year ago when he had been so starry-eyed, so full of hope for our sunny future together.

Richard and I caught sight of each other across the bar and he nodded and smiled. I feel weirdly flattered he recognised and remembered me, but my emotions were so jumbled I felt numb. Jo had to get back to her own family and I went to the bar to pay the bill. I felt a light tap on my shoulder.'

The Diary went by the board for a bit, Steph recalled, but she could remember all too well how rapidly their relationship grew. Richard seemed keen and pursued her, taking her to expensive restaurants, presenting her with gifts – and successfully seducing her into his bed. She knew she was vulnerable but was in no position to resist his considerable charms. He seemed rather quaint and old-fashioned, really almost too good to be true, as she later discovered. They had not even moved in together, but after a few months she accepted his offer of marriage. His apparent ardour, the idea of a splendid wedding ceremony with all the trappings; his ability to pay the bills and enable her to be a 'proper mother', as he suggested to her, was altogether too much to resist. He seemed close to perfect, certainly beyond the standard she was likely to achieve in the circumstances.

She wondered if Faith would understand all this? Would it perhaps help her not to fall into the same pitfalls in life? Would she say, *But Mum, did you love him?*

As Steph drove along towards Bloomstock, she was beginning to feel that her load was lightening bit by bit, like baskets of lead yoked around her neck being emptied, or floating away, one by one. This physical sense of relief also allowed one or two clearings to open up in her foggy head. Her top worries had been dispersed, but the space they left allowed other matters to invade – there was a name for this, wasn't there? Ha-ha, the irony of it. Parkinson's Law! Perhaps she was just a born worrier. She could sense them, these other matters, marching in, marking out their territory: the computer club and the possibility of Greg finding out what she was up to; Barnaby's agreed visit to Jackson's home; the mystery of Gloria's son, which she must fathom, even though it was, possibly, none of her business …

Was she becoming a busy-body-do-gooder? Oh dear. But there was something else that was rumbling away in the back of her mind, something hard-hitting and truly bothersome. Something to do with Jackson. Yes! His family! Justin had lightly mentioned that Mr Jeffrys was expecting *a visit from his family*! Well, he must've got that wrong, for a start. For sure, Jackson would have told her if that were the case, wouldn't he? But there, he hadn't mentioned the school talk that Faith had planned for him. Sometimes he forgot, it was only natural at his great age, ninety next month she had noticed the other day from his file.

She felt sulky and realised that this was wrong. It was almost like being in love, a kind of obsession driven by the heart instead of the head. But of course, it was not like that at all because Jackson was, after all, old enough to be …

A shutter slammed down inside her head to divert her thoughts to Justin, as she drew up in the concrete multi-story car park in Bloomstock. She almost wondered how she had arrived there, as if on automatic pilot. It was quite scary how that happened sometimes; she worried that she might have exceeded a speed limit or run over a cat without noticing. At least the route was not a complicated one so she would not have gone through a red light.

She reached for her mobile to check for messages and was horrified to find that she had forgotten to switch it back on after leaving Willem Hardrop. Oh well, she then thought, burying her guilt over breaking the rules, I guess no one will ever know. She quickly switched it on and thrust it in her pocket, before making her way swiftly to her assignation with Justin with just two minutes to spare.

She need not have worried, as there was no sign of him. After about ten minutes she then doubted he was going to come. The coward! He had ducked out. She might have known. Well, he really was not her problem; she was sorry for the two women in his life but it truly was none of her business. It was a distraction she could ill afford; SSS could ill afford.

As she stood up, deciding to get herself a sandwich from a nearby café to silence her rumbling stomach, he appeared, striding manfully towards her, waving as if all was well with the world, carefree and with a conscience as clear as the blue sky above. Prat!

He extended a hand. Now he was here, she sat down with bated breath. She really did want to hear his story. Who wouldn't?

"I understand that what you heard was, I think, probably, something that ... er ... must've sounded quite bad. It was only ages afterwards, when my foul temper had died down a bit I realised that maybe someone had overheard me?"

Idiot.

"I should imagine more than a few heard you. You were shouting, for pity's sake!"

He closed his eyes and did an airhead, what-am-I-like, Hugh Grant thing with his mouth.

"You probably know what I said better than I do myself. God, how embarrassing," he said, with a little snorty laugh as if she might just find him rather cute and winsome.

This was too painful and she needed to get back to work. "Look, Justin, it's your life, but I do feel some concern because I know what I heard. You have two women and a man friend. Right?"

He jumped. "What!"

"Adrian?"

He laughed. He had the temerity to throw back his head and emit positive guffaws. "No. He's totally made up," he said as if she were the stupid one for thinking otherwise. "I ... I ... er ...use him as an imaginary flat-mate, such an unsavoury character, that it keeps ... er ...Tracy away from my living-quarters."

"Oh, Cowslip Lane? Keeps her away from the other one, you mean?"

He studied her slowly and she felt a hint of menace. The smile had gone. "Ye-es." There was a momentary pause. "You know where I live then?" A slight rush of guilt surfaced but she promptly brought it under control. "Where I *actually* live."

"So the flat and Adrian are in your head only?"

186

"Ah-ha." He nodded.

"Are you going to tell your wife, or girlfriend, the other one?"

"Mia *is* my *wife*." He said through gritted teeth, showing signs of anger. "Tell her? What do you mean?"

Obtuse numbskull. "Tell her about Tracy. The pregnancy?"

"You're kidding."

"What happened to Marbella?"

"She decided she didn't want to go." Now he sounded like a grumpy child. He was a complex personality, she was beginning to see, able to switch – or rather, unable to stop himself from switching from one persona to another as if with a flick of a handheld remote. He was answering questions, almost as if it were a welcome release. "I haven't … resolved the situation yet. I am trying to escape the clutches of Tracy, although to be frank I'd rather be with her … but Mia is 'the Bank'." He stared down at the ground between his feet.

"What, you married for money?" she asked. Then memories of those testing times with Richard flooded through her head. What right had she to judge, to criticise?

He raised his head, still not meeting her gaze. "The last few years have been tough for estate agents. I realise they never win anyone's sympathy! But, you know, hardly any houses on the market. I'm not qualified for anything," he whined. "She succumbed to my charms all too willingly … well, *she* is the one who wanted to get married. She's gorgeous in her own way, a stunning head-turner, she's Daddy's little rich girl and she was the one doing all the running. I mean, how the hell was I supposed to resist?" Never his fault is it? At least, thought Steph, I had the guts to take the blame for

187

marrying Richard, my one really mammoth mistake in life.

"But you don't love her."

He shook his head slowly and miserably. Turning now to face Steph, he replied, "I don't even fancy her. She hardly eats. She's a fashion model. Tall, thin, you know?"

She got the implication. Not his preferred bodacious type.

Steph looked him straight in the eye and, from bitter experience, with sincerity from the bottom of her heart. "You must finish with your wife, Mia. Support Tracy." How could she be saying this! She had shocked herself. Yet she felt it was absolutely the right advice, not that he would want her advice. Why would he? Why was she dishing it out, anyway?

Just as he stood up, she caught sight of Greg, who was sitting on another bench just six metres away. What the hell was *he* doing here? He looked up at her. He was *watching* her! She looked at Justin, then at Greg, then back ... Men! Honestly, men! She hated them. They were all rotten, devious bastards to the core.

"If you don't tell Mia, then I will," she shouted, feeling herself spiralling out of control. Now Greg knew that she knew he was watching her, but still he sat there just quietly observing. How *dare* he? This was her lunch hour. She flicked a glance at her watch; actually, it was a quarter to three already. She was late for her meeting.

"Fuck you!" shouted Justin. "Who the hell do you think you are, you interfering bitch!" Then he noticed that she was looking over his shoulder and he turned to see Greg who was now standing up and clearly about to come over. "Have you set me up?" he hissed. "You fucking, fucking, cow!"

25

With the help of a few people in the area, Greg had found the full address of the clients listed on Steph's work schedule. Heigh-ho, so much for data protection, he thought. He double-checked their names – Astrid and Arthur Kersham.

After going through their thorough security procedures, by which he was duly impressed, for it showed they may have read and acted upon advice given in the SSS leaflet, he was eventually invited in. Once he had produced his card and said he was looking for Steph, the atmosphere changed; he was welcomed and offered tea and a slice of Banbury cake.

"She left just ten minutes ago – on her way to Bloomstock to meet a friend for a picnic," explained Astrid. "That's what she said, wasn't it Arthur?"

Her husband nodded. "She seemed a bit anxious to get away to be perfectly honest – I was in the middle of telling her about …"

"Perhaps it was her boyfriend!" interrupted Astrid, laughing.

Greg frowned. What was happening to Steph? Leaving her phone switched off? Engaged in all kinds of unnecessary activities? Now rushing away from a client – an unforgivable sin, far removed from the SSS mission – for a picnic lunch with a friend?

As he drove off to Bloomstock, on her tail, he felt deeply disappointed and puzzled. She was a warm-hearted person but normally conscientious and efficient too. Ted Devonish had hand picked her after all; I was a mere afterthought, appointed by the Trustees, he thought. A lovely, caring young woman, everyone said so, and very capable, although as her boss he had to be somewhat restrained in his praise of her. She might take it personally. He had already overstepped professional boundaries by sending those flowers. She had never thanked him or even referred to the gift; presumably he had really embarrassed her. He would not make that mistake again.

He had planned to ask her to lunch, as he really wanted to have a relaxed chat with her. Since seeing that sign up on the village notice board and the article in the local paper about the Simulac classes, he wondered why she had kept the Internet coaching idea from him. It had prompted him to bring himself up to date with possible risks in using the Internet, and ways to protect your personal data. He may as well stop this pretence that he never uses email; he would always be wary, but he had good reasons for that.

He would let Steph know she could email her schedule and reports through to him. He also wanted to celebrate with her some other news, but would scrap the lunch now and set up a more formal meeting. Much as it aggrieved him, he would have to take her to task and haul her over the coals, then smiling at his penchant for old-fashioned metaphors. He hoped it would not get as far as a verbal warning.

Where, in Bloomstock, might anyone have a 'picnic'? Perhaps this was just a sandwich outside somewhere, a quick chat with a girlfriend. She was entitled to a lunch break after all. There was a small green area by the council offices, he knew that, and decided to park near

190

there and take a look around. He was beginning to feel like a snooping investigator and did not like this bit of it at all. Finding her to check on her safety was one thing, but spying on her was entirely another and made him feel distinctly shabby.

He soon spotted her. There was a man with her. They were talking to each other hard, heads intimately close, engrossed. Perhaps Astrid was right! About to walk away, feeling somewhat voyeuristic, he then did a double-take. Wasn't that the shifty-looking guy at Willem Hardrop's? He had been easy-going enough, apparently helpful, to advise him that she was going on to see someone in Appley Green but just had not thought to mention that he was actually meeting her later for lunch. There was something about that Justin … and why *was* she meeting him? Away from their own territory? It was a cold, windy day for August. There was no sign of food being eaten either. It just did not stack up. Was he married? Was he having an affair with Steph? The idea of him and Steph possibly … he shuddered.

He decided to sit on a nearby bench under a fluttering silver birch where he could watch, just for a minute or so. The conversation seemed quite intense, like an argument was brewing. He started. Oh, yes! Raised voices. Swearing. What the …?

Now Steph had a defiant yet scared look on her face. Even at this distance he could tell. Arms folded, raised chin, but stepping back – for both she and Justin were on their feet now, locked in verbal combat, it would seem. She looked across and clearly spotted him, then Justin turned and also registered his presence.

Greg decided to go across boldly and come clean. Yes, he had been following her, but for all the right reasons - surely.

191

26

Justin scuttled off – like a rat in a sewer, thought Steph.

"Greg! Is this a strange co-incidence?" she asked, forcing an awkward smile, a businesslike courtesy towards her colleague. They had only met at meetings, maybe six times in all, so she rarely saw him out of context, certainly had never before randomly bumped into him. He looked younger than her mental image of him always suggested. Taller, too. He was wearing an open neck blue check shirt and dark moleskin trousers and she realised, as a male of the species, he was passable. His pace had reduced to a leisurely stroll, hands in pockets. She sensed he was trying to appear casual.

"No, Steph. I've been searching for you. All morning."

"Oh? Is there a problem?"

Greg paused. "I'm not sure. Perhaps *you* can tell *me*." He was giving her one of his looks. How *dare* he follow her around. This was some kind of harassment, wasn't it?

"But why …?"

"In the first instance, your mobile was switched off and I was concerned. I did try your landline too."

She could feel herself blushing. "Oh. Yes. I was in a meeting but it was only short and then realised later I hadn't switched it back on. I'm *sorry*." She said it in a way that might convey she was anything but.

"Well, you know the rules."

She bit back the retort that wanted to sprout from her mouth.

"So, you've found me now. Was there something else?" He would be wondering what the meeting was, but did not ask.

"I had to, you know. If something had happened to you, and I had taken no action, then I could have been held accountable in some way."

"Please, don't feel you have to be responsible for me."

"I am your manager, Steph."

Memories of Brodric were stirring, that feeling of being treated as an incapable subordinate when she knew she deserved better. Summoning all her strength she kept her lips tight shut, turned around and walked away. She did not want a war with Greg to add to her list of concerns. It seemed that as fast as she rid herself of one worry, another sneakily slotted into its place.

Now he was trailing after her! Really, this was too much. He must have been to Astrid and Arthur's house to ask them questions. Of course, she had let slip where she was going next.

"We need to talk," he said, as he caught up with her and walked by her side.

This was the kind of thing spouses would say to each other. *We need to talk*. It was more typically about an infidelity, money problem or communications malfunction.

"Well, I have a meeting to get to. I …" she broke off, about to confess to being already an hour late. In fact, the meeting would be nearly over and she had not let them know to apologise.

"According to your schedule, you should be visiting Elsie someone."

"Yes, yes. I know. Look," she swung round to face him suddenly. He stepped back as if aware they were a little too close for professional comfort. "Today has been a bad day. Things have not gone well. Maybe even *you* … have days when something goes wrong early on and then the whole thing collapses in a total mess? Yes?"

He just stood there and she could have punched him. "I'm really not at all sure what to think," he replied at last, prefaced by something like a grunt. "That's why we need to sit down and talk properly. I'll email you with some dates and times. I can see you're upset and don't want me around you, so for the moment, goodbye Steph."

With that, he just stood still, presumably thinking she would walk on. For some reason she did not. She felt so alone, as if she would actually like to tell him about everything: but he would not understand. Not in a million years. Lending a shoulder to cry on, or even a listening ear, was certainly not in his job description or even in his nature.

But after perhaps ten long seconds, she did walk away, quite calmly, hoping he wasn't standing there watching her. She certainly was not going to be caught out by turning round to check if he was. Then something he had said reached her brain and she thought she must be going mad. He said he would *email* her.

Once back in her car, Steph first called the residential home where she should have attended a meeting about setting up a group session, and then Elsie to apologise for her tardiness. It was only when she was finally lying back in a steaming hot bath, blissfully in danger of sinking into a coma, that she did this thing that was becoming a habit. She ran through her mental to-do checklist.

She added the new actions, freshly accrued today. Firstly, she must decide whether she should carry out her threat to tell Mrs whatever-her-name-was, Mia, and get herself further enmeshed in that madman's life. Then, she must check her emails.

Tomorrow was the next session of the computer club. Oh joy! She could guess what was going to happen there.

Was she right to tell Justin that he should leave Mia? His wife? My God. What had she done? She had no right, but … she would remind herself of what it was like to be trapped in a marriage for all the wrong reasons tonight.

'My Wedding Day!! Yesterday, the wedding was a golden autumnal dream, ceremony and reception at Hunters' Lodge Hotel, my childhood dream fulfilled. It was a bright frosty day, with oaks and beeches gilded in stunning coppery shades and I am just filled with hope now for a shiny new start for me, and for the children. Richard lavishes me with the best of everything and I am willing to be spoiled! As we stood side-by-side exchanging vows, a happy shaft of sunlight beamed down on us through a picture window that overlooks the grounds. I am so bloody lucky to have such a charismatic, good-looking husband. The whole thing happened so fast! He is what Mum, with a sigh of satisfaction, would have called 'a bit of a catch'. A voice deep-down somewhere whispers to me that I am shameless and shallow but I can't listen to this voice. It was such a beautiful day - friends hugged, kissed and congratulated, the champagne flowed and Barnaby and Faith have a father once more.

Family came from both sides – except for Dad. Richard's close and distant relatives were there. In fact, they outnumbered my family by what seemed about fifty-to-one and they seemed to carry themselves like royalty. To me, Dad's absence was an achingly huge, gaping chasm at the top table. An occasional wave of grief – as if he'd died – rolled through me from time to time, but no-one else seemed to give it much thought.

He couldn't make the effort to travel from Somerset! When I heard he wasn't coming I thought I would die from the sorrow of it all …

I took Faith and Barnaby to see him twice, in the early months after he left, but he seemed distant and unwilling to play with his grandchildren or even be taken out to lunch. He wore a sad look about his features and seems to have become one of those people who grimly resolves to never recover from the grief of losing the love of his life. He had even given up painting, he said. I thought he was made of sterner stuff.

I tried. "Look Dad, give us a call or write a letter some time," I said, when we left him sitting forlornly by his mock coal-fire. The bungalow he bought was very small, as if he was all out to be a martyr for some reason. It irritated me, to tell you the truth. "Easy to look after," he reasoned, with a wry smile and I thought that just sounds a bit lazy. And no way was his little place big enough for us to stay over. He'd never thought about that.

His miserable stubbornness really has made me cross, even a little bitter.'

Steph closed her eyes. She had forgotten that all this stuff about her father was wrapped up in the Richard bit.

"Come and see us!" I urged him, trying to speak brightly, but through gritted teeth as my patience ran out. It's not as if he is truly too old to travel. "You know we can always find a spare bed for you. Faith and Barnaby miss you." This was not strictly true, as the children had adapted to him not being around. "I miss you, Dad," I said.

Since then, never a letter, never a phone call. He just seemed to want to cut himself off. I know he has his sister and brother and other friends within reach, so I just steel myself to the fact that it was just him and me that were losing touch. It was his choice.

So I'm married to Richard now - a new phase of life. I know deep down I do not love him as I did Lucas (in every waking moment), and still do in my dreams. Determined to make a go of it. A different kind of attachment, a sort of love, will grow in time, I am sure of it.

I silently vow (for my children's sake) that I will not be like that, like my father, stuck in a mire of grief. We rarely speak about him now, although I do dream about him sometimes, as he was years ago, when I was his 'little princess', his 'number one helper'.'

'A few weeks have gone by. My new husband does not expect me to work, of course. Sounds wonderful, but I am not sure how I shall be with this new status. What am I? A housewife? A full-time mother? Certainly his house, gated and barred, secreted away in woodland with grounds encased in wrought-iron fencing to keep out both fallow and the little muntjac deer, requires some looking after. He does not employ a cleaner, or a gardener. It is a little strange. Whilst I have said goodbye to the independence and self-reliance I had before, I have absolutely no financial worries! What a relief!! I do feel a bit like Daphne du Maurier's Rebecca, but without the staff.'

'I sometimes wonder if Richard has told me everything about his past. "My previous marriage failed. An error of judgement on my part." This was pretty much all he said. He told me he divorced his first wife after a couple of years – or perhaps she divorced him? Not sure. A childless marriage came to an acrimonious end, either way, and he makes it absolutely clear he does not wish to remember it or talk about it, or other ensuing, short-lived relationships, further. I'd like to tell him more about Lucas, but there again, he would not want to hear about that either, I'm quite sure of that.'

'Well, we are settling into our new environment, in the heart of this vast wood. With a bit of encouragement from me, Faith and

197

Barnaby have taken up birdwatching and listening for their calls and songs all around. We've heard nightjars and, unmistakably, owls at dusk. Faith found an apparently lame song thrush with speckled breast, creeping amongst some brambles when we were picking blackberries, but I thought it was too small and decided, from my bird book, that it was a perfectly healthy dunnock. Jays, magpies, woodpigeons, collared doves all became part of our day; we put out seeds for blue-tits and get so close to a robin we can almost touch it.

How lucky we are! Really. I count my blessings and know I can make this new life work ...'

December. It is freezing cold. This house is not cosy. Richard is more driven than I realised prior to marriage.

"I shall be late most evenings this week," he announced, flatly, almost out of the front door on his way to work on Monday. His office is in London – the exact nature of his business he rarely discusses, as if it would be beyond my comprehension. It has something to do with imports and exports.

Indeed, I am beginning to realise we rarely discuss anything! I've been trying to pin him down to plan Christmas, but when I broach the subject, he just shakes his head, "Don't usually make much fuss to be honest. Not as if I'm religious. But get the usual fripperies and baubles, as you like." He gave me a smile as if to placate me; there was no depth to it. His tepid approach does not exactly fill the house with excitement! Perhaps I am expecting too much of this marriage.

When he was 'pursuing me' he was lively company and attentive, even laughing at my jokes. He assumed the body language of a captivated listener – the slightly tilted head, lingering gazes that confirmed his love for me. But he has changed; he has won me and now perhaps he thinks he no longer needs to try. I guess all married couples are like this!

'I suggested to him, "Perhaps we could do something together next week. Or, at the weekend, with Faith, and even take Barnaby along?" Faith and Barnaby do not figure in his life **at all**. I can only assume this will take time. "Go ten-pin bowling or something?" Yes, a toddler might be troublesome and would be confined to spectating from his stroller, but this is what family life is, isn't it? Compromise. Muddling along. I remembered he claimed to have achieved an astoundingly high score at this – the bowling, that is. Apparently he did it once when he was a teenager. I was trying to meet him halfway.

"Mm. Maybe!" he replied shortly, with a brief peck on the cheek.

Oh well, we'll see.'

'Richard told me he has booked a ski-ing holiday for us all. Something he does every year. We've never done it so guess we'll all be split up on different slopes!'

'Last night he did not return home. I got a brief text as I was going to bed: Meeting still on. Will stay at flat here. Speak tomorrow. Richard.'

'Last night we planned to go to the theatre in Bloomstock. It was some kind of a mystery-crime-thriller and Richard said, when the brochure came in the post advertising the winter season's programme, that it was the only thing he would be interested in seeing. No Panto, no ballet for Faith, no chance to see my favourite actress … I'll go with friends, or perhaps do the Panto just with the children. Richard won't mind in the slightest. I feel I am back to being a lone parent!

Anyway I was happy to go along and enjoy his preferred choice of play. Of course, I was, and all dressed up and ready, the babysitter there, when the phone rang.

"Tomorrow," came Richard's rather breathless voice, without so much as a hello. He sounded like he was pounding the pavements.

199

"Need to entertain clients." My heart sank. "I'll stay here tonight
…"

He had forgotten. He had simply forgotten. And we've not had a 'date' since the wedding. Is this it? Is this how married life is going to be – till death do us part? I keep his large house reasonably clean, despite hating housework with a vengeance; give him functional sex when he wants it, rarely wanting it myself although I am eternally hopeful of achieving an orgasm; (must make sure I keep this diary hidden away) iron his shirts for God's sake, not even complaining when he simply drops his clothes on the bathroom floor assuming that some kind, invisible, laundry-maid will deal with them. What is happening to me? Am I becoming a total doormat?

I said to him, "I take it you won't be here to go to the play then? That's a …" I was about to say, "that's a shame" laced with some sympathy, but he cut me off mid-sentence.

"Oh, never mind that. You go. Look, tomorrow, I'll be bringing home three or four clients, big players, need to look after them. Push the boat out, you know?"

I almost squeaked with shock. I've never done anything remotely like this before, not even sure where to find the best table linen.

"What? What kind of people are they?"

"What do you mean? They're important!"

"Are they English, for example?" English-speaking, even, I wondered?

"As it happens, no. Japanese, but I think they are quite fine with English food. I'll let you know."

He put the phone down.

Somehow this little scenario told me what I was beginning to suspect already - our marriage is not destined to last. I cannot stomach it. Yet, what can I do?'

'For the sake of my children, I'll stick with it for as long as I can. I will service his needs, involve myself in the village activities and just use the marriage as a kind of convenience, pro tem. This feels so very wrong, little better than being a mistress, prostituting myself as a 'kept woman', but life has not been kind to me for a while; so that's the way it will have to be until I work out a better option.

As for men, never again will I be seduced. All they ever do is let you down. I - and my children - are better off without them.'

'Maybe he thought he could use me as unpaid provider of various services, or perhaps he wanted the married status for social, professional or family reasons. I shall probably never know. Richard continues to have no real interest in me or my children but, oddly, seems keen to keep the good ship marriage sailing.

My shiny new captain usually leaves the house early, considerate enough not to wake any of us. On the evenings when he is at home, he enters the house, draping his cashmere coat and scarf over the banisters as if some valet were standing by ready to sweep them up, brush them down and hang them in a cloakroom. Almost obsessive in his expectations of tidiness and order he rarely puts away anything himself. By habit he then pours himself a large drink and either goes into his study or turns on the TV. Sometimes he buries himself in a copy of Horse and Hounds, which I can never understand, since he has contact with neither animal.

I ask, "Good day?" A cheesy question, but I struggle to think of something that might not cause offence; for another thing I've twigged about Richard is he can be defensive and easily upset. (My old school friend, Paula had a husband like that; it soon turned to violence.)

"Complicated," he replies, condescendingly, or "Busy, busy." Assumes I'm unable to grasp the heady challenges of his business world! Sometimes he just nods wordlessly. He rarely returns the question so then I'm left to think of something else to ask him. If I *just launch into an account of my own activities, he picks up a newspaper or his magazine, or closes his eyes suddenly too tired to even keep them open. For this, he seems to expect sympathy.'*

'Perhaps he has real deep concerns at work that he seriously cannot discuss. Perhaps it is tied up with client confidentiality, financial or legal issues. He won't talk to me. Can things possibly improve?'

'The thing is I have the chance here to be the 'perfect mother', with both time and money to give. Whilst often falling short in his self-inflicted, newly adopted role of stepfather, Richard never quibbles over me spending on whatever I need.

I think Faith is unaware of the rift opening up between me and this remote man who, to kids, is still a bit of a stranger; whilst she wouldn't be a normal child if she didn't sparkle with delight at the leap in material comforts this new 'parental coupling' brought with it – a frilly, marshmallow-pink bedroom, pretty clothes, toys, games and the (unfulfilled) promise of a puppy from Father Christmas whose bulging sack was a bit heavier than last year. Barnaby is still too young to care, just as happy with a few twigs and a cardboard box to play with, as with the brand new toy car Richard insisted on giving him. (His generosity is strange.) But of course, with time this toddler will learn and take luxuries for granted.'

'There's a blackbird's nest Barnaby has been watching closely while Faith is at school. It's lodged in the woody tangle climbing up one side of the west wing.

"Look Mum! Is that the Daddy bird or the Mum one?" It strikes me he's learning the concept of fatherhood in an unconventional way! We are watching the parent birds go back and forth with twigs and feathers and Barnaby is looking forward immensely to the day when the eggs will finally hatch. (All down to good parenting!) We can look down into it from Faith's bedroom window and count the speckledy-blue-green eggs. I explained to

Barnaby today how the tiny baby birds would be fed for a while before they could begin to fly. Barnaby runs around the house flapping his arms in a keen display of empathy.'

'Small events help bed in my initial seeds of doubt. (I am turning poetic). This morning, Saturday, Richard decides to do a spot of tree pruning and casually mentions that he came across a nest that had fallen down with the detritus of branches resulting from his task. I wanted to beat him over the head with the axe still in his hand, as he stood there on the back terrace. I was sure I'd told him how excited Barnaby was about this nest, but he could not have heard or been in any way interested. Barnaby's tears were hard to bear and, for Richard, rather tiresome.'

'Last night, we lay in bed after having sex – it could hardly be termed making love as the act involves no affection from him, and no passion from me. He seemed content with this arrangement. Usually he turns straight over and slips into an untroubled sleep.

So it came as a shock when he said, "How long will it be before we have a baby, I wonder?"

I am on the pill. Absurdly, in retrospect, it never occurred to me that he would want to have children with me. His question came as more than a bit of a surprise, although see now I am naïve and really pretty stupid; we're married, he has none of his own and in theory the question was entirely natural. But we're both living under different, unspoken, assumptions. He has never raised the subject before and he seems entirely lacking in paternal instincts, scarcely exchanging more than a few words in passing with either Faith or Barnaby. I could kick myself for being so blinkered, not appreciating this particular shortcoming of his before accepting his proposal - blindly, rashly, naively. I can detect no evidence of him understanding what children are, or are for! He must have been one himself, I tell myself.

*I hesitated in my reply long enough for silence to supply a clear
answer to his question.*

*I now fully realise that my own identity is slowly shrivelling,
being eaten up and swallowed whole by this deceptively demanding
husband of mine. My overall strategy must take a different course.*

*I shall go back to work. Eventually I'll escape this marriage
from hell. How could I ever have entered into it'*

Well, reading this she could see how it happened, how
easy it is to slip into the wrong thing. That was *her*
experience though. The solution she eventually found
may not apply to Jason and Mia ... she must leave them
to sort themselves out. She would back off.

The following day, Simulac's Nick phoned her late
afternoon full of apologies.

"I just realised, looking at our schedule for tonight –
we've promised our equipment and trainers to another
venue?"

It took a moment for his words to sink in. "What?
You've double-booked?"

"Kind of."

"So, you'll have to cancel them, won't you?"

"I would, but they are an actual customer. One of our
top clients, in fact. No way would our directors want to
let them down. I'm afraid that, as you're non-paying, we'll
have to let this one go tonight."

"But ... it's too late to put people off," she protested
fiercely, thinking of the members.

"So sorry."

It was half-past five. The computer club people would
come along and be disappointed, probably angry with
her, quite rightly so. Some of them, like Jackson, and the
older, less mobile members would have arranged

transport, had a nap in the afternoon. They would be even more put out if their outing was cancelled.

She racked her brains for what they could do instead.

It was Sod's law, she thought, that tonight promised to be a full house; outstripping what the usual quota of equipment could satisfy anyway.

Sure enough, word had spread bringing new members to sign up and join.

The catering team valiantly came along to each session with their tins of cakes, wrapped trays of sandwiches, pastries and platters; the array of food seemed to grow each week and now people were giving a donation towards their costs, she noticed, quite voluntarily. Quite right too, even though it probably breached some food safety regulation once money exchanged hands.

Once the stream of people stopped, she closed the doors and stood up on the dais to speak. In the sure knowledge that some people were hard of hearing, she had managed to hook up an antiquated audio system and tapped the microphone to make sure it was working. She estimated she had an audience of about fifty. It was a few moments before they noticed her and she had to bang on the table with the metal heel of her shoe to bring the chatter to a halt.

"Good evening everyone." There were a few squeaks from the loudspeakers and she patted the microphone again, hoping this might help. They all replied in a cheerful chorus - what lovely folk. "Thank you all so much for coming. And what a crowd we have tonight! You may've noticed there's something missing." Some of them, she observed to her dismay, actually began looking around them. "Yes, the computers and our lovely

Trainers from Simulac couldn't be here tonight." She expected one or two groans but none came. "So I've asked my good friend and neighbour, Lettie, to come along, at *extremely* short notice, and talk to you about what it is like working from home in Appley Green. She is, amongst many other amazing things, a graphics artist and a website designer."

Everyone clapped politely and Lettie came up to the podium. She had her dark curls tied with a red and black silk scarf, and was wearing make up. Wearing a poppy-red tunic-dress made of soft fabric that swirled as she walked and sparkly black leggings with high-heeled boots, she looked stunning. It was like welcoming a celebrity.

"I began using a computer as a child in a remote part of Snowdonia and have never stopped. I can't really imagine not working with one every single day of my life, for lots of reasons. Not all bad! First off, it now enables me to earn a living, without having to fight the traffic every morning to get to an office …"

Considering she only had her own laptop running on its battery to demonstrate anything, Lettie made her talk fascinating. You could have heard a pin drop, except when she made them laugh. Steph looked out onto the gathering and heaved a big sigh of relief. There had been no complaints yet.

She was about a third of the way through the forty minutes they had agreed with beforehand, when the outer door opposite where Steph was sitting, slowly and quietly opened.

Greg slipped in, gave her a little wave and funny sort of smile, then silently, rather stealthily, took one of the only two spare seats at the back. She squinted at him, unsure what his motives might be. Was he checking up on her?

Lettie ended with the words, "I hope what I've shown you has helped. Good luck with your browsing, emails, digital photos and whatever floats your boat. Perhaps you'd like to have a go at designing birthday cards, or ordering your groceries online like I do. I'd love to hear about how you get on. Stick with it!"

The audience's appreciation was so enthusiastic that mere clapping was not deemed to be enough; some were stamping their feet and whistling.

Steph stood up to thank Lettie. "Thanks so much for coming along tonight, Lettie. All that applause speaks for itself. So now please stay on, everyone, and chat about what you've heard, help yourselves to refreshments in the usual way. Next time, the computers will be here, as usual."

All the while as she walked down the middle aisle to welcome Greg, she was thinking what a blessing in disguise Simulac's failure was, in so many ways.

She decided to be pleasant although, with the memory of Bloomstock still recent, she felt awkward. "Greg! You seem fond of surprises this week."

He extended a hand quite formally. "I saw your class advertised on the notice board and thought I'd take a look," he said. "It was mentioned in the local paper too."

"I see. Well I did tell you about it."

"You did. Although you omitted to mention that you were encouraging people to use the Internet," he replied in an even tone. Steph could not tell if there was implied criticism in the comment or not. She had been dreading the possibility of him finding out for weeks, but never imagined the discovery would be quite like this.

She raised her chin. "It's all part and parcel of using a computer these days, isn't it?" she said, smiling, keeping her nerve. Even you must see that now, you stubborn man.

His poker face was so annoying she had an urge to poke him indeed, to provoke some kind of reaction. Instead she mirrored his expression, or rather lack of it; two could play at this game.

"Let me introduce you to the speaker," offered Steph, as a way to break the tension.

"I've met Lettie before."

"Oh, really?" Steph was surprised. It's not as if he lives in Appley Green and it was only a few months ago that Lettie and her husband, Angwyn, moved in next-door.

"She seems to have been quite a hit this evening. Very persuasive. I'll go and say hello," he said. With a little excuse-me wave, he sallied forth in her direction.

She felt strangely abandoned, but not letting this show, she looked around her with purpose. Jackson was not here; maybe his family had turned up. Where was Gloria, she wondered? She was always so keen on the project, her number one supporter in fact, but she did not appear to have come along this evening.

All around people were sitting in groups or weaving about with plates of food. Those who were a bit unsteady on their feet congregated around the tables that usually held the computers and others were ferrying cups of tea and coffee to the more sedentary folk. The place was buzzing with *bonhomie* which had made Greg's expressionless face all the more out of place. His eyes, though, she noticed, were alive and somehow – smiling, maybe mocking.

27

As soon as she blinked her eyes open, Steph felt vaguely aware that today was something special. Yes, this was the day Barnaby was coming with her to see Jackson. She could not fully understand why this was such a pleasurable thought, particularly as she had initially fought against allowing him. One reason for that still stood: he might form an emotional attachment, as she suspected Faith had, adopting Jackson as a kind of surrogate grandfather, or even great grandfather. Yes, Jackson was actually old enough to be *her* grandfather.

But she wanted to see Jackson's delight in having a young visitor, a boy who would probably be awestruck by his house, books, garden, the man himself. She knew Jackson now well enough to know that he was mentally and emotionally stronger than his physical appearance suggested. She no longer feared that he might become reliant upon such visits and then suffer if they stopped.

It was scheduled for half-past four, to fit around Barnaby's school day. Jackson would have had his post-prandial snooze and would most probably enjoy them sharing with him an afternoon cup of tea and slice of his favourite Dundee cake. It was all arranged; he would come to the door at four o'clock. Barnaby had his laptop with him and had combed his hair.

"Have you decided which websites you're going to show him, Barney bear?" she asked in the car on the way.

"I've got a few ideas, thinking about what you've told me, but d'you know what Mum? Probably best to be flexible and hear what he says first."

Flexible. Bless him. Steph smiled and nodded. How wise children can be sometimes. She could not remember being so sensible, or sensitive, at the age of eleven. Ted Devonish would have liked that.

"Phwaw," he cried, as the car crunched to a halt in the gravel driveway. "It's huge!" His reaction reminded her of how limited her son's experience of large houses was; he had no memory of Richard's even larger mansion – or Richard, thankfully. "It's … it's like it's been caged, like some monster from space swooped down and wrapped lianas round it."

"Lianas?"

Barnaby threw her a disdainful look. "What? Mum. You don't know what lianas are? At your age?"

She laughed, admitting nothing and promising herself to consult a dictionary later. It was a good thing she did not rely on her children for self-esteem.

Jackson opened the door, almost as soon as they had rung the bell. His routine was to sit on a window-seat in the hallway at the appointed time; to avoid keeping visitors outside for too long.

As predicted, he gave Barnaby a warm welcome and had already pulled out some old books, jigsaws and games for him. Barnaby secretly gave her an amused look, but was mature enough not to scoff. How sweet, that an old man had these things to hand, even though he never saw his own grandchildren, or great-grandchildren. They were covered in a thick layer of dust; she hoped Barnaby would not let his guard down and comment on this. Children could be uncompromisingly honest sometimes.

"I asked my lunchtime carer to set out some refreshment on a trolley in the kitchen," he said, once the introductions were over and they were sitting down in his study. It seemed to be the only room he used now.

"Would you like me to put the kettle on, then?"

"No rush, my dear. Perhaps in a few minutes." He would be thinking Barnaby may not like to be left alone with him until he had familiarised himself with his surroundings.

"How are you today?" She always checked on this first thing, as he rarely mentioned a problem unless she asked.

"Not too bad at all." He nodded and placed his right hand over his left to help still their tremor. Then a wry smile, "Apart from the usual."

"I heard you have family coming to see you. Is that right?" Why was her heart pounding in her chest? Why did a part of her want him to deny this?

"Oh, yes. Indeed. All coming. That'll be a bit messy!"

"Messy?"

"Chaotic! There's so many. Don't see them from one year to the next and then they all come at once. Like proverbial buses!" He chuckled. "Is that a computer you've brought there, then, young Barnaby?" Barnaby opened it up at once, needing little encouragement. "You must show me a few things." Then he turned to Steph again. "Yes, they will stay in a hotel, of course. They will."

"Oh really?" Steph could see this was practical. "I guess even this house might burst at the seams …"

"I've told them it'll be convenient for them to stay at the place where the party will be, of course."

"Party?"

"Well, it's my 90th, you know!"

Of course, why had she not put two and two together? "But your birthday is not for a while yet."

"You think it's easy to get a date when twenty-six people are all free to travel round the world?"

Steph raised her eyebrows. "Must take some organising."

"My dear daughter, Estebel ..." She felt the blood rise to her cheeks, embarrassed, confused, as if she were ... what? Jealous? This was ridiculous. That Estebel was stealing her thunder? She should be happy, very happy for Jackson ... This was a thousand times better than anything she could offer to bring his family closer. "... who lives in Aberdeen and has done all the work – using the email I believe. Wonderful thing, eh, Barnaby, the email? We used to think the wireless and telegraph were miracles when I was a boy!"

"Did you have a phone though?" asked Barnaby. "One of those old wind-up ones like you see in black and white films? In westerns?" Bless him. She loved her boy so much she wanted to give him a squeeze, but he would not appreciate a show of affection right now, to put it mildly. If only Lucas could see him; each day as he grew, she saw something of Lucas in him. Lucas would have liked Jackson too.

"I think by the time our family got a telephone, technology had moved on one stage from that, but it was a big, black heavy old thing with a rotary dial. If you look in that book there ..." and he pointed to a row of heavy volumes that luckily was at ground level, ... "the one, I think third from the right in that section."

"Labelled 1930s electronics?" asked Barnaby on his knees, with his head twisted so he could read the spine of said book.

"I'll put the kettle on now, shall I?"

212

Jackson smiled. "That would be splendid. We can have some man-talk," he said with a boyish mischievousness that Barnaby, to her surprise, seemed to understand perfectly. It was a bit sexist, but she would bear it, in the circumstances.

With ears like a bat, she listened as she went about her kitchen duties. She could hear laughter, the unbroken boy's voice, the soft tones of a man with Parkinson's that almost reduced to a whisper at times. Their gentle murmurs made it all seem rather conspiratorial, cloaked in secrecy. It warmed her heart though. They were getting on famously.

His laptop had almost been forgotten, but once tea and cake were done, Jackson requested to see it. Perhaps he was guessing that Barnaby was keen to show him; so thoughtful, so typical.

"Well, what kind of thing would you like to see, Mr Jeffrys? My Mum did suggest perhaps some houses where you could go and live?"

"Mm. How about, first of all, some games? I always liked to play games and I have some small boys coming to visit me soon. I'd like to know the kind of thing that boys of today enjoy playing ..."

Though not superstitious, Steph now kept everything crossed. She had not anticipated this. There was nothing she could do now but trust to Barnaby's discretion. Why did she have a sudden sinking feeling in her stomach, compounding the strange emptiness already there?

28

The email from Greg that lay among about twenty others, stood out to Steph like a flashing sign in the dark; not as a signal that help was coming, more like a disaster warning light. Greg Mason. An uninvited guest. Never before seen in her Inbox. A fitting surname for a man whose middle name should be Stone, she thought, huffily.

It was set out rather formally, like a letter. He would learn, she mused, maximising the window, though quickly realising there was no need. It was concise. Why did that not surprise her? *Dear Steph, Here are some proposed dates and times for us to meet* ... she reached for her work diary ... *Please allow a couple of hours. There are a number of things I wish to discuss as a follow-up to your Performance Appraisal. Please suggest a venue that will be time-efficient for you. Also please note that from now on you can submit to me your daily schedule, any subsequent amendments, and monthly reports by email. With thanks. I look forward to hearing from you, Greg. Greg Mason, Special Support for Seniors.*

Huh! Heaven forbid that he should in any way appear friendly. No mention of how well the computer club went last night, when he dropped in unannounced to spy on her. No little joke to acknowledge that he must have done a U-turn on the email embargo. She quickly emailed back to demonstrate how brilliant email was for instant communication and getting things done. There were no gaps in her schedule until next week, so she picked the

Wednesday on his list, 11.00 am at her house. She could scarcely find a more 'time-efficient' venue than that!

But what exactly did he want to discuss?

Faith appeared from upstairs. "Morning!" she said, "Early bird catches the spam, uh?"

"Morning, sweet. Actually, I don't get much, with all the junk email filters and firewalls now. Do you?"

"Nah! Well, just the usual. You know."

Steph wondered. "Mm. Tell me if anything bad … you know …"

"What! Penis enlargements and stuff like that?"

Steph's pupils dilated. "Hm. That kind of thing."

"OK. Well, I don't get those any more."

"Oh. I'm glad to hear it." She wondered if she should be monitoring her daughter's online activity more closely. "Anyway, how's you? Finish your story?"

"Yeah. I emailed it to Jeff … er …Mr Smallwood. He said I 'done good'."

"What! He actually said that?" asked Steph, wondering what English teachers were coming to these days. "Is he American?"

"No. Course not! Mum, you are funny sometimes," she commented lightly and breezed off to make herself some breakfast. "And I mean funny odd!"

"Oh, ha-ha!" One of these days her offspring would say something to make her feel that the effort of rearing them was worth the trouble, that she was in some way a good human being – in their eyes. Steph might have queried Faith's rather disparaging observation but her attention was diverted by another email pinging onto her screen. From Justin. Steph held her head in her hands and whispered some very bad language.

She read it, almost covering up her eyes, as if afraid of what she might see, like when, as a very small child, she used to half-watch *Doctor Who* on TV.

It was stiff and formal and she was immediately suspicious. *I have some suitable properties, ideal for your Mr Jeffrys. Also we have received so much interest from prospective buyers for The Hideaway we would suggest putting it to auction. I assume you wish all communication to go through yourself. Please contact me to arrange a meeting.*

She supposed there would be no harm in meeting him at the Willem Hardrop shop, although it would be extremely awkward. She would need to check this out with Jackson first; Justin had been the one to tell her that Jackson actually wanted to hold fire until his family visit was over.

The doorbell rang and she jumped. Not Justin surely. Or Greg, possibly? Who could this be, so early in the morning? She needed to grab some breakfast and get out to her first appointment. With this meeting with Greg on the near horizon, she must carry out her duties to the letter and make sure she was always at the right place at the right time. Huh!

Faith had beaten her to it and she heard, "Hi Lettie. Come on in!"

"Lettie! Star of stage!" said Steph, rushing out to the hallway to give her a hug. "Thanks so much for last night. It was just fantastic. You will never know how much you saved my life!"

"Sounds a bit dramatic!" scoffed Lettie.

"Sorry – I'm prone to exaggeration. Come on in."

"It was my pleasure. And to tell you the truth I think your little gathering was just as happy to sit and have a chinwag over tea and cake!"

Steph laughed. That was one of her Mum's words, *chinwag*. "Not at all. You made their evening. Sit yourself down. Would you like a coffee or something? I haven't had breakfast yet."

"Thanks. OK. Just straight black for me."

Instead of taking a seat, Lettie followed her out to the kitchen. As Steph put some strong Italian coffee in the cafetiere and slices of brioche in the toaster, she said, "I hope the fee was OK. Enough I mean. We have a fairly limited budget for emergencies."

Lettie shook her head vehemently, black curls bouncing around her face. "No. Actually that's what I came to see you about."

Steph had wondered if it was enough and felt a bit mean, but this would not look good on her expenses. She would gladly give more out of her own pocket ...

"I really enjoyed doing this and as I was chatting to these people, I thought what a great thing to do as a change from working with a screen all day! You know sometimes I feel a bit of a recluse. Days and weeks can slip by and I don't actually speak to anyone workwise – not in the flesh!" Steph loved her sing-song Welsh accent; she was such a joy to listen to. "I don't want paying, see, not for this one. Call it a test run."

Steph wanted to wrap her arms round her and plant enormous kisses on her cheeks! "Absolutely, I can totally see that, but you gave up your time and we agreed ..."

"No," Lettie cut in, "No fee, but ..." and she gave Steph a cheeky look.

"Yes?"

"A massive favour?"

Steph was intrigued and worried in equal measure now. "Whatever. I am in your debt. So much." She held her breath.

"Would you be kind enough to write me a reference, or be there for others to contact, so that I can have a go with other organisations?"

She breathed again. "Oh Lettie, of course I …"

"It's such a great way for me to put a feel out into the community. You know, I can really get to know people, use my speaking voice which sometimes goes mad for the lack of an audience that actually lives and breathes, and as if that isn't enough, I can promote my free-lance work and hopefully pull in a few more customers … You see? In the long-term all that's worth much more to me than a fee. Oh, I'd be so grateful." At last she paused, looking hopefully at Steph with her huge alpaca eyes.

"No problem at all. Sounds like an enterprising plan. Do you have a card?" Lettie nodded. "Let me have a few and I'll spread the word around as I go on my rounds. I see all kinds of people, other than retired folk I mean. Professional people, other charities and societies, all sorts."

"That's a lovely job you have. I'm really grateful for this. Look, as a kind of thank you, I've been meaning to ask you round for supper one evening but Angwyn is usually there … well, I wondered if you and your colleague, Greg, would like to come round?"

Steph gasped at the idea. Lettie went on, "I mean … you don't have a … you know, anyone at the moment do you? Sorry, that's a bit rude isn't it, I mean, if you do then …"

Steph smiled. "No. There are no men in my life, if that's what you're struggling to say." Nor ever likely to be, she thought. Never again.

"He seems so nice. He knocked on my door when he was looking for you. I didn't realise who he was and may have put my foot in it, as usual, but anyhow, last night he came over and chatted to introduce himself properly and I had a chance to put things right ..." Steph was wondering what on earth she had previously said to Greg, but Lettie carried on mischievously. "I tell you," and she whispered, "if I wasn't happily married myself, I'd ..."

"What! You'd give him one?"

They fell about laughing and Steph suddenly realised that it was a long, long time since she'd really had a good laugh with a friend and it felt so good – she nearly burst into tears.

Faith was putting on her coat ready for school. "What on earth's wrong with *you*?" she asked, dryly.

Steph liked Lettie so much she had no alternative but to accept the invitation, but after her meeting with Greg, she suspected she might be forced to change her mind.

29

For days, Steph avoided the final section of her Diary –
because she knew where it ended, that point where she
stopped recording her thoughts and feelings; so it was
with some trepidation that she finally picked it up again.
She knew she must decide whether Faith could read it
now, later or never.

*'The job market this winter is at a low ebb, stagnating, with
employees hanging on to their jobs like grim death. Finding part-
time work to fit in with family life is not easy, even with my proven
track record and glowing references, not including the one that my
last boss, Brodric McTavish, might have supplied.*

*I've explored blind alleys and hit brick walls! So am going to
enquire about vacancies at the council Leisure Centre in Bloomstock
where I last worked. It holds bad memories of bullying but I'm
desperate.'*

*'Today I gave them a call and got through to the Human
Resources department. The recruitment manager remembered me
and sounded really cheerful about it! And, as it happens, they have
something. He said how lucky it was I called because jobs are so few
and far between just now, but there is something in Accounts. My
heart sank when I heard that. Accounts! Not my favourite things,
book-keeping and spreadsheets … only worked with them in the
past as a small part of managing House of Fitness when I had to
keep a sharp eye on profit and loss but much of the paperwork I*

delegated to other staff members. I learned how to interpret statistics, but am the first to admit I'm not ahead of the game with routine number work.

But I (half-heartedly) asked them if they could email me a job description and an application form. Little other option at the moment, so I'll go for it and hope that with a foot in the door, it could be a stepping-stone to a more fulfilling position.

The guy said, "Sure I can. You just get it filled in as soon as you can. Interviews are next week, so be quick! Good luck, Steph." It was so good to hear a really warm and friendly voice, making me acutely aware of what was missing in my life. I feel hopeful that this could be another new start that might turn my life around.'

'Today I got the job offer and straight away broke the news to Richard. Imagine his reaction!

"Why do you need to work?" he cried, his face contorted with anger, as if I had confessed to pushing drugs on the streets. "Don't I provide for you well enough?" He took it as a personal insult, his pride badly dented. We come from different worlds; I can see that now.

"Of course you do, but I need to get out and work with adults, Richard. It's what I'm used to." (Felt as if I'd stepped into the 1950s!)

"But you told me, as plain as day, how you had struggled to work and bring up your children on your own. I thought this life at home was what you wanted!"

He's right of course. In fact he sounded so reasonable, my actions were hard to justify. Our row continued until we reached a point of silence, one of the worst kinds of climax in any marital conflict, I think, short of violence.'

'Richard has stopped talking to me completely, it's been days now, nursing his grievance like a wounded bear.

I know more than ever I must make this job work and release myself and my children from his subtle, but tyrannical, hold. He's never raised a finger to me, nor even shouted or cursed, but somehow he makes me feel worthless, a mere appendage, a satellite to his sun. It'd be a challenge to convey my reasons to a third party. A need for divorce would be hard to plead and I need to be sure of my financial footing before I make the break. After such a brief marriage, I would not expect a share of his income in the settlement; I will not be beholden to him for any longer than I must.'

'Barnaby is settled in a pre-school Nursery and with the part-time job, I can pick up both him and Faith after school. It's all beyond Richard's comprehension but I must amass some savings before we can leave him.'

'I've been in the Accounts job a few weeks now. I've made superhuman efforts to bond with colleagues and be productive, but today who should walk in and lean heavily into my desk, but my old buddy, Brodric McTavish. I nearly handed in my notice, there and then.

"Ah-ha. So you're back with us are you?" he said. I never noticed before quite how much his breath stinks. He has this way of leaning forward, invading my space, crushing his manhood against the edge of my desk. I have no idea why he does these things, but his old ways came flooding back.

I took a deep, calming breath, looked up briefly from my computer screen and somehow smiled. "As you see."

"Ah. Agency, is it?"

"No. Permanent. Full-time," I replied, knowing he likes to stick with facts. Short, sweet, to the point. No time-wasting.

The corners of his mouth were turned down, his thin wet lips forming a perfect inverted U shape. He was so like a pantomime villain, I had to stifle a hysterical giggle. "Now that does surprise me," he commented, and with that he walked away in the direction

222

of my new boss's office, no doubt to offer them some enlightenment on my past negligence.'

'That was the day I got the terrible news - like a body blow. In the evening my landline phone rang, as I was describing the scene at work to Faith in a slightly expurgated form. It made me feel better, although I was not sure a nine-year old was really that interested or understood the implications of my story. In fact, it's as well she did not - unsuitable stuff for young ears. I glanced upstairs, hoping the phone hadn't woken Barnaby who finally went to sleep halfway through a third bedtime story. He's really into anything to do with jungles, bears and dinosaurs and forces his eyes to stay open with fierce four-year old determination. But I am delaying what happened next.

It took me by surprise to hear my aunt in Somerset on the end of the phone. We've lost touch for so long, (she didn't come to the wedding) I didn't even recognise her voice at first.

"Is that Stephanie? It's your Auntie Carole here, love," she said. With her West Country burr, she sounded so friendly. My first thoughts were along the lines of why I hadn't seen her in about ten years. How time disappears ...!

"Yes, of course. How are you? And everyone?" I said, you know the automatic response, but then it shot through me, painfully, that I haven't seen Dad for months, nearly a year. He hadn't called, written or indicated that he wanted to see me or the children ... 'out of sight out of mind' made this unbearable truth easier to bear. And I was so absorbed with my own problems.

"I'm so sorry. It's your father, dear Giles, he passed away just an hour ago. In hospital."

I couldn't believe it. Still can't. Had no idea he was ill. "What? I mean, are you sure? In hospital?" So many questions. She told me he'd been in hospital for a few weeks. "Look, Steph, you'll be coming down, why don't you come before the funeral – and no worries, we'll sort all that out – and I'll explain properly. I'm so very sorry. He didn't want you to know, you see. He made me

223

promise." That was what she said, more or less. **He didn't want me to know. He made her promise.**

I cannot bring myself to tell Faith. I knew she was listening to my side of the conversation with a tiny mouth and wide eyes, trying to understand. I had no idea who it was when I lifted up the receiver. It must have been clear to her, though, from my face that something was very wrong.'

That was where the diary ended.

Steph looked through her schedule for the next few days. She had just emailed it to Greg. Already she could see there would be an amendment; she wanted to fit in a visit to Gloria, her stalwart computer supporter, but was not sure if Greg would approve. She did not, after all, fit the SSS profile. She was a strong, independent woman who wanted to help others; she was not a lonely, isolated, in any way housebound person in need of their services.

But it was rather odd that she did not turn up at the last class. She was not to know there was no equipment and she had attended all the other sessions. A sixth sense told Steph that she should find out if all was well. She would call her.

The phone rang about six times before the answer-phone cut in. Steph left a message, but then wondered how Gloria would react if she dropped by her house without forewarning. Some people were fine with casual visits; but with others it was such a no-no she would put a note in their file to remind her never to do this. She would wait a day to give Gloria a chance to get back to her. Maybe she was away on holiday, but something still niggled with Steph; Gloria was so efficient, she would have passed on apologies for her absence.

On her way home at the end of a busy day, fitting in five home visits, she drove back around Appley Green down the lane towards home when she wondered whether to nip in to Willem Hardrop. It was nearly their closing time, so this would ensure the meeting would be kept short and businesslike. She wanted nothing more from it than the brochures Justin had mentioned in his email. For the rest, she would just forget, ignore, put it behind her.

She swung the car into Heathfields School driveway whereby she could turn round and go back the half mile into Appley Green. Once she had parked behind the village shops, the timing was perfect. She could be in and out in ten minutes max.

What she had not anticipated was that Justin would be leaving a few minutes early and would happen to be entering the narrow alleyway leading through from the shops to the car park.

Greg was typing a simple agenda for 'Meeting with Steph'. Seriously rusty in computer skills he was cursing at the cursor, shouting at the mouse, and almost wanting to kick the keyboard at times, but eventually ended up with a list: Weekly schedules – priorities; Problem Areas – time management; Future Projects; Liaison with Other Agencies; Financial Matters (GOOD NEWS); Any other Business. He then deleted the '(GOOD NEWS)'; reserving it for another occasion.

His cat was wandering across the desk threatening to cause complete cyber-confusion. "Long time since you saw me doing this, isn't it Bill?" he muttered to his pet. It sat down neatly, like a china ornament, and appropriately on the mouse-mat, and blinked at him.

After emailing the document to Stephanie he spent the rest of the day updating his software and persuading more of his recalcitrant fingers to take part in the typing. He also checked his incoming mail. Two from Stephanie, to confirm a date – oh, not till next week, why so long? Then the schedule. "Ah, now I see why," he muttered.

When Justin saw her approaching he stopped dead. As if realising this made him look guilty, furtive, nervous, all those things alien to his adopted persona, Steph could practically see him pull his bootstraps up and his shoulders back before striding on towards her.

"Steph!" he said, with a hideous smile. "Those brochures!"

She did not return his smile. "Yes. I was about to collect them." She felt very vulnerable. His gaze was penetrating and he now stood close, a little too close. Then she heard him whisper, "I have told Mia. Everything. So there's no need for you to do anything, say anything. OK?"

"Yes. Yes, of course." She could tell he was lying; there was something about his manner of speaking that she could now read. It was just his way to get her off his case. Well, he needn't bother! She wanted nothing more to do with him.

"You won't contact her then. Right?" She was even more certain that his persistence proclaimed his deceit loud and clear. He doth protest too much.

"Have you a moment to go back for the property details? For Mr Jeffrys?"

He looked at his watch, clearly torn. "I have to be somewhere. An appointment. I'll get them to you."

Without a further word, he walked away towards the car park where Steph now needed to be. She waited a moment, giving him a chance to get well ahead of her.

Tapping her foot with impatience she decided to go back to her car. She tried not to notice Justin standing in the car park, talking to a young pregnant woman. It was none of her business.

Gloria did not return her call. Steph left another message and waited a further day. When she was passing by between visits she decided to slip down the driveway to her mansion. It was such an easy thing to do and in no time she was standing in the porch, waiting for the heavy oak door to creak open.

Gloria, wearing what looked like pyjamas, appeared, looking half the woman Steph remembered. In droopy clothing and very evidently, wearing no support garments beneath, she was transformed, not in a good way.

As soon as she saw it was Steph, she stood up straight, as if somehow caught out, and affected a cheery expression. "Stephanie! Oh, dear. I couldn't think who it might be. Perhaps a courier. Please excuse my state of undress. Come in, though, please do, come in, come through …" Steph followed her, closing the front door behind her.

They sat down in the room, as before, but how different this woman was from the one who greeted her on that first visit she made a while back.

"Are you well?" She looked at the baggy eyes, the bedraggled grey hair that hung limply around her shoulders, usually pulled back in a neat French roll. "I mean, are you *not* well? You don't look yourself, Gloria."

She grimaced a little, as if searching for words, unable to explain. "Stephanie, in your job, you will understand perhaps better than most. I am not ill. So my doctor assures me at regular intervals. No, not ill. But I get these moods that come and go …"

Steph recognised the signs of depression instantly. She hoped it had not gone too deep. "Are you sleeping well?"

She sighed. "Naps mostly. Keep me going. Powernaps. Hah! Not much sleep at night though."

Gloria was normally a straightforward, no-nonsense kind of woman, who would not prevaricate so Steph decided to get to the point.

"Is there something worrying you?"

"No more than usual, my dear."

"So usually there is something?" There was a pause. Steph allowed this to happen; she could see Gloria was weighing something up, deciding whether to spill it out. "I am a good listener."

"I know."

"You know?"

"I hear it from others." She tapped her nose. "Village talk. And," she stressed, "I remember Ted Devonish used to say how he had chosen you for the new charity he was planning, just in his mind at that time, but not that long before that awful, fatal accident." She shook her head at the memory of it, momentarily distracted. "So tragic. Such a waste."

But at least he had it all set out in his Will, though Steph. "Yes, indeed." Steph smiled and tilted her head. "So? I can listen. If you like. If it will help." It would make her late for the next visit, but just this once, so be it. She felt Gloria was, at this moment, even more in need of a friend than her next client was. It would not be the end of the world if she arrived late.

228

"You probably think I ... I am a strong, happy woman. On top of things?"

"You certainly appear to be on top of the world, and with all your extraordinary past achievements ..."

"Ah! Now that's the problem isn't it? What you do in the past can sometimes be irrevocable. Can never be put right. Never. No matter what." She gazed to her left, her face tense, avoiding eye contact. She was staring out of a window, absently following the antics of a couple of grey squirrels darting up and down a monkey-puzzle tree. Her hands were clasped together tightly.

"Is there something you would like to put right? Gloria?" Steph was sure now that she really wanted to unburden herself, to let something fly out, but was finding it almost impossible to face, let alone express.

"Yes. But I cannot." Her chin trembled and her eyes filled with tears. What a sad, sorry sight she was. Steph, quick to empathise, felt a lump in her throat.

"Is it so terrible? What happened?"

"I didn't know at the time." Another long pause. Steph resisted the temptation to look at her watch or reach for her phone. Maggie and Jim would have to wait – at least they had each other; another partnership of the Arthur and Astrid kind.

"It must be something very painful to you ..."

Gloria cut in, her composure apparently recovered. "You are right. I was always strong, full of life – like my mother, who was never in any way soft with me and my siblings. She was never really there, except for formal meetings now and then."

Steph raised her eyebrows. "Really? Meetings? With children?"

"Oh, yes. We had a ... a Nanny, you see. Nanny Rudge." Another pause. "Anyway, I enjoyed my work, although I never really needed it in the financial sense. As you know, my husband was a Colonel serving in the British Army, usually posted abroad, and I bore him a son. He seemed very content with this. The one son and heir was all he really needed. I buried myself in my work, you see. People thought I was clever, lavished praise on me. Our son, Maurice, ... he had a Nanny, just as I did. I knew nothing of real motherhood, but ..." she broke off, something like a sob catching in her throat, "Stephanie, I could have learned. Yes. I should have. Could have made the effort to be a proper mother." The term 'proper mother' was always going to be a confusing concept for Steph. "But I never did. I turned my back on my little boy, even though a part of me was jealous of his Nanny, Nanny Bernadette."

"So, your son? Where is he now?" Steph found herself looking around for evidence of any family by way of photos or portraits, as she had before.

"He is fifty-eight now and lives with ... with Bernadette. Bernie he calls her, so they tell me. He has nothing to do with me. It's as if something has turned him to stone. He can, I suppose, never form a bond that should have been formed years ago."

"I see." Steph, now armed with this knowledge, felt unsure of what to do with it, how to react. "And you blame yourself?"

Colour now rushed to Gloria's cheeks and she threw her arms up in the air. "Of course I do!" It was, at least, good to see some animation, some fight, some of the old Gloria.

Steph considered this. "I feel maybe it's not my place to pass comment, because I can see this is a sensitive situation, and very emotional, but ... please don't be too hard on yourself. Maybe your husband could have been around more, more supportive when he was at home. Did he ask you if you wanted more children?"

Gloria pursed her lips and shook her head briskly. "No. Never. My opinion did not count – not with him, you see. I adored him, right until the day he died five years ago. Still do – the memory of him. But ... he was, you know, the boss. Absolutely. Military man." She sliced the air with her hands to indicate something – a kind of precision, Steph guessed. "He appointed Bernadette. Yes I think I would have liked a noisy houseful of naughty, lively children, of course I would."

"Then you would have had more purpose at home?"

"Maybe. But it doesn't excuse me selfishly putting my own needs before that of my only child."

"So he was unhappy?"

She thought a moment, pulling back her hair deftly into a kind of knot at the back, making her look instantly more groomed. "Actually. No. He wasn't. He's never mentioned that he was in any way unhappy. Of course, he always adored Bernadette. She played with him, fed him, sang to him, saw him take his first steps, read him stories, pushed him round Appley Green until he could walk ... Everything. I was just a stranger. But he was never unhappy, I would say."

"Well, that's good at least. It's just you that's unhappy. Perhaps you have no need to be."

"But it's as if I never had a son! He loves his Bernie. They live together," she repeated. Steph now wondered how almost-incestuous this relationship was, but thought it best not to probe. "Sometimes I see them. In Appley Green. Can you imagine? It's like a knife going through me." She got up and went over to the window, her back to Steph. She was wiping her eyes, Steph could tell.

231

"I know how it feels to hand over a baby to another person," said Steph, going over to her. "I had to do the same thing, but my little girl never suffered as a result of that. She is a happy, altogether lovely teenager, really quite a young woman at the age of sixteen. My story is different from yours, but I can see how it was. And you shouldn't blame yourself. Actually, did the Nanny do the best she could to include you in bringing up Maurice?"

Gloria considered this. "It was up to me. I should have made it clear that I wanted to be there at certain times. Bedtime. Bathtime. But I didn't. But, now you mention it, no, she was very protective of him, almost as if I were poison, and as a small boy, he would shrink back when he saw me. Later, he went away to boarding school. No question. That was the way of doing things …"

Steph could not help but wonder what poisonous thoughts Nanny Bernadette might have been feeding her small charge, but this was pure speculation and she did not voice this idea. It would be uncharitable. It was as if Gloria had read her thoughts, however.

"I did overhear her telling him a story where there was a wicked Mother – rather like the more stereotypical wicked stepmother of pantomimes and fairytales – so unfair in reality, especially these days …" Gloria stopped to turn and smile. "She would hold him back when I approached. Yes, she did," she added dreamily, as if picturing it all too clearly in her mind. "And, of course, he would turn and cling to her knees, as if … as if, in fear. And can you believe it, *I too* was intimidated?"

"Shall I make us a cup of tea?" asked Steph, realising that she must somehow bring this traumatic visit to a close.

Gloria slapped her thighs. "My goodness me! Whatever must you be thinking of me? I shall make us a very quick cuppa and you, my dear, must be on your way. I know how busy you are. I feel … so much better. You can't imagine how much. Please come again and I shall lay on a small feast for you. I really will …"

30

Even though it was term time, Steph still had to plan carefully. "I have a work meeting here tomorrow," said Steph, "so when you come home from school, just slip in quietly, say hello politely and …"

"Evaporate? Keep out of sight and sound," replied Faith. "I know." Then there was a sharp intake of breath and Steph saw colour rise in her daughter's cheeks. "Gah! Faggots! I forgot to tell you." She reached for her school bag and began a desperate rummaging in its depths and pockets. "Last week we were given a letter. I'm sorry, Mum. Tomorrow is an Inset day so Barnaby and me'll be here, or around anyway. Didn't they email you?"

"Hmm. Don't think so, but …" I've been a bit distracted lately, she might have added. Steph tried not to over-react but was thinking that too much domesticity at a meeting with Greg would not look professional or be businesslike enough for him. "Barnaby. Hmm. Well, hopefully he has enough homework he can get on with …"

"And computer games. I'm sure he'll amuse himself," said Faith with cheerful optimism.

When Greg arrived promptly at her door, Faith and Barnaby were both upstairs in their rooms. After her short lecture to them, full of warnings, silence reigned.

When she saw his jeans and navy Guernsey sweater, she felt overdressed in her pewter-grey trouser suit teamed with a crisp white linen shirt. He handed her two warm paper bags exuding bakery smells.

"That's nice. Ooh! Mmm," she said, despite herself, peeping inside to see various Danish pastries, fruity, apple, spiced and chocolaty. "Thank you, Greg. Coffee?" Barnaby could smell food he liked from a considerable distance, she thought, doubtfully. This would surely test his curiosity to the limits.

"Please."

"It's ready." With a gesture, she offered him a seat facing away from the stairs that issued straight into the room.

"So! Where are your children?"

"Oh, well …"

"I wondered why there were so many school-kids hanging around the village. Sarah in the bakery told me they were all off today."

"I didn't know this until yesterday. They're upstairs. Working."

"Cruel mother! Child slave labour in the garret?"

He was trying to be funny. She suppressed a smile. "Homework, of course. I received the agenda," she said, realising how stilted and awkward they were with each other, "attached to your email." Resisting the temptation to quiz him about his change of heart regarding emails, she simply poured the coffee, passed a cup to him and put the pastries on a plate.

"Before we work our way through that … Steph. There's something, possibly more important. Ex-agenda."

Her heart gave a little thump. What was he going to say? Something horrible. Some criticism. She could feel it coming like a towering, irresistible wave she was powerless to rise above.

"I don't quite know how to put this, but, working as we do, just the two of us, it's terribly important that we get on. Isn't it? We need to understand each other a bit more than we do? Professionally – and personally. Would you agree?"

She looked away and shrugged, feeling like a wayward teenager who was being upbraided by a teacher or parent for breaching some petty house-rule.

"Perhaps, it is. Are you saying we don't? Get on? Understand each other?"

"Yes. I am." He bit into an apple and cinnamon Danish. She watched crumbs fall from his mouth, and the way he delicately licked his lips and fingers, enjoying every mouthful. He showed no signs of the queasiness she was experiencing. He had very shapely lips, she noticed. What might be described as sculpted, and even, white teeth. Not that such things mattered, but she had never really studied these particular features before. His nose was straight but not beaky, more fleshy ... "Are you having one of these? I can't eat them all, you know ..."

"In a while. They look delicious, but I had breakfast not that long ago ..." Steph looked up to see Barnaby appear at the half-way point in the stairs, where they turned back on themselves. He was visibly sniffing the air like a bloodhound. She glared at him and he retreated.

"I'll tell you a bit about myself," he said. "You may not be interested and that's your privilege, but we need to do this. Then you can have your turn."

Steph froze. She was not at all sure she wanted this therapy session, the unveiling of her personal life. She thought of her time with Gloria the other day, how a simple chat led to emotions running high, secrets, revelations. After all, she too had gone through very dark times that were best left alone.

236

"Could we deal with some of the things on the agenda first ..." she suggested, feeling slight panic. "Then perhaps half-way through we can have this ... chat." Or maybe not, she hoped.

"Oh. Well, as you like. I can't force you to listen, or to talk." He seemed a little affronted, as if this had spoiled his day. His easy-going manner was replaced by a frown hovering over sad eyes and she immediately regretted her procrastination, or perhaps refusal, to enter into his plan.

At that moment the doorbell rang. Steph excused herself quickly to pre-empt Barnaby rushing down. Probably the postman, she thought. She opened the door, only to see Justin, confronting her. He looked at her blankly, pushed a pile of property brochures into her hands, turned on his heels and left without a word.

When she returned to the room, Greg was standing at the window looking out, hands in his pockets. He looked pensive as he watched Justin disappear out of sight.

"Sorry. Where were we?" asked Steph, putting the brochures on a side table.

He came back to the table and sat down. "Unfortunately, if we do it your way we shall start on a negative footing. First item: Problem Areas. What do you see as the problem areas in your job Steph?"

She thought for a moment. "I think the greatest problem is always time. Or lack of it."

He nodded, looking down, his face serious. Then he gazed up at her in that very direct way of his.

"This is clear even to me. Do you feel you lack focus sometimes?"

She felt herself bristle. She worked hard, she did everything she could for her clients in the time available.

"Possibly. It's easy to go down the wrong tracks sometimes," she admitted.

"If time is the key problem area, there is no place for getting derailed down sidings and dead-ends. Is there? Would you agree?"

"Yes, but it's not always simple to stick to the mainline fast-track." Perhaps, she thought, anger rising, you would like to spend a few days doing my job. Role reversal! How great that would be!

He took out some hand-written notes. "There's the question of the Gemstone shop. The people there said you are helping them with their website. All part of your job, is it? Do they fit the profile? Ted Devonish's model?"

Steph blushed guiltily. He had been talking to people in the village – about her? What right had he got to do that? She could be helping them in her own free time as far as he knew. Keeping a cool head and even tone she replied, "They came along to the computer class and I thought their enthusiasm and success on the Internet would be a good example. Extremely motivating for the others …"

"Hmm. Helping clients find property? Is this in your job description?"

"Not exactly, but it might be essential to their future wellbeing."

"Hmm." He was stroking his chin and she could not help noticing his neat finger nails. "Not sure how involved you should be in that. You seem to have a relationship with Willem Hardrop that could be … distracting?"

How could she explain herself? "That Justin … he …"

238

"Is an attractive man? With whom you have to meet away from prying eyes, possibly because he is married?" This was becoming like a police interrogation. He had bothered to find out Justin was married!

"No, no. Oh you've got it so wrong!" she cried. There was no way she could explain all that now. It was history as far as she was concerned.

"And the fact you had your mobile switched off was … unfortunate."

"Yes, well, I didn't expect you to go on some massive chase across the country to find me!"

"No. And since then, I took a call from a couple who told me you simply did not turn up."

Maggie and Jim. "I was held up elsewhere. These things happen."

"Now I know you called them later, they let me know. But that's not the point, Steph. They were expecting you and the gentleman in question was very stressed about you letting them down. Actually, I think they were worried about what had happened to you, but, you see, it could have been them in serious need of something."

"I felt the person I was with was in greater need at the time."

"Who was that? The previous client I assume." He consulted the printed version of her schedule.

She sighed. No. Not a client. Gloria. "No-o. It was … someone … not actually a client on file. She helps at the computer class and, as she failed to turn up and respond to my messages, I called to see her …"

"Just like that! You called to see someone, for whom there is no record, no contact details. This is not a safe way for a lone worker to be working, Steph. Can't you *see* that?"

She was close to hating him and found it difficult to defend her actions after the event.

"She is, in fact a depressed lady, very lonely. With issues."

"Name?"

"Gloria Whittaker."

"OK – let me have her address and telephone number, open up a file."

"Is that it?" asked Steph, growing weary of his analysis of her problem areas. "Perhaps we should move on to Future Projects."

He raised his eyebrows and looked at her. "No. That is not *it*. There is the matter of Mr Jeffrys?"

She shifted about uneasily on her seat. This was too much. She hated this, she hated Greg and felt close to tears, quite at odds with the situation and her extremely smart appearance.

"I was looking at the number of hours you spend across the week with clients. Why so much time with him?"

"His needs are great. Isolated, physically incapacitated …"

"Perhaps he requires referral to other agencies."

"I think he relies on me …"

"While others may suffer and be left out altogether." He closed his file, as if to say 'I rest my case'. "All I can say, Steph, is that this way of working must change."

"You don't understand …"

He then put his head slightly on one side and offered her what seemed like a genuinely kind smile, a small olive branch. "I know I don't," he said, softly. "Isn't that what I said in the first place?"

Steph had an irrational, irresistible need for him to take her in his arms and hug her hard. A non-sexual, avuncular type of hug. This was ridiculous and rather shocking. She must be going insane. She loathed him and his sniping. He would be the last person in the world she would go to for comfort; no more than a minute ago she felt like punching him somewhere it might hurt, and yet … he was offering that most wonderful of things, a listening ear, a wish to understand. Isn't that what SSS is all about? Now suddenly she felt something of what it must be like to be on the receiving end.

It was a lucky, or perhaps the unluckiest, interruption when Faith and Barnaby both tumbled down the stairs together in search of sustenance, claiming to be starving, staking their rights to a share of the Danish pastries. Steph's pulse was still racing from the grilling she had just endured.

"I guess we are nowhere near finished yet, are we?" she asked cautiously but also rhetorically, not waiting for an answer. "Perhaps I should make us all some sandwiches or something …" The suggestion was greeted with a unanimous chorus of approval. "Then we can share the pastries." An even louder cheer.

Barnaby stepped forward and held out a hand to Greg who took it and shook it with manly panache. "I'm Barnaby," said her son, with simple good manners that made Steph feel proud.

"I'm Greg. How're you doin' then, young man? Is life treating you well?"

Barnaby shrugged, nodded his head. "Not bad, not bad. Been working pretty hard this morning though. You?"

Greg was smiling but not laughing. Gauged about right, thought Steph. "Yeah. Busy the whole morning through … lots of work, lots to do."

Steph declined all offers of help in the kitchen. It was too small and would be easier and quicker, she decided, to make a unilateral decision on the sandwich fillings than to deal with orders, preferences and quibbles. She needed a moment to calm down anyway.

"Is there anything you really can't eat?" she checked rather grudgingly with Greg.

"Oysters, snails, slugs …" Barnaby creased up with laughter. "That's about it, I think. Oh, and broccoli. Sorry."

"Well, I think you're safe then."

She could overhear them talking about favourite foods which happened to be one of Barnaby's special subjects. How different Greg was from the rather humourless authoritarian he could be. Even this morning he was ruthless enough to make her angry and close to tears, yet she realised that much of what he was saying had an element of truth, and she could see how he had picked up a false picture of the truth about her and Justin and her apparent lapses. Of course he had been right too, that they should have established the foundations of their relationship before they could move on. A frank one-to-one was now going to be difficult with two other pairs of ears in the house.

Faith had now joined in the conversation after briefly excusing herself to read a text message on her mobile; Greg was asking her questions about her interests and how she liked school.

"Do you think you'll stay in Appley Green?" he was asking Faith, when Steph walked in with a tray bearing a selection of tasty sandwiches. Barnaby had brought in some glasses and a jug of iced water.

"What a sumptuous feast!" commented Greg. Hardly, thought Steph, but at least the comment was positive.

242

Faith set out the plates and paper serviettes without being asked. "I would like to. It's the best village you could ever imagine, I think, sort of countrified but not far from London really and you can get to cinemas and stuff easily. Plus all my friends are here …"

Greg nodded. "It can be difficult once you need to think about where to earn a living. Are you going to University?"

"Oh definitely," she said. "I think I want to become an architect."

How wrong it is the way teenagers are unerringly portrayed as a grumpy, moody lot, thought Steph, feeling proud of her daughter.

"If we can afford it," she put in, quietly. Money would not be a problem but she did not want Faith to know that – yet.

"It's a long haul, I believe. Many years. And higher education not so easy to fund as it was in our day – sorry I mean *my* day. Two different eras!"

"Are you a lot older than Mum then?" asked Barnaby, scrutinising Greg's face from across the table.

"That's so rude Barnaby!" Faith chided.

He looked genuinely wounded. "Why? Why is that rude? Mum, was that rude?"

Greg responded quickly with a chuckle, "Of course not. No offence meant and none taken. Just an honest question, eh? I am a few years older." *A few?* Steph raised her eyebrows, actually thinking this was a gross underestimation. "If my sums are correct, there is a gap of fifteen years, so when I went to university there was no problem with getting a grant and pretty much everything paid for."

"Well, even in *my* day, if I'd gone to university I think it would have been less cost for my parents than how it is

243

these days," said Steph. So he's barely past fifty, not that old. Why is he semi-retired, she wanted to ask?

"Why didn't you go to uni, Mum?" asked Faith. "You've never really said."

Steph shifted in her seat, unsure if she wanted this. "I … preferred to get a job. Didn't work hard enough at school either. Not the best of ideas necessarily, but for me it worked and I … I had … help … in making it work. My father, your Grandad, he was able to give me a lot of advice and business knowledge."

She felt a little uncomfortable with what she saw as a confession; an admission that her incredible success in building up *House of Fitness* was partly due to her father.

"Lucky for you, but you are the kind of person who would do well anyway," put in Greg supportively. "Your Mum is a go-getter, a do-er and a finish-er! Did you know that?" Steph thought she must have misheard and her mouth hung open for a second. Big compliments.

Faith and Barnaby said they did. They seemed to understand what he was saying in his office jargon and, as the four of them sat munching sandwiches and putting the world right, Steph felt more loved, more complete than she had for years and years.

"Although, going back to the career thing, I certainly would *never* want to be a mother raising children on my own," said Faith suddenly, uttering apparently unfiltered thoughts. The honesty of children could let you down sometimes.

31

"I'd like you, Faith and Barnaby to come round and meet my family when they're here, you know," said Jackson. "Essie will arrive first." He reached for his diary and spectacles; jittery fingers flicked through its pages. "Next Thursday, I think. Then Jacob and his tribe from Pretoria, and finally the Auckland contingent."

Steph sat opposite him in his study in the usual way. They had been going through the property brochures. She had made sure his hearing aid was on and that he was looking directly at her.

"And the party is on the Saturday?"

"Yes, indeed. Just a family gathering, though. Nobody else will be there. It would be a little … overpowering to have a huge crowd."

"I imagine so."

"Hah! Most of my old buddies are dead anyhow. So would you be able to pop round perhaps on the Sunday sometime? If you have a spare half an hour?"

"How kind. I'll check with my two at home and let you know."

Her heart was beating hard, trying to cope with some inner conflict. She actually did not want to meet his family, his daughter, and all the others, all these strangers, these … the word 'imposters' came to mind. What was *wrong* with her? She wished they were not coming! This was madness. She was going insane. This was what the computer class had been all about initially, to get him there, to enable him to contact his family more easily. Now they were physically closing in on him from all corners of the globe and she did not want to be a part of it. The very idea made her feel sick.

She gathered up her things and consulted her watch. "I'm afraid I have to go now, Jackson. I ... I'll let you know. About the weekend, but I'm sure I'll see you before the party anyway, one day next week. We have another visit booked in, don't we? Is there anything more I can do?"

"No. No thank you my dear. I think Essie has all the travel arrangements in hand, taxis, pickups from the airport and so on. She sent me a letter."

"You ... you must be ... very excited."

Jackson shrugged and smiled at Steph. "To tell you the truth, my dear, I rather get used to them *not* being here. Their lives are so far removed from my own now. They will speak of people, places, events ... ah, things of which I know nothing." Her heart gladdened when she heard this and she felt her mouth twitch into a genuine smile that she knew was terribly wrong. "Frightful thing to say, but you know, when so many years have elapsed, I'm not sure if I shall cope well with all the emotions that will, undoubtedly, be running high. Mmm." He stopped to reflect on this for a moment and Steph's spirits plummeted again. Emotions would mean laughter, tears, hugs. Her own emotions were telling her something and she did not like what they were saying. She was jealous. This was not right.

That evening she checked with Faith and Barnaby. "How do you fancy a visit to Jackson this coming Sunday?"

Faith nodded. "Fine."

"Ye-ah!" cried Barnaby.

246

"I think it's best we keep out of the big family reunion. He did invite us to meet them on Sunday week, but …"

"Oh? *That'd* be cool," said Faith.

"Oh yeah. He *said* there was a boy coming …"

Steph cut in. "No, I really think it best we don't. I'm going to tell a little white lie and say we can't make it that weekend. Then offer to visit this Sunday instead."

"I don't understand," said Barnaby. "I think a lie is a lie. White or whatever."

"I'd like to meet them. Aren't you curious, Mum?"

"Look, I've decided it will be for the best …OK?"

Jackson was sorry to hear that they could not make it to meet his family but accepted this. Nothing really fazed him.

"Please do come this Sunday then. That'll be splendid." Steph was happy when he said this. It would be cosy, just the four of them.

Lettie reminded her that the dinner party was set for this weekend too. She had made contact with Greg and it was all arranged. Steph was unsure whether she was actually looking forward to this or not. He had such a way of blowing hot and cold; one minute offering a smile that made his treacle-brown eyes twinkle with an honesty that she so much wanted to trust; the next an intimidating, reproving glare that could freeze hell, as if he might be harbouring an axe behind his back.

She thought of the key men in her life and what woeful disappointments they had been. Lucas, the love of her life, had accidently killed himself. Obviously, she could never blame him for that and never would; he was just trying too hard to make a life for them and their babies, and in so doing had pushed himself too hard. No, the *accident* had killed him. But his tragic death was probably the cruellest disappointment in her life. Ted Devonish was a much revered, elderly gentleman, an entirely different case in point, but he died before his time and, bless him, left her with this enormous legacy, a challenge she must fulfil for his sake and for Appley Green. And Richard? Well it was her own fault for being so naive as to marry him! Brodric, he was just a hateful specimen of male office low-life, a bully, a coward, a nasty piece of work. Then there was the villain Justin, who had entered her life uninvited ... and even her own father ... she really struggled to think of a single man who had not failed her in some way or the other. Jackson, of course, vulnerable and sweet, was the outstanding exception.

She would never be caught out again. She and her two children were a team and that is how they would stay, until such time as they grew in numbers by accretion. Faith would settle down with someone worthy of her and they would have children, she felt sure. Barnaby ... it made her smile to imagine him as a man with his own offspring. How amazing that would be! But this would be enough. No man could ever fill the huge space she felt from time to time. Better by far to leave the vacancy empty.

She pulled out hanger after hanger from her wardrobe, biting her lip, exasperated as she realised she had nothing, but nothing, suitable to wear to her neighbour's dinner.

Faith appeared, leaning casually against the bedroom doorframe. "What's the big deal? Jeans and a sparkly top, surely. Yeah?"

Steph threw her a grateful look, as she surveyed the discarded evening dresses and skirts now strewn on the bed, like a well-rummaged jumble sale table-top. Most of them she had not worn for years. They were outmoded and much too fussy.

"Or that long cream linen shirt with black leggings? You're only going next-door." She went off shaking her head.

She opted for a feminine violet silk tunic top with charcoal-grey jeans. Lettie was a colourful arty-type, unafraid of red-pink, lime-green-maroon, purple-orange mixes and she did not want to appear too dull alongside. Tasteful yes, but not entirely boring. Above all she did not wish to appear overdressed. Not again. Especially as this was the first time she had really been with Greg socially. She was still not quite at ease with this concept, but at least he could not beat her with harsh words in public. Could he?

She was not sure whether to arrive first or wait until she saw Greg's car. It had not been made clear whether he would come and pick her up first. A phone call from an old friend, who could really talk, took the decision from her and by the time she knocked on Lettie's door, people were standing with drinks. She was taken aback to see a roomful, though the room was very small. Two other couples: Babs and Tony and another couple she did not recognise. No Greg, it seemed. She felt a stomach-roll of disappointment that took her by surprise.

"Hi Steph! Why haven't we done this sooner, I keep asking myself? You look very lovely," said Angwyn, as he took her the few short steps it needed to join her to the throng. "Now. Do you know everyone?" Maybe someone such as he could restore her faith in the male of the species, thought Steph. She handed him a bottle of Chateauneuf du Pape and a box of chilli chocolates, hoping he would recognise the expense involved. His eyes lit up and she was duly satisfied.

Babs and Tony called across in unison and Steph instantly suspected she might need a few stiff drinks to get her through this evening, if Greg *did* show up. The other couple shook hands, introducing themselves as Sue and Eddie, looking like a nice normal couple, thought Steph, and clearly American judging from their accents.

"Don't think we've met have we?" said Sue. "Although I'm just *terrible* ..."

"Easy to offend, honey..." said Eddie, giving his wife's arm a squeeze.

"Wine?" asked Angwyn. "Red or white?"

"Red please. Lovely," responded Steph, then turning to the others, said, "Well I think you must be new to the village, as I don't recognise you either. Do you actually live here?" asked Steph.

"Yes, we do. Moved here just a couple of weeks ago. Adorable little place," said Sue, twitching her nose.

"So British and kinda quaint, yet real close to London town," added Eddie.

She soon established they had come from Brooklyn, New York, although they originated from some rural place in America Steph had never heard of. Having tired of city life, they sold up and made the bold move to come to live in Appley Green where an elderly housebound aunt and uncle lived. Apparently Steph had visited them and they had spoken highly of her. "Your visit much cheered them," said Eddie, "this was before we gotten here. Even in a friendly village like Appley Green they could feel pretty lonesome." It struck Steph how clever Lettie was, weaving them all together.

Lettie came over with a tray of canapés. She was wearing a white short smock-top, very understated, with lace panels, over some flared deep-teal trousers. The stretchy satin fitted around the hips but hung with a simple elegance.

"You look like a model – I mean that in a good way, not half-starved. Stunning!" Now she wished she had gone shopping for something new. "Is Greg coming?"

"Oh, sure! He called. Got held up with road works near Farnham."

Steph took a large glug of wine, feeling an absurd heat rising to her cheeks, which she fervently hoped nobody had clocked. Why had he not called *her*, she wondered, rather peevishly?

He soon arrived and was duly ushered through. What mood was he in? Her heart gave a thump and she clutched her glass, which she assumed was due to her fear of him turning on her in some way. "Hi Lettie! Steph!" He kissed both, just one cheek each. His arm just lightly caught her shoulder, she noticed. Introductions were made over again.

Lettie explained, "Now Babs and Tony say they met you already, Greg, so we thought that would be nice. Lovely to make connections with people, isn't it? Proper match-maker, me." She winked at Steph.

Once at the table where seating was arranged boy-girl-boy-girl so that partners, heaven forbid, did not sit next to each other, Steph began to relax a little. Greg, apparently laid-back, seemed to fit in easily; chatting to Lettie on his left and to Sue on his right. They seemed to be enjoying his company and Steph remembered what Lettie had said about him before. She was positioned between Angwyn and Tony and looked across from time to time.

When offered more wine, Greg closed his hand over the top of his glass with a polite shake of his head. Of course, he was driving. She lost count of the times Angwyn refilled her own glass. Everyone seemed to be talking at once, and Steph did wonder if there was much listening going on.

"How did you get to know Babs and Tony, then?" Steph asked her host.

"Well, to tell you the truth, Steph, I've never spoken to them before," he said, quietly in her ear. The noise levels were now such that they would not be overheard. "But they needed help with their website and brochures and suchlike stuff for their business and …"

"Ah, so Lettie …"

"Well, they contacted her, in the first instance about the website they'd planned, but Lettie had some other ideas for promoting their business, which she threw in for free."

She looked across to Lettie and Greg. Lettie was tossing her curls about, very animated. She was flirting with him! Giving him coy sideways glances, responding to his every word and laughing. Well, the little slapper! What her Grandma would have called 'a cheeky minx'. Angwyn seemed oblivious. Greg looked entirely smitten, with her husband just the other side of the table! Well, Greg, don't take the moral high ground with me ever again. Not that he needed to. The entirely ridiculous Justin suspicion was something going on in his imagination only, thank God.

Lettie suddenly called across. "You okay Steph? My husband looking after you, is he?"

Steph nodded, merry and carefree, an alcohol-induced illusion. "Totally, thanks Lettie. Totally." She knew she sounded dozy but nobody noticed. They all sounded even more inane. Greg was the only sober one, the only guest who was not going to stagger back home.

Steph was vaguely relieved the subject of *The Gemstones* website had not been a major topic of conversation across the table, just confined to Angwyn and herself. Some ghastly debate might have ensued on the pros and cons of the Internet and profitable use of time. She dipped her spoon into the rum chocolate mousse. How strange that Lettie had produced what used to be her most favourite dessert, one she had not touched since Lucas used to make it for her all those years ago. It had such strong associations, the idea of eating it always seemed like a betrayal. She took a tiny spoonful of the gorgeously rich pudding and savoured it with her eyes closed.

"Hey, Steph! Are you having an orgasm?" cried Eddie, with a loud laugh.

Bit crass, thought Steph, but it did have the effect of swiftly pulling her out of her trance.

"Almost! Sorry, it … it just takes me back. To when my …" no, not husband, "well, the father of my children used to make this for me."

"Wow! Husband to die for!" said Sue, which had they not all been drunk would have been cringe-worthy on many levels, enough to reduce the gathering to an awkward silence.

"Never my husband, unfortunately …" responded Steph quickly, with a little forced laugh, not wishing to make anything of this. It was not Sue's fault. Then she heard herself adding, entirely against her better judgement, "He did die though." How could she have said that? It was the wine talking. Now there was, indeed, a pregnant pause.

Steph could hear Lettie rushing to the rescue. "Not Richard then? The ex who sent you the flowers?"

She shook her head vehemently. "I never knew who sent that absurd bouquet! I don't think it would've been Richard. Quite out of character and out of place, really, now."

She saw Greg take an unusual interest in this exchange but he said nothing. She knew what he would be thinking. It would be that Justin, wouldn't it?

32

Greg accepted the spontaneous and warm offer from Lettie and Angwyn to stay overnight, so he could catch up with the rest on consumption of alcohol. He made up for lost time with admirable speed, noted Steph, smiling to herself as his speech grew a little slurred and sleepy. By the time they got to coffee and an array of quite 'vintage' liqueurs Angwyn said they needed help with using up, he was positively *slumped* in an armchair. Steph wished she had her camera. She could use a photo as evidence he was but human after all.

The evening came to a close, Steph had said all her thank-yous and goodbyes and was about to leave. Greg caught her elbow as she stepped out into the night air. Suddenly, they were both standing outside alone together in the moonlight. She shivered.

"Steph. Before you go, I … I …" he faltered and stopped, running a hand through his short, fairish-going-grey hair. Then, hands in pockets, staring down at the ground, he rocked back and forth on his heels as if this were somehow helping him to form words. Whatever was the matter with him, wondered Steph? Finally he carried on. "Oh, never mind. Look, I wondered if you could well, maybe have dinner with me some time. Soon. I … well, you know, what I said before."

She assumed he meant they still needed to cultivate some kind of mutual understanding.

"Well, I certainly cannot take time out during the working day, so …"

"Quite, quite."

"… that makes sense. Just email me."

"How about Monday?" suggested Greg.

She thought. "Mm. I'll check my diary and email you."

"Or I'll email you. I thought we might go out and find somewhere quiet where we can talk."

She raised her chin. "Away from prying eyes?"

"No. I didn't mean that. Just so we can hear ourselves, I mean each other, speak. You know."

Steph nodded. "Goodnight Greg."

He gave her arm a squeeze and she felt his lips lightly brush her cheek.

"Goodnight Steph. Say Hi to Faith and Barnaby for me. They're great kids."

He could be quite amenable under the influence of alcohol, Steph thought, and if there was one way she could be persuaded to warm to another human being, it was through praise of her children. However, she decided to wait for him to email her first; for sure, she did not want him to think she wanted this quiet get-together he had in mind.

Barnaby and Faith were ready to visit Jackson, actually looking forward to it immensely. They decided to walk. It was a bright sunny day with an autumnal nip in the air and no hint of a breeze. Bracken growing on rough ground all around Appley Green was tinged with gold. On the higher ridges, Scots Pines were silhouetted darkly against a powder blue sky. Soon there would be frost in the mornings, coating Appley Green and its heath with a sparkle. Steph loved the changing seasons.

She was very happy today. Walking through Appley Green with her two beautiful children to see a person she cared for and who wanted to see them in the most genuine way possible, it made her spirits soar.

They had tea and cakes there and Jackson somehow managed to artlessly share his time between the three of them, so there was no jealousy or vying for attention. He then urged them to stay a little longer and everyone readily agreed to that. Steph could not help thinking this visit had turned SSS on its head. It should be her giving *time* and *attention* to him! But she could see that their company was making him happy too. His symptoms were less noticeable, eyes shining and voice stronger than when he was down, stressed or nervous about something, which was not often.

At one point she sat back and just quietly observed, as Barnaby, Faith and Jackson sat at a table in his elegant dining-room where they had convened. She could imagine his children and wife from the photograph, sitting around discussing artists of their era or Ban the Bomb protest marches, as they passed round the gravy and took roast potatoes from the cream bone china still displayed in 1950s cabinets.

Now her children and Jackson, between them, had spread out a number of tomes on architecture, engines and all manner of things and they were each absorbed, in their own way. She could have done handstands in the nude and they probably would not have looked up. Instead, Steph sat quietly in a state of peace and contentment, on a cushioned window-seat, the sun comfortingly warm on her back and the top of her head. She found herself floating off into a kind of daydream. Lucas appeared to walk into the room. He joined the happy group, ruffling Barnaby's hair, hugging Faith, giving Jackson's hands a gentle stroke as if to say he understood the pain he sometimes bore in silence. The old arthritis, the Parkinson's. The image then stilled, like a Dutch painting; a snapshot of a frozen moment in time. The warmth, compassion, empathy and love that permeated the room and spread through her were so very good, so addictive she wanted to hold on to the magic. The illusion must not end. She closed her eyes to capture and trap the moment, to keep it there so she could tap into it when she needed to. This was how life should be, always …

Then she heard a voice. It was calling. "Mum! Mum, are you all right?" She opened her eyes to see three pairs of eyes all gazing at her. "Are you all right?" Barnaby was close to her, on the brink of poking her in the ribs, she suspected.

She sat up straight, as if coming out of a faint or anaesthetic, putting her hands to her head.

"Yes, yes," she replied, "I'm fine."

"We were talking to you!" said Faith.

"Mum, I thought you'd died!" said Barnaby, solemnly.

She pulled him to her and, to his consternation, gave him a tight hug – in public. "Oh bless. No, my loves, I think I just dozed off for a minute."

"You must be worn out," said Jackson.

"No, no. I think it was just the late night and too much brandy!" confessed Steph.

"Well," said Jackson. "That sounds jolly good, I must say. But a little powernap is always good for the constitution. That's my experience anyway."

"How right you are," said Steph, softly. "It's so lovely here, Jackson. I mean, the whole visit has been … a treat. How wonderful it will be for you to have your real family here."

Time went by in a restless blur for a few days. Unable to relax properly, she focused on her job, sticking to her schedule fastidiously as if world peace depended upon it, checking and double-checking her emails for some reason, perhaps afraid of missing something important that she should attend to. Soon Jackson's family would be with him and she accepted she was undeniably jealous, which was quite inappropriate, she knew that, but there was nothing she could do to fix this. Reason does not conquer the heart, she decided, sure that Shakespeare or Byron must have a take on that.

She vowed not to put a foot wrong before the next meeting with Greg. At last an email lay in her Inbox, bold and unopened, from Greg Mason. Her pulse quickened, always wary of what he might say. She read: *Would the Hops and Barley suit you? it's on the road between Bloomstock and Farnham. Not too busy during the week but does good food. Hope this is not too much out of your way. If you prefer somewhere nearer to your home please let me know* ... He then suggested some days this week. To have dinner with him some place where he was anxious to be discreet was a disturbing prospect; she hoped he did not want to speak too privately. She hoped he was not looking for an opportunity to 'read the riot act' to her 'one-to-one', as he might put it.

33

Greg had had a dull meeting with the Trustees. As he pottered about in his kitchen, adding the last touches to a chicken Caesar salad, he wondered if Steph might like to be involved in these rather stuffy conflabs. Initially, the first time they met, she was offered the chance, which she instantly turned down.

"Best I use my time to get on with the job, I think. These financial meetings don't need both of us." Steph could be very decisive, he noted, a good thing on the whole, but not all decisions were irreversible. She was quite correct when she said this, of course; duplication of effort was basic inefficiency. But he now wondered if more involvement at strategic level could be motivating – besides which her presence would liven things up a bit. However, he could hardly stress the importance of time management on the one hand, while diverting her into other extraneous activities on the other.

He could not wait to see her reaction when he told her the altogether good news.

As he sat down to eat, with a newspaper for company, his thoughts reverted to her again. How could he get her to open up a little? He always felt there was something going on inside Steph's head – *something else*, that is, as if she were operating at two levels. She could be quite defensive; he felt that he could so easily 'press the wrong button' and he would be 'out on his ear'. He must stop thinking in clichés; this lazy use of the English language was no way to win her over.

She was quite complex too, he mused. An enigma of paradoxes and contradictions! On the one hand she was soft, caring, kind – rather like a good quality hand cream, he mused, a balm able to smooth out the wrinkles in people's lives. This fellow-feeling was achieved by listening and always putting others before herself. It was the side of her that made others love her, worry about her, rooting for her to do well; he had spoken to enough people to know this. But sometimes she was unfathomably prickly; she could wound with words, without meaning to. She was determined and conscientious, highly intelligent and capable – all those harder qualities that, combined with her softer traits, made her the perfect person for the job. Ted Devonish had been so right!

He was beginning to realise he cared for her – very much.

But when he examined her working days, he was perplexed. There were many aspects to her time-management that really did not stack up. She seemed to stray off, lose sight of the key SSS mission, get involved with people and activities that were not part of it. It was no good firing questions at her that simply rebounded. He needed to tease it out … no, he needed to understand. That was what he had said, and that, fundamentally, was what he meant.

And, yes, he thought, I will mention the flowers, but not until the end of our chat. Must not put the entire evening at risk.

Would she be in the car park or waiting inside the pub? Some women were funny like that, even in the 21st century. They did not really like to be seen on their own

261

in a bar. To be waiting for a friend, especially a man, perhaps looking at your watch now and then, could appear un-cool, a bit desperate. Others, he thought to himself with a wry smile, were very different, usually much younger than him and very clear on buying their own drink and probably texting as they sat, apparently fully occupied, though actually waiting for someone. This posture signalled they were in demand, in control, with a take-me-or-leave-me attitude. Where did Steph fall, he wondered?

He arrived on time. There was no sign of her in the car park, so he decided to wait a couple of minutes in his car. Five minutes went by and he went inside. She would see his car anyway.

Once inside, he got himself a beer and asked the barmaid to set up a tab. He checked they had spare tables and were serving food this evening, since they did not take bookings. His questions were somewhat risible, he realised, as there were only four other people in there; a couple of old geezers propping up the bar and a young couple in a far corner, who it seemed had eyes and hands only for each other.

Fifteen minutes later, Steph flung open the door, clearly discomposed. Her glorious head of fine blonde hair was a windblown mess, her cheeks pink.

"I'm sorry. I left my mobile at home, had to go back. Charge it every other evening and …"

Greg put a steadying hand on her shoulder. She twisted her head to look down at his hand as if a seagull had dropped a deposit there and he quickly removed it. Oh! It was going to be like that tonight, was it? Prickles already! "You're here. That's the main thing."

"Yes, but I don't like to keep people waiting."

"Even me?"

He wanted her to say, *Especially you, Greg.* But no such luck.

"Hmm. Even you."

Steph said she would have a sparkling mineral water, but he persuaded her to have just one proper drink. Probably that was wrong, debatable, but he did not want her stiff and tetchy for the duration. They ordered food at the bar and settled themselves down at a table for four to give themselves some space. It was by a window. Outside it was dark already; the evenings were starting to draw in. It was peaceful.

He decided to let her speak first. How long would he have to wait?

After looking around her for no more than a few seconds she commented, "You seemed to enjoy yourself on Saturday evening." He could feel the intensity of her critical gaze on his face.

"It was good. Nice people. You?"

"I had a lovely time. Drank too much, but that doesn't happen often these days, so ..." her voice faded.

"No harm now and then."

She nodded.

He had to make good use of the time available. Once the food arrived, speaking would inevitably slow down.

"Steph, tell me a bit about how you met Ted Devonish. I never knew him. Was he a real character?"

Her features immediately softened. "He was. One of the best. Anyone in the village would tell you that, those that can remember him. His family were always the patrons of the village. Well, you can find details about his ancestry in the Appley Green museum ..."

"Yes, I did that. But, I mean, what was your relationship with him, that he entrusted you with his dream?"

Then she really began to talk. It all came spilling out. He heard about her time at *House of Fitness*, how Ted used her as a kind of agony aunt, but in the nicest way. She was his close friend, someone he could turn to, because she cared about his problems. His wife was having an affair and finally left him. He feared he would lose his daughter, Natalie ... Then Steph told him more about her boss, Brodric, fairly typical sort of heavy-handed manager of those times, not yet embracing the new spirit of empowering employees and delegating responsibilities. Thought he could get the best out of staff through fear. He had met plenty such egotistical bullies in his business life; a kind of confrontational authority that would clash with Steph like a bulldozer ramming an articulated lorry; which might stand its ground, but would ultimately buckle a little under the strain. Somebody else could probably articulate this better, he thought, but it was the picture that flew into his head. Brodric would have soured her view of anyone who might presume to know better than she in the workplace. Ah, right! That explains a few things.

Moving on ... "So you were married at that time, were you?"

He then heard more about Lucas, father of both her children. So they never actually married. He watched her put her knife and fork down and float off a bit as she described their time together, the birth of their two children, his tragic death. Such a terrible thing to happen ... Then everything changed. Her face, her voice. He could sense real pain.

"I'm sorry ... but if you can bear to tell me, I can listen."

She paused for a moment, as if considering her options. She told him about her mother dying. Bloody

264

hell, thought Greg! Poor Steph, what a tough time she must have had at such a young age. It was when she began to talk about her father that she was most agitated, he noticed. She held her hands tightly clasped together.

"So he left! You must've been devastated."

"I was." She stared down at her plate, maybe remembering, or perhaps wondering how to reply, how much she should reveal to him. "I was also very ... bitter. Hurt. At the time, totally unforgiving." Then she went back in time again, recounting how her father had steered her away from leaving home to go to university, and advised her on growing the *House of Fitness* business. "I was really much too young, you see, to take on such a commercial challenge. But I'd always got straight As, as they say, so Ricky, the owner of the gym, could see ..."

"Had you always been close? You and your father?"

"Mm. Very. No daughter was ever closer than I was to my Dad. When I was little we spent hours together. His real passion was painting ..."

Greg listened, feeling he was entering the core of her being. His understanding of her grew by the minute. She had lost touch with this wonderful father who had left her when she needed him most.

They had long since finished their meal and there was still so much he wanted to find out. He felt encouraged to see previous inhibitions melting away; she seemed quite willing to talk.

"So, when your father died, did you go to his funeral, even though ..."

Understandably, there was the hint of a tremble in her chin. He was, after all, churning up memories of the death of her father whom she once idolised and then possibly hated because he had deserted her. She felt somehow spurned – was that the appropriate word? It

265

was, he reflected, a strange way for a close father to behave. Indeed, it was.

"I think," she said, looking at her watch, "I'd better be getting back. Barnaby will be asleep, but Faith … she's probably staying up. She finds it hard to go to sleep if I'm not there." He had pushed too far.

"She'll have to one day!" replied Greg, realising instantly this was clumsy and flip. "No, I'm sorry Steph. She's still young – and she has school tomorrow."

Steph smiled, but threw him one of her sharp looks. "Yes, and I have work. Don't I?"

She was holding something back. Would he ever get her to pick up this conversation and delve further into the past?

After they had driven off their separate ways, he thumped his head. He was going crazy!! So absorbed was he in her quite heart-rending tale, he had not told her the *good news*; had failed to ask her about that shifty character at Willem Hardrop; and, who was it, Richard? Didn't Lettie refer to an 'ex' called Richard? He had not even confessed about the flowers. There was so much more to talk about. Another 'meeting' must be fixed asap.

Did she like him, he wondered? Was there any hope at all, that she might grow to like him? If not, their professional relationship was set for a rocky ride he was not sure he could stand, indefinitely. Something would have to give.

Steph lay awake that night, head buzzing, heart racing. Was this final cathartic release of memories composting in her head a good idea? Indecision rocked back and forth as she tried to drop off to sleep. Was it healthy for the soul to distil one's past? Such focus usually involved some kind of distortion of the truth. Greg would be seeking out 'issues' with the idea that he could help her to solve them. Well, he couldn't. There was nothing anyone could do.

Able to recognise a natural talent for counselling when she saw it, however, she was seeing another side of Greg. What would he be like the next time they met in a normal working day? Would he revert to normal, cold, hard, critical, analysing every action, every deed to the nth degree? Or would he greet her with a benign smile and warm eyes that made her want to nestle her head in his chest …

Her eyes snapped open. What? What did she just think? No. She must not entertain such weird ideas. Absurd. She turned over and, after a few moments of deep breathing, fell into a sound sleep.

It was not long before they met again at her house. He had checked with her 'to pinpoint a slot' in the day when she could spare a little while, during the school day.

As before, Steph tried to make it businesslike. She had set out the table conference-style: small bottles of water, some biscuits, even a thermos jug of coffee; so there would be no domestic interruptions.

Greg sat down and after establishing, rather Mr Darcy style, that they were both well and that there were signs of a cold winter ahead, he said, "I have some very promising news about SSS. I clean forgot to tell you at the pub." He thumped his head, rather endearingly it had to be said.

"Well, good! Always open to that!"

"It's actually terribly important, for SSS, for us and for all our 'clients'" He said the word indicating quote marks. She knew he hated the word as much as she did, but they had as yet failed to come up with an acceptable alternative. People? Too vague. Patients? No, SSS was not a medical team. Customers? No, they were not charged, or served. Friends? Not quite. Members? No they did not subscribe. Cases? Sounded too clinical and impersonal. The debate would go on and on; meanwhile they were stuck with 'clients'.

"Ye-es?" Steph leaned forward. He seemed to be pausing for dramatic effect.

"The indications are ..." another pause, "we shall not want for funds." He sat back in his chair, smugly offering titbits of something apparently momentous.

"We shall not want for funds," she repeated slowly to make sure she was understanding this properly. "How so? Nobody has funds these days! Oh come on, Greg. This is tantalising."

"I'm sorry. Just savouring this moment. How I didn't come to tell you before, I ..." he shook his head slowly and pursed his lips. "OK. So, one of the Trustees did a little publicity about SSS, just an awareness thing, and it has resulted in an excellent return on legacies and bequests!"

Steph greeted this with mixed feelings. "What? You mean people have died and left money? And you are celebrating?"

"Well, they would have died anyway. Don't look at me like that. I didn't personally polish them off. The fact is that it is clear that there is huge sympathy and goodwill toward our aims out there and already senior citizens in other parts of the country are planning to leave money to SSS."

"So it's money that is promised to SSS in Wills?"

Greg nodded. "And donations before death from those who are more tax-savvy. Already we are in receipt of ... well, a substantial amount of money. Anecdotal evidence suggests that many elderly feel there is a huge need for what SSS offers, so those who can afford it are leaving, or giving, funds to help us set up in their area. Projections are staggering, considering the state of the national economy. The spread is from as far north as Middlesborough to the Lizard in Cornwall."

As Steph understood the significance of this she felt her cheeks burn with excitement. "I see. Yes! This is really major news. It'll affect all our future plans ..." Her mind was already leaping, scurrying, exploding with ideas.

Greg stopped her there, putting up a hand, and reaching for his diary from his briefcase.

"Totally agree. But let's diarise some meetings for that and you must also come and meet the Trustees again. This really does change everything, as you say. We can plan forward to recruit."

"We can expand nationwide! This is wonderful. If only Ted were here to know."

"Perhaps he was shrewd enough to foretell this would happen!"

Once they had put in some dates, Greg said, "I'd like to finish our chat, you know. The other evening."

"Oh."

"Just bring me up to date from where you left off, so I don't have to fall into interrogation mode. I really don't want to do that."

"How about ... you tell me a bit about yourself?" Steph suggested, in an attempt to change track.

"That won't take long!" he scoffed. "University. Married. No children. Ran a couple of construction companies. Widowed. Would love to meet right lady. Good sense of humour. "

Steph could not help but laugh. "I feel you could expand a bit on that!"

"I will. I will." He leaned forward slightly and met her gaze. "There'll be plenty of opportunities for that. But let's ..."

"... finish me off first? Is that what you're thinking?" she blushed. This was a term she and Lucas used in another context entirely ...

"Exactly."

Steph stood up, feeling suddenly cross. It was not so simple. Perhaps she was neither willing nor able to finish up her own story, tidy up all the stray bits, the wiggly threads that wanted to escape and refused to be woven in nice and neat. Life is not like that. It's an all-round messy business.

She made her way to the kitchen, just as an excuse to leave him for a moment, and as she passed by his chair, he caught her arm quite firmly. He seemed to have a habit of doing this, as if he wanted to control her, pin her down in some way. She snatched her arm away.

"I'm sorry," he said, immediately. "Oh Steph, please. Sit down. Tell me. Please. Come on. There is something, isn't there? Something you don't like to talk about."

She stopped still. He was very insistent. Decision time. Tell him to get stuffed or talk?

She sat down slowly. "OK." She took a deep breath. "I'll just 'finish off' my love-life, if you like. Let's kill that one, shall we? I married the wrong man. I don't particularly want to rake over that. My mistake. It was a miserable marriage and I got what I asked for. Soon I escaped and am the better for it. No regrets on leaving him, but it has left me very suspicious of men." She did not need a shrink, or Greg, to tell her that.

"What about the estate agent?"

Steph laughed cynically. "Oh, you'd never believe it ..."

"Try me."

She did. She told Greg every last detail of the overheard conversation on the train as she remembered it and what subsequently transpired.

"I don't really know why I could not just let it go. I was incensed by him." She wondered now if it was simply because his looks at first reminded her of Lucas and he then turned out to be *such* a disappointment.

"I'll tell you why," said Greg, unexpectedly. "Because you care for other people. You were imagining the hurt and pain he was causing others, and the fact that he could perhaps groom children on the Internet, be violent towards his women." Above all, thought Steph, it was the threat he might have posed to Jackson. "All this was possible. In fact, he is still a potential danger to others, isn't he? He is a bit of a loose cannon, if ever there was one."

She shrugged. "I guess he could be. But I've drawn a line under it."

Greg nodded. "Your choice – but if I ever see him again, I might just take a swipe at him and re-arrange his face."

Steph knew this was so far from being possible, she found herself laughing - again. "By the way, in case you're wondering, Justin did *not* send me flowers! No way."

Greg smiled uncertainly it seemed. "I know that," he said. "And I know you know. Why would you tell me that?"

Steph shook her head, not understanding. "Well, I don't know who did send them, but he certainly would not be the one. That's all."

"You really don't know? Wasn't there a gift card? I distinctly gave them a message on the phone to put on a card."

271

Steph's mouth fell open. "You? Really? You? *No*! But why?"

Greg looked embarrassed. "I'm sorry. It was perhaps inappropriate. Unbusinesslike. I just thought it might cheer you up. We'd just had a meeting and you seemed a bit down. Thought I might have been partly the cause of that. My clumsy attempt to make amends."

"But I had no idea."

"There was no card?"

"There was a message, *Just to brighten your week, Steph,* but no name."

"Ah!"

"You should get a refund from the florists!" suggested Steph, lightly. "All the trouble they caused."

"Oh. Did they cause trouble?"

"They were a terrible distraction! A mystery. They sat there challenging me to work out who on earth could have sent them. Lettie was convinced I must have a secret lover!" There was a short silence. "They were beautiful flowers."

"I'm sorry. I did not intend to confuse. It was impulsive nonsense."

"I never thought of you as the impulsive type, Greg."

"There we are then. You don't actually know – or understand me at all."

They both smiled, collecting their thoughts independently.

"Thanks, anyway. For the flowers."

"And your father's funeral?" asked Greg.

She paused, looking down at the table, fiddling with the corner of a folder. "It was a small family affair. Relatives I hadn't seen for years, and others I've never even met. As an extended family, we were never that close. But my aunt greeted me, took me to one side, said she had something she must tell me." She swallowed.

"There was no chance to have a chat until after the funeral. It was a sad and confusing day. I thought I would never get over it. People I did not know were looking at me strangely and turning away. Even relatives I hadn't seen for a long time seemed unsure whether they should speak to me. I felt unwanted, a stranger … it was so painful. I wondered what he had told them to turn them against me. "

Greg seemed to be listening with real concern in his eyes, and watching her wrestle with the torture she was putting herself through. Should he have encouraged this?

"Then when everyone had left, my aunt and I were alone, sitting outside on her patio. It was late, a balmy summer evening and we'd watched a display of starlings swooping en masse in the sky, like they do. We were so tired and drained, it was hard to think straight, but, as she said to me softly, there were things she needed to clear up with me before I went to bed, or she would never sleep. She told me, very gently, that my father had left us because … even before my mother died of cancer, he had been diagnosed with a horrible wasting disease. It's quite rare. He'd told my aunt *never* to tell me his reasons for leaving, but she was always very torn."

She stopped for a moment, thinking back, but Greg did not interrupt. "You see, when my mother was terminally ill, the pressure was on for us, for Lucas and me. We were struggling over money and I, naturally, as any daughter would, made time to be with my mother and Lucas had to take on extra work. You know, I told you before … but the thing is my Dad could see that I did not need the extra burden of another parent who might need 24/7 care, for possibly years and years. He could see that I would never be able to cope. At least, that was his thinking. He just didn't want me, or the children, to see him or to know. And, you see, he suffered, really suffered. People I spoke to at the funeral said that he had been incredibly brave. He battled on at home, so frail, living modestly with the minimum of care from outsiders, but was practically paralysed by the end. My aunt would pop in and see him now and then but he refused help from family. He neglected himself. He … gave up. Of course, he died in hospital, with no family."

She closed her eyes, going inside her own head for a moment. Eventually, Greg gently prompted, "And you loved him, and he loved you."

Her throat tightened and tears filled her eyes. "He … he stinted himself, living modestly so he could leave Faith and Barnaby some money when they reached adulthood."

"He obviously thought things through very carefully."

She put her hand to her mouth and looked away. After a pause, she replied huskily, "Yes, he did. He stipulated that they should not know until then."

"A difficult secret to keep."

"But I must. He kept *his* big secret from me – with the best of intentions, and at such personal sacrifice, so I … Anyway, yes, it was special. What we had. You know, when he hugged me, as a child, I felt all my little petty fears would just dissolve, like someone wrapping a big duvet round you when you are facing a biting wind – well, I imagine …"

"But Steph. These things happen. Elderly parents die. Often they do not have much in the way of family support. You, of all people, know that."

She jumped up out of her chair. "Yes, I do know! Don't try and make little of it, Greg. But this was *my father*. He had lied to me. He had concealed the truth."

274

There was nothing she could do to stop herself now. She would say what she really thought! "He should have trusted me to make the right decisions. I …" there was such a lump in her throat she could hardly speak. ".. would have managed. Once he had moved away, we would've at least gone to see him, to visit. Rather than tell me, he hurt me so … how could he *do* that?" Suddenly she found herself sobbing. "I was hurt, I … I hated him and left him to die a horrible, lingering, lonely death …" Now her words were barely audible. "I should have made more of an effort. Oh, God, I should have gone to see him, whether he wanted me to or not …"

She closed her eyes, trying to blot out what was happening here. Then she felt a warmth close around her and she leaned into Greg's firm, welcoming chest and allowed him to gently rock her as a father might rock a distraught child.

Yes, everything had changed all right.

34

There was an item in the local paper about Jackson's visit to Heathfields Comprehensive in Appley Green. A portrait photo taken when he was perhaps in his fifties, held central position on the front page. As she stood in the Post Office come Newsagents, his eyes seemed to gaze straight at her. *Hideaway Local Celeb Goes Back to School.* She quickly picked up four copies and went to pay for them.

She called in to see Babs and Tony on her way walking back home. She thought they might be interested, although there was no real connection for them.

As she entered the shop, she gasped in wonderment. They had seriously revamped the shop, grouping paperweights together, with locally woven scarves draped as a backcloth for beads and rings. Lumps of rock – stunning ornaments in their own right, beautifully cut and polished, were spaced out, displayed like priceless sculptures in an art gallery, some on pedestals. Everything was gleaming and the walls had had a lick of white paint that seemed to flood the whole shop with light. It looked ultra modern.

They were more interested, however, in speaking of other matters.

"It's all kicked off now," said Tony, subliminally kicking the oak boards of the shop counter. Steph assumed the worst.

"In a good way," put in Babs, reassuringly, a steadying hand reaching out to Tony's leg.

"Lettie came up with all kinds of suggestions for promoting the shop. Leaflets, talks, workshops, we're going to get people to come in, even whole groups to have a go on the carborundum tumbler to see how gems are polished. Yes, like your man there," and Tony pointed to Jackson's picture in the newspaper. "Visits to schools. And colleges."

Steph was relieved. "Did the website not really work for you then?" she asked, tentatively, feeling guilty for having encouraged them in the first place.

"Well," said Tony, doing that seesaw gesture with one hand. "Yes …"

"… and no."

"The postage and carrier costs were going to be prohibitive. Customers need to come to us. Although …" he wagged a finger knowingly before tapping his nose even more sagely, "we shall develop a new line of lightweight…"

"…dainty …"

"…items, for that purpose, but the thing is the Internet is wonderful for spreading news about events and suchlike."

"We can publicise all the more traditional sales and marketing campaigns we've got planned."

"So the whole website venture didn't fall on *rocky ground* then?" Steph teased.

They both laughed as Babs shook her head and Tony nodded. "Definitely not," said Tony. "It's opened up all sorts of possibilities. It's made us think – er, well, quite …"

"…strategically. Like proper business people, you know."

"I'm sure you always were businesslike, but you must have a bit of a niche market."

"That's what we'd always thought, but you know we can appeal to a mass market if we approach it cautiously."

"What? Creep up on it and take it by surprise?"

Babs and Tony laughed again. "You're very cheerful today, young lady," commented Tony, making Steph aware that they had spotted a change in her demeanour.

"Well, it's a lovely day, isn't it?"

Back home, she decided to give Jackson a call. His phone rang and rang and the answer-phone was not switched on, which was altogether unusual. They were bound to be staying on after the birthday party, some of them anyway. People do not come from the other side of the world just for a party. Do they?

She got on with other things; there was always paperwork and ironing to do. It was late evening when her landline phone rang.

It was the Cottage Hospital just outside Appley Green.

"Is that Stephanie Perriman of SSS? We found your card amongst Mr Jeffrys' belongings, with a note saying to call you in an emergency?" said the female voice.

Steph put a hand to her chest. "Yes. Yes? That's me," she replied, softly.

"Sorry to call you so late. He had a suspected heart attack. In view of his request in his wallet, perhaps you would like to come along tomorrow - if you can get to the hospital? You may be able to help. Some family members are here, but seem to know very little about him."

Already, with a shaky hand, she was scribbling a note to Faith who was asleep. She would just have to leave them.

"I'll come right now." Her heart was thudding so hard, she thought she might have a heart attack herself. Trembling, she found her bag, car keys, pushed her arms into a jacket and wound a woolly scarf around her neck. She knew it was cold outside; winter had arrived early and suddenly.

Running through her mind were some cases a few years ago where medical staff had removed medication from patients with Parkinson's. They would be assessed, diagnosed, medical records would be found and doctors notified, but meanwhile, the person would be in desperate need of their pills. All that – in addition to a heart attack! She shuddered.

She stepped outside only to find it was snowing. She had no idea. Just what she needed! It was coming down quite thick and fast. Snow could be very stealthy; silent, soft, busily laying down its white fleece as people slept. It struck her hard, Jackson could be dying. The word 'emergency' was ringing in her ears.

She turned on the ignition and allowed a minute for the ice on the windscreen to thaw. She needed gloves, but there was no time for that now. After spraying all the windows with defroster, she sat in the car blowing on her red fingers, waiting another long, long minute for the glass to clear so she could see out.

At first the snow was just soft and pretty, but the gritter lorries had not been out and tracks on the roads were very few. Appley Green was renowned for its enviable lack of traffic, but now this meant she was carving through almost virgin snow, if there is such as thing as almost virgin. Her attempt to focus on the task helped blunt her sensibilities of where she was actually going. She felt the wheels skew off now and then; clearly there was a layer of ice beneath it and the tyres were slipping. Jackson too could have already slipped away by now. No. He would be fine. She gritted her teeth and stared at the blurry view of the deserted road ahead.

In her sleep, Faith had heard the front door close, but it was not until she heard the revving of her mother's car engine that she woke up. It had a distinctive sound, more of a cough. She blinked open her eyes, glancing at her bedside clock. It was coming up to eleven o'clock. What on earth was her crazy mother up to now? She lay still waiting to hear the front door close again, wishing for some reassurance that her mother had come back indoors. But no such sound came.

She went to the window and saw something like a Christmas card. It was so pretty, she wanted to cry out and tell somebody, to share this moment of beauty. She loved that first fall of snow, still undisturbed, 'deep, crisp and even' – just like Barnaby's favourite pizza. Already the tracks left by her mother's vanished car were covered up. Where on earth had she gone? This was so bizarre she pinched her arm to make quite sure she was not dreaming.

Now she would never get back to sleep. Though yawning noisily, she decided to slip downstairs to watch TV for a bit. Hopefully her Mum would soon return. She would not want to get stuck somewhere in the snow, especially at this time of night. Driving alone in the dark. Had she gone completely mad to even set off? Imagine the rollicking I'd get if I did something that dumb, thought Faith, with a little grunt.

Once she switched on a light in the living-room she saw the note. She snatched it up and read: *Faith – Had a call from hospital. This is just so you know where I have gone. Jackson has had heart attack. Felt I must get there in case …* She had not finished the sentence, but it was clear to Faith what she meant. She stood very still, tears quickly filling her young eyes. No, this cannot happen. She realised how very fond she was of the old chap. He was not only a charismatic celebrity-type figure, he was like a grandfather who cared for her. He was very special.

She tried to call her mother's mobile, but she was not answering. She felt she must do something. She wanted to see Jackson too. He was far more than a 'client'; he was a family friend. How could she possibly get to her mother and Jackson at the hospital, in the snow? It was too far to walk and she had no transport other than a bike. A taxi would cost a fortune and might not even come out. And, anyway, what should she do about Barnaby?

She opened the front door and was astounded to see how quickly the snow was piling up. She plunged a finger into it just beyond the doorstep; it reached up a couple of centimetres already. As she peered down the row of cottages, there seemed to be no lights on that she could make out, just a couple of streetlights at either end. Lettie and Angwyn were away in Wales, she knew that, of all places in Snowdonia.

35

The Cottage Hospital was about two miles from Steph's house and, although unsuitably shod, she decided to park her car on the side of the road and walk the last half a mile in the snow, now about three inches deep. Every twig of every tree was coated with a white mantle of fluff.

The drive so far had taken so long, this would save time, even if her feet would end up wet and numb with cold. She could feel the freezing air nip her nose as she turned to look at her car that she had simply brought to a halt, rather than parked, since there was not much of a verge. Its red hazard warning lights blinked hazily through the still falling snow, now turning fine like icing-sugar.

As she trudged along in the darkness, she began to think of all the things she had not asked on the phone. But maybe it was best that she had not wasted precious time. Normally someone with a heart attack would be rushed to intensive care at Bloomstock District and General, but perhaps the weather conditions had made that difficult. She could have told the caller about the Parkinson's, but was in such a state of shock she could not collect her thoughts fast enough; she hoped that by now the medical team would have worked that one out. But she had no idea when or where the heart attack had taken place; how long it was before he was discovered; how truly severe it was. They did use the word 'emergency' on the phone though, didn't they? Her heart was both pounding and racing and she was breathless from the effort of walking as fast as she could uphill in now ankle deep snow.

She reached for her mobile. When she had the phone call from the hospital, it had been turned off for the night and she had not switched it back on. It was not in her pocket. She frisked herself; jeans, the jacket's inside pocket, then felt around roughly amongst the contents of her shoulder bag. This was just slowing her down; she may have left it on the passenger seat. It had probably slid off the seat and in haste she had forgotten about it. Never mind, she would retrieve it when she repossessed her sadly abandoned vehicle.

The hospital's small reception area was surprisingly calm and quiet. The lighting was subdued, as if the very building had nodded off to sleep. She rang a bell at the desk as lightly as she could. Someone came very quickly, and once she explained her reasons for being there, a nurse from the right ward was found.

"My dear! We didn't expect for you to come so fast. And in this weather?"

"How is he?" was all she wanted to know.

"Oh, Mr Jeffrys? He's sleeping now. He's had his medication and should be fine to go home in a day or so."

Steph grabbed the side of the counter-top and heard a loud cry that seemed to echo in the peaceful lobby. She felt an arm go round her shoulders and guide her to a seat.

"You've had a shock, I see. Are you another relative, or a friend? Mr Jeffrys said very little - he missed some of his pills and his speech was very slurred, very poor." The entire Appley Green world did not know about Ted's challenge and her mission, after all.

283

Another relative? "I am with SSS – *Special Support for Seniors*, but … he has become a friend, I would say." She sniffed. "My own children are very fond of him."

She realised she was sounding very unprofessional. What on earth would Greg say to this appalling display of weakness. She drew in a deep breath, sat bolt upright in the plastic chair and reached for some tissues.

"I'm so sorry. Tell me about what happened, could you please?" she asked, determined not to let tears of relief get the better of her.

"His daughter called us." Steph felt herself go rigid. "There was some kind of big family reunion, apparently .."

Steph nodded. "Yes, I knew they were coming."

"Maybe it was all a bit too much. Who will ever know? He may be able to shed some light on this when he wakes up. Maybe it was just something that was waiting to happen. But at least they were there when it did. The daughter is still here actually, she stayed to make sure he went to sleep comfortably and planned to leave soon, but … with the snow, I'm not sure what will happen. In fact, we are all wondering how we shall get home. Most staff are local but …"

Steph had been hanging on to her words.

Estebel was here.

Did she want to meet her? She would be angry with her, she knew that. She would want to blame his family for leaving him all these years … then for invading his space en masse and causing him to have a heart attack. Rage against his entire family burned through her.

She bit back the words and pushed down ungenerous thoughts. Then she looked up and thought she must be hallucinating.

284

There in the Entry lobby stood her two children. Faith and Barnaby were looking at her, suddenly rushing towards her, flinging their arms around her waist. "Mum, oh Mum. Is he all right? Is he OK?"

"Did he die?" asked Barnaby, wearing his normal sleeping apparel, boxers and tee-shirt, under his school coat.

"Oh my goodness! How on earth …? What …? Yes, they say he is still alive and ticking, my loves. He's OK." She hugged them both tight, then ruffled Barnaby's hair, a gesture of affection that usually made him wriggle away in disgust. "He's OK."

Through the glass door, she saw Greg stamping off excess snow from his sensible, sturdy boots. He then strode in.

"I didn't know what to do," said Faith. "I saw your note and thought – who can help? Who can I call? You know, I'm sorry if I panicked but I wasn't sure who to turn to, with you gone, Mum."

Steph felt a lump in her throat as big as an egg but was determined not to break down.

"So, you called Greg. How did he get here so fast?"

"He's got a four by four with *massive* tyres!" replied Barnaby, quick as a flash. Clearly Greg had just gone up many notches on his hero-of-the-hour scale.

"And – I found his mobile number scribbled on an SSS card that was stuck up on our kitchen notice-board," explained Faith. "It just so happened he was already on the road …"

Greg at last spoke for himself. "I was out rescuing Gerry over there." He indicated a robust, elderly gent with ox-blood cheeks and white, bushy eyebrows, who had taken a seat in the far corner. Steph had not realised that, when this man came through the door, they were together. "He'd gone adrift, trying to drive home from a Rotary do at the Hunters' Lodge." Steph looked across and the chap waved across tentatively, no doubt aware that he might be on the edge of a very solemn situation.

"These two were – so worried about, well everything! You, dangers on the road, this man they call Jackson. He's one of your clients, yes?"

"Yes." She looked down, embarrassed. "More than that." She felt her chin wobble.

"He's great," put in Faith. "And he's all right, Mum says."

"Yeah!" cried Barnaby. Steph urged him to keep his noise down. "I would remind you this is a hospital," she whispered.

"Sorry." She squeezed his shoulders and leaned her cheek into the top of his head. Barnaby gave a furtive look around to make sure nobody saw this. A nurse was coming across to them accompanied by a tall, smart woman Steph guessed must be his daughter, Estebel.

"I suppose the heart attack must've been a mild one, or …" began Steph.

"Ah, just caught that. This lady here panicked a bit, but perfectly understandable. The paramedics soon sussed it was a very minor stroke, mixed with indigestion pain from too much rich food … but the kind of stroke that people get over. That's why they brought him here, not Bloomstock."

"A warning though?"

"Of course," replied the nurse. "A bit of a wake-up call for him, I think."

Steph wanted so much to see Jackson, to make sure he seemed normal. Would he be affected by the so-called minor stroke? With his daughter standing there she did not like to ask outright?

"Do strokes make people go all lopsided?" piped up Barnaby.

The woman who Steph deduced was Estebel, replied to Barnaby, kindly. "He won't be, apparently. Hello, are you Steph? I've heard so much about you from my father. It's lovely to meet you in person," she held out a hand. Despite the resentment she felt, Steph took the offered hand and shook it firmly.

"Yes. I am with SSS, *Special Support for Seniors.*"

"It's quite American that. Isn't it?"

"What?"

Estebel smiled. Jackson's daughter really was trying to be friendly, but Steph was unconvinced so far. This grey-haired woman seemed almost detached from the reality of the situation. "Seniors? The term seniors? I mean people tend to use 'senior citizens', elderly, pensioners, retired, lots of things …" Her accent was very slightly Scottish mixed with urbane English. Of course she had spent most of her life in Aberdeen. Steph prayed Barnaby did not interject here, adding some choice contribution to her list of terms.

Estebel's cool curiosity did not match the anger ablaze in her own chest. At this moment, who the devil cares about names? She felt like shouting at her. Greg stepped in diplomatically and supplied, "It makes the name catchy. Needs to be memorable."

"I see. Clever. And implies a kind of SOS too."

Greg simply nodded. Steph realised that Estebel had had more time than she to readjust to the fact this was not a life-threatening situation.

"How is your father?" asked Steph, anxious to cut to the chase.

"He's fine. Mind you, there's been a huge change since we all last saw him. It was quite a shock ... if only he had told us, you know ..."

Then something happened to Steph. She was determined not to, but she felt herself sway slightly and thought she might faint like some over-corseted heroine in a Victorian novel.

Something snapped into place in her head. This, she was thinking, with sudden clarity, is how other people must have viewed *me* at my father's funeral; the hard-hearted daughter who never had time to visit her own lonely father, suffering in silence.

Her anger cooled a little. "Yes," she replied softly, touching Estebel's arm gently. "I do understand. Don't feel bad about it, though. It must've been his choice not to tell you. To not cause any worry."

Estebel's eyes suddenly turned wet and glassy. "We had no idea! All three of us. He does so well, he was always a fighter – whether pleading a cause, making his opinions known, or dealing with a common cold. He would never give in to anything ..."

"And he still has that same fighting spirit," said Steph, wary that Estebel was lapsing into the past tense. "He'll pull through this."

"Oh, no question."

Greg was observing all this quietly, piecing things together. He could see the glaringly obvious connection that Steph resisted facing. Jackson was a substitute for her father and it was a deeply buried guilt that was stopping her from admitting it.

With snow falling thickly again, like goose-feathers, visibility would make driving home hazardous, he thought. They had better wait it out in the hospital for a while. He saw Steph glance towards the glass door.

"As we're a bit stuck here, could I … just take a look at Jackson? I mean Mr Jeffrys?" he heard her ask the nurse. She did not ask Estebel. It was almost as if she did not regard the daughter as a blood relation; as if she saw herself as the real daughter. "For peace of mind."

Faith overheard and Barnaby cottoned on. "Can I go too if I really creep, and whisper?" he asked in a small voice. "I really like Jackson. I want to make sure he is actually all right. You can't always believe doctors, you know Mum."

Steph looked across at Greg and smiled at him, sharing her amusement at her son's worldliness, probably picked up from watching too many soaps.

The nurse hesitated as she considered this unusual request. "Well, rest assured, he is sleeping soundly, but …"

Estebel put in, "After all you've done for him, I'd be happy for …"

"Well, in that case, then, just a quick look," said the nurse.

They formed a motley crocodile procession as the nurse led the way for Steph, followed by Faith and Barnaby, with Greg and Estebel bringing up the rear. They tiptoed along the highly polished linoleum floors of dimly lit corridors, to the right and then to the left, up one flight of stairs.

"It smells of …" Barnaby began.

"Shshsh," went Steph and Faith.

Greg wondered at the power this elderly gent had over Steph and her children. Her devotion had clearly rubbed off on them; their concern was real and sincere. Kids, thought Greg, do not fake such things. Even though he had none of his own, he knew that much about them.

He was in a small room as a private patient and the door was ajar. Greg hung back as there was not enough room for all of them and he felt very much on the sidelines. He had never met this person and was only there to support Steph and her kids however he could.

Steph pushed the door very gently. He could sense her anxiety, as if she would not take the nurse's word for anything. She had to make sure for herself he was breathing. Faith and Barnaby just stayed at the door as Steph approached his bed and Greg could just make out her figure, as it bent close to his face.

After a moment, she came back, apparently satisfied, nodding to her children. The three of them held each other and, strangely, he wanted to add to this mutual hugging. He wanted to be involved.

Steph had looked at the old face on the pillow and thought of her father, at how she had missed his death and all that had gone before. Avoiding any risk of waking him, she resisted the temptation to touch his face, squeeze his arm, kiss his forehead or whisper words of comfort. He was breathing comfortably and looked all right so she tiptoed out quietly, feeling now overcome with relief.

Without thinking, she went towards Greg and slipped an arm through his, and his hand closed over hers. This is how it should have been, her and Lucas at her father's bedside. If only, if only, if only.

36

By about half-past one they were able to leave in Greg's car. The snow had eased off and now the skies were a clear ink-black, twinkling with stars; the moonlit heath and wooded copses around Appley Green looked like Narnia. He drove slowly, heavy-duty tyres crunching the partially compacted snow. She sat in the front, at Gerry's insistence who had gratefully waited for the lift and was now squashed between Faith and a sleeping Barnaby in the back.

As he drew up, close to Steph's row of cottages, Greg said, "We'll see how the roads are tomorrow and try to get your car back. Hopefully by then there will be some grit to help clear the way. And I could always tow you."

Barnaby's eyes blinked open. "Yeah," he murmured.

After a solid six hours sleep, Steph and her brood rose, each happy in their own way. After some yawning, groaning and stretching, both Barnaby and Faith went off to school, assuming that it had not closed. She got the call that went from one parent to another, after they had left but decided not to go racing after them. They would find out soon enough. Some teachers, they said, were unable to get in from further afield; so Heathfields would be closed at least for today. At dawn there had been a further fall, raising the overall depth to about five inches.

She rather relished some time to think alone. It was even more peaceful than usual in Appley Green, with the snow blanketing sound, the birds subdued, and the absence of traffic.

She would be seeing Greg today. It made her feel glad. The very idea of him lifted her spirits. When he turned up at the hospital last night she felt something new, an awakening of something that had lain dormant for so long she thought it was gone forever. He had brought her two children, and she was feeling the relief of Jackson's hopeful prognosis, but the pleasure was down to more than that.

She saw him as the man she wanted by her side. In fact, very surprisingly, she wanted him. This had happened fast, perhaps too fast. But he was her colleague. He had given her comfort at a time of distress and shown a gentle side she knew nothing of before, could not have even imagined before. Above all he had given her a dose of her own SSS medicine – a listening ear. That's probably all there was to it, from his angle. Professional support.

And yet, there was still something not quite right. She could see now that Jackson was in some way a substitute for her father; a concept she would have denied to the death had someone else come up with it. When she thought him close to death, it had been brought home to her. Yes, it had felt good to give him attention because it helped allay the consuming guilt that had eaten into her conscience for so many years. He was her penance, perhaps; to help him was redemption.

Still hot tears sprang to her eyes, still her stomach went into knots when she thought of her own father. He was, in some weird way, her first love. Now that sounded odd. That sounded very odd. But as a child and a young woman when they worked long hours on making a success of *House of Fitness*, she loved him to hug her, to spend time with her. They had a spiritual connection; a bond that was not the same as the love she had for her mother. When he left her in the way he did, it was just unacceptable, and even though she tried to understand his logic, in the cold light of day, it was still totally impossible to accept. There was something extreme about the decision he made, the actions he had taken.

Still puzzling over this, but pleased that she could now rake it all over in her mind, instead of pushing it down, out of the way, Greg arrived.

She checked her appearance in the mirror on the way to the front door; a bit pale, but a new light of happiness in her eyes. Even she could see that.

She opened the door; he was busy kicking off his snowy boots. "Never mind about those," she said. "Take them off inside. You'll freeze." The morning was icy cold. "What are the roads like?"

He stooped slightly as he came in through the door. "Hm. No sign of gritters and not many vehicles at all. Even in my car, it was tricky this morning."

He came in and kissed her cheek, as a friend might. She could smell his shower gel or soap.

She poured some coffee. "How was it getting back to your place?" she asked.

"No problem," he said, sitting down at the table, where she joined him.

How could she tell him she had misjudged him as a person? He was not the cold-hearted man of stone she had thought. He was not resistant to reason; inflexible – none of those things. "I really … appreciate … well, everything," she faltered, feeling so much more than gratitude.

293

He looked at her and her heart nearly stopped. "So all these years, you've kept this guilt to yourself? I take it that was what this Jackson obsession was all about. I mean …"

"It wasn't an *obsession*!" she retorted.

Then he reached across for her arm. "Well, it seems to me that you allowed your dedication to Jackson to take over in an … irrational way."

"It was perfectly rational."

"What, the number of visits? The wish to please him, to win his approval, his gratitude, his … love? The attachment you have formed? Perhaps at the expense of others. Steph?"

This was not how she wanted today to go. He was just being thoroughly objectionable. Oh welcome back, she thought. The old Greg is alive and well.

She stood up. "Don't worry about my car," she said, stiffly. Practical thoughts battled it out with the emotions rippling through her. "The battery will be flat but it'll come to no harm for a while and I'll arrange a pick-up service. For today, I can re-arrange some of my visits and just do those within walking distance …"

Greg came over and suddenly grasped her shoulders and gave her a little shake. "Don't do this, Steph. Don't shut me out. I want to help."

She stared at him, unsure.

"I … I don't even understand myself, so how can you possibly understand me? And if you can't understand me, how can you help?"

"Just let me try," he said, looking at her, now gently stroking and squeezing her shoulder. She let him, it felt good. She wanted him to hold her close, but not in a way that was normally appropriate for one colleague to embrace another.

294

She tentatively put her fingers around the back of his neck. His skin felt cool, still fresh from the freezing outdoors, but quickly warmed under her touch. The heat of desire flooded through her; the first time since Lucas. If this was the wrong thing to do, then she was unable to stop herself. It had been so many years since she'd had the slightest wish to touch, to explore or be intimately touched. She may have once hated Greg, may have resented his analysis, his observations, but overall she knew he was usually right, and most importantly, he cared. She could trust him, she was certain of that. He would always listen; always try to understand – this had become his mantra.

"You see," he said, "I think I may have fallen in love with you. I'm sorry, but it can't be helped." His fingers lightly tilted her chin and his lips were there, suddenly, firmly on hers. She felt their gentleness turn to something stronger and she found herself responding. This was not just any kiss, joyous thought it was. This was a kiss of great significance and they both knew it.

Suddenly the back door burst open, a whoosh of ice-cold air rushed through – or more correctly hot air flew out - and Barnaby rolled in bursting with snow news. When he saw the two of them locked together, he stopped in his tracks, then a smile crept over his face as they stepped apart rather guiltily.

"Oh, yeah. Great. Wait till I tell Faith!" He rushed back outside as fast as he could.

37

That Christmas everything seemed to be going so well. SSS was going from strength to strength; new branches opening up in pockets of adjacent counties, sending out ripples far beyond.

Jackson was back to normal, the Parkinson's a little worse, but his medication adjusted accordingly. The hospital referred him to a Parkinson's Society support worker, who would visit him from time to time. When Steph heard this, old feelings of jealousy rose up, but with Greg's help, she knocked them back. Jackson was now a family friend; everything had shifted. He invited the four of them, Greg, Steph, Faith and Barnaby over to *The Hideaway* for mulled wine and mince pies on Christmas Eve. Then they all squashed into Steph's little living-room for Christmas lunch, exchanging presents, love and laughter.

In the holiday between Christmas and the New Year, they had visits from Gloria and from Ted's daughter, Natalie, who came to congratulate them on the admirable progress SSS had made.

"It's hit the media and is on a roll," she said, hugging Steph. It was an emotional moment, both women thinking of the SSS founder in their separate ways and how proud he would have been. Natalie came along to the SSS Christmas party in Saviour's Hall, postponed to January due to the December weather conditions. She gave a little speech, when the generation well able to

296

remember Ted as a younger man, shed a few tears. Sharing the moment, feeling a community spirit that had been the dream of Ted Devonish, made this Christmas feel like no other had for many years for Steph and many other residents of Appley Green.

Faith now learned from her mother that she had the financial means to go to University.

"Your Grandad wanted you to be sure of your dream; and not to take this for granted," Steph explained to her. "He tried to explain in his Will that you should know about the money he set aside for you, at the right time. This is the right time."

"Does this mean I'll have the same?" asked Barnaby. It was impossible to hide this certainty from him.

"Only when you're old enough to know what you want to do, and I approve your plan!" She just needed to retain the option of nipping in the bud any wild ideas of her future eighteen-year-old son living on his wits as a beach-bum-cum-rock-star-cum-computer-games-wizard-cum-footballer ... with money in his back pocket, courtesy of Grandad.

Future plans began to fall into place. Greg decided he would move house to Appley Green. Jackson chose to move into a modest bungalow overlooking the Green within easy reach of everything he needed. He would employ a regular day-nurse and a night-nurse and was riding high on a wave of optimism that this would work out for as long as he could stay to enjoy it. He knew he was fortunate to have the means for such luxury.

It was the third week in January when a registered letter arrived for Steph. Fortunately she was on her own at the time. She signed for it, feeling it, peering at the writing on the envelope and the postmark.

She could never have imagined what was inside; not in a million years would she have guessed this one.

The envelope contained a brief note from her Auntie Carole enclosing another envelope:

Dear Steph

We hope you, Faith and Barnaby are all well and that you had a good Christmas.

New people moved into your father's house – a young couple. They found a box of stuff up in the loft. How it got there I cannot imagine – he must have had help – and he must have forgotten about it as his end drew near. It is hard to be sure. Anyway, they passed this box to me and it was mostly old documents of little interest, although I will get them to you to sift through. There may be some keepsakes.

However, the enclosed …

Steph saw an envelope clearly marked in her father's handwriting: 'STRICTLY CONFIDENTIAL – FOR STEPHANIE MY DAUGHTER ONLY, ON MY DEATH'.

… is for you and looks more urgent. I do hope this is nothing but good news.

Happy New Year!
Auntie Carole

Steph's heart was thumping hard as a bass drum, as if it might at any moment burst from her chest. What was this?

She slit open the envelope and took out quite a long letter. It must have been written a while before he died, for he was unable to pen so much as a sentence in his latter months.

She sat down on the sofa and read:

My dear Stephanie

I hope this reaches you at the right time. I wanted it kept securely away from others' eyes. This is for you only – that is, no other family members need to know about this.

You may still be saddened and hurt by the way I moved away – just at a time when you needed your father the most. You have no idea how much of a wrench it was – for me, that is – or the pain I went through.

You see, Stephanie, the love I felt for you was more than is perhaps normal for a father.

Steph gasped at the implication, feeling the blood drain from her face. What was his meaning?

To find the right words now is unbelievably difficult.

Let us go back to the beginning – always the best place to start perhaps.

You know that when you were born I was still in the army; I had been in the army for years. When I came home on leave, your mother and I did everything we could to … well, you know, we wanted to have children. Of course we did. But nothing happened.

Until one day it seemed our luck had changed. Your mother was in England and discovered she was pregnant – she sent me a letter – I was in Germany at the time. I cried out to everyone within earshot. 'My wife and I are going to have a baby.' And they all shouted back. 'At last'. There was much teasing.

You were born. Our little angel. How we loved you and spoiled you. After a couple of years, as we were rather old to be parents, we wanted to provide you with a little brother or sister, but of course, once again, nothing happened. As biological time was running out for your mother, we went through various tests that had become available. It seemed the problem lay with me. I was unable to provide the necessary – apparently.

Steph put a hand to her mouth, reading faster …

So you see, Steph, I am not your biological father. Of course, it made little difference to how we loved you and the way we brought you up. Your mother never confessed there had been another man and I never asked her. Only my doctor and I know how impossible it was for me to make your mother conceive. I was 'firing blanks', if you know what I mean. Oh dear, this is all so distasteful no matter how I try.

I could never blame your mother – after all, I was away so much, the temptations must have been great. And I could not give her what she needed so much – a baby.

I treated you as any father would treat their daughter I hope. But as you grew into a lovely young woman, my fondness grew into something close to … well, a different kind of love. Please forgive me, Steph. I struggled in vain to stop my feelings …

Steph's head was whirling. She was aghast. She felt sick. No. No. This could not be. Just as she had come to terms with her own guilt, her father's generosity and self-sacrifice, everything was turning on its head. She could not bear this. He had persuaded her against university, he had spent so many hours with her, close by her side … how would she bear *this*?

… and of course never would make you aware of them, in any way. But now I feel you need to know, to understand how hard it was for me to see you with Lucas, your love for each other, your babies. You did not need me any more. You will probably know, by the time I pass away, that had I stayed I would have been an

300

unspeakable burden to you. I never wanted for you to feel that you should give up your precious time and energy caring for your old Dad. That is all so, so true. I made Carole and others swear to secrecy so never blame them.

But there was a little more to it. As you probably guessed. Perhaps, you knew that we had something special too. Something quite unacceptable. Something nobody else would want to know. But you were young and innocent.

I could not die without making sure that, at some point, you will know the whole truth.

I am sorry to be a disappointment to you, but, believe me I love you with all my heart and leaving you was the hardest thing I have ever done in my entire life.

Steph was shaking, sobbing, unable to read his signature through the tears.

The shock was subsiding as the whole shift in their relationship sank in, drip by drop. She had shuddered, almost retched as she read his words. But now, she was thinking that he was the one who had suffered all along the way, and he had really done nothing wrong. Nothing. Reason does not conquer the heart.

Could she admit to herself that the strength of her love for him was more than it should have been? Had he been her first love without her realising it?

Oh my God. Was this incestuous? She balked at the word. She had heard of stepfathers making unhealthy moves on their stepdaughters, but this ... this was something else. All kinds of questions came up in her head.

Is it the natural or the formal father-child relationship that stops ... she put her head in her hands. Was it nature or nurture that wrote the rules? How would she be able to keep this to herself? He said he did not want family to know.

Steph read the letter through four or five times, examining every word, every nuance. So who was her real, her biological, father? At the moment, she did not want to know.

She left it alone for a while doing a few mindless chores around the cottage, mulling over its contents. She came back to it and thought about the days when he worked with her so closely, for long hours at *House of Fitness*. But by then, she was already firmly attached to Lucas. He was the love of her life. No, she had never felt what her father may have fondly imagined. She loved him as a father, her real father.

She thought of Greg. He would be Faith's stepfather! How did that sound now? No. Dark thoughts belonged to the past. She loved Greg for all the right reasons and he loved her. Above all he would listen, he would understand. This was closure. She needed so much to tell him and she would. After all he was not family, but she had his unfailing support.

Now she would get on with the rest of their lives together. Happiness was the only thing on the agenda.

44

As time passed, Easter approached and Steph wondered if the annual remembrance of Lucas' death would be any easier to bear this year. She had always thought about him quietly, privately and in silence, unable to ignore the mark in her diary.

This time she shared it with Greg and he held her tight. To an outsider this may have seemed too much to expect from a partner, for that was what Greg was now. But there were no boundaries to the love and comfort he gave. He far away compensated for the villains of her life, tipping the scales way in favour of men overall. She realised that even Richard, Brodric and Justin must have had some redeeming traits to which she had become blind, her memory of men soured by her father's rejection. She could see all that now, but only through talking to Greg.

It was her birthday when Greg took her away for the weekend without Faith and Barnaby. They went to Paris. Paris in the springtime!

"It is no co-incidence that we are in the most romantic setting I could think of," he said, as they sipped cocktails within view of the River Seine, watching people go by. The sun was going down in a marbled pink sky, but the air was warm.

"Steph – would you do me the most amazing honour of becoming my wife?" he asked, simply.

She felt herself being stroked gently by his loving gaze. She had no reason to hesitate. There was nothing that would make her happier. She accepted.

It was impossible to push away the memory of Richard suddenly springing the question on her about having children together.

"Greg, may I ask you something?" They ambled along the embankment, nightlife now twinkling and throbbing all around them.

He laughed. "You're asking me if you can ask a question? This must be big!"

"It is."

"I am very afraid."

"Would you want children?"

He stopped still. "Steph. I've *always* wanted children. Sandra couldn't and since she died, there has been no-one … No, I am so thrilled to become a step-dad to Faith and Barnaby. Don't doubt for a …"

"No. I mean, would you want us … to have a baby?"

His face filled with light, eyes turning large, but somehow as if he did not dare to hope. "This would be up to you …"

"Well, if I wanted to, which I do …"

"If *you* wanted to, which you do …?"

"Yes."

"Then I cannot think of anything that could make me happier than I already am." For the first time, Steph saw Greg's eyes fill with tears – of joy.

"There's something else, too." Steph took her father's letter from her bag, which she kept with her at all times for fear of someone else finding it. They sat down on a bench. "Once you're family, I won't be able to show you this, strictly according to my father's wishes. It came quite recently. I need to share this with someone, though. I cannot keep this to myself for ever. It's just too much for him to ask of me."

She passed him the letter and he read it more than once, just looking up at her now and then.

"How did you feel when you got this?"

"At first I thought I would be sick. I mean, the idea …"

"I wonder what he thought was to be gained by throwing this brick into the pond."

"It's the truth. He held onto it for long enough. It must've been hard."

Greg nodded. "Did it help you? Knowing his other reason for leaving? I mean the full story?"

Steph nodded. "Yes. I feel loved rather than abandoned and despised."

Greg smiled. "Good. Then I would put this behind you and look to the future."

"It helped to share it."

"I'm glad you did."

Back in Appley Green announcements were made amidst profuse congratulations. Everyone was so utterly delighted with the news, it seemed that an impromptu party was called for, quickly arranged at the *Fox and Rabbit* in their events room that long ago took carriages and horses. Even Jackson made it along for an hour or so.

Faith, Barnaby and Faith's boyfriend, Max, who had suddenly appeared on the scene, helped make sure he was comfortable in a quiet corner, protecting him from too much noise and bustle.

Sitting nearby with Greg, Steph overheard Faith say to Jackson, "Do you know, when I am filthy rich and a notoriously famous architect I'm going to buy *The*

Hideaway and have lots of children." She guessed she had had a couple of glasses of cider.

"Ah, my dear, it's always good to dream. And who knows? Your dream may very well come true." Jackson patted her hand kindly.

Greg had heard this remark too and looked at Steph. He raised his eyebrows.

"Why had we not thought of this before?"

"What?"

"Well, why don't we buy *The Hideaway* between us?"

"And keep Jackson in his own home, as it were? Is that what you mean?"

They put the suggestion to Jackson there and then.

"Hah! Oh, you lovely people. If you want to put in a late offer for the old ruin you are more than welcome. Both garden and house need work … but I am moving out. That is for sure. I am looking forward to my bungalow, I really am."

Steph and Greg considered this. Steph said, "But would you enjoy visiting it? You could come and check on progress. I think we would want to restore it …" She looked tentatively at Greg.

"… to its former glory?" said Jackson.

Greg put in, "Exactly."

"Well you must both give this some more serious consideration," advised Jackson.

Faith was nearly exploding. "This is just great!"

Barnaby was also taking a keen interest. "Oh yeah! I could build a tree house."

It seemed a plan was hatched.

"*I'll* go to Willem Hardrop tomorrow," said Greg, with a knowing smile.

"In a moment I shall pinch myself and wake up," replied Steph.

Then suddenly Faith stood up. She seemed grown up to Steph. A young woman, mature enough to read her old Diary, she decided, warts and all. She made everyone go quiet.

"Apart from what we are celebrating tonight, and we can toast the lovely couple in a minute, I just wanted to do something. I heard today that I won a little writing competition."

Everyone clapped. Steph was delighted but frowned that she should stand up and apparently congratulate herself so publicly. It was the first she had heard of it.

"I would not normally have mentioned it," said Faith, as if reading her mother's thoughts, "but it seems to fit tonight, so whether you want to hear it or not …"

Greg whispered in Steph's ear, "She's so like you." Steph stuck an elbow in his ribs.

"… I'd like to read it out. It's called 'What makes a Parent Special' and I had to keep it to 250 words, which was *really* hard." She paused and checked she had everyone's attention. You could have heard a pin drop.

She read aloud:

"I can only speak for the parent I have and she is special. My Mum had me when she was four years older than I am now. When I am twenty, she will be forty. When I am forty she will be sixty. When I am seventy and she is ninety we shall be two dotty old ladies sharing memories.

I cannot yet imagine myself as a mother. By the time she gave birth to me, she had a successful career and the love of my father. I dimly remember going to his funeral but I know that my mother remembers him always.

At a very young age she had also won the admiration of Appley Green's most respected man, Ted Devonish.

She is compassionate and rarely a taker. She gives of her time and her love and her energy.

My Mum has always been my best friend, always there when I needed her. Sometimes she looks tired and can be snappy but that shows me she is human. We all feel like that sometimes.

I know how she has sometimes gone without so that Barnaby and I could have things we wanted. I know she put us before work. Now I grow closer to the age she was when she lost my father, her mother and, in a way, her father, I can see how strong and wonderful a Mum she is.

To me she is as special as a parent can get."

After a few sniffs, people clapped again.

"Now, I would ask everyone to raise their glasses. To my Mum and her gorgeous man, Greg. We love him already. To a very happy future!"

END

Gypsies
Stop
tHere
by
Miriam Wakerly

Will uprooting herself from London to live in the country help Kay escape guilt-ridden memories of her husband's death? Far from finding a quiet life, she is caught up in an age-old village conflict where passionate opinions on Romany Gypsy Travellers divide the local people.

A young woman, Lena, enters her life, unwittingly putting Kay's plans on hold as Kay struggles to not only come to terms with her emotional past but to resolve Lena's problems, those of the village and the Gypsies.

And another relationship blossoms that she would never have dreamed of …

Available from Waterstone's bookshops or Amazon.
Also a Kindle Ebook.

No Gypsies Served
by
Miriam Wakerly

Two years have passed since Kay successfully campaigned for the Appley Green Gypsy Site, and four years since her husband was murdered. Life in the village was going so well, until the phone call and letter. Then comes the disastrous site opening. Worst of all, Dunstan, whom she realises is her best friend and ally, is giving her the cold shoulder for some unknown reason.

Dunstan is taking an emotional trip down memory lane, into childhood as a Gypsy on the road, and his eventual break from his people. Why is he so angry with Kay that he keeps away from her?

Chances of a longed for reconciliation look slim …

A sequel and prequel to **Gypsies Stop tHere**.
Available from Waterstone's bookshops or Amazon.

About the Author

Miriam Wakerly has had short stories and articles published in magazines. Her first novel, **Gypsies Stop tHere** was launched the day after she retired in 2008; **No Gypsies Served** followed two years later. These two books are also set in Appley Green.

Her career history includes teaching, public relations and marketing in the IT industry; and community work. Now retired from work other than writing, she lives in Surrey with her husband. Their three adult children live and work in London. Before retiring she worked for two years with the Parkinson's Society, visiting people in their homes to offer information and support.

Miriam Wakerly has a BA Degree in Combined Studies (English, French, Sociology, Politics) from Leicester University. She is a member of the Society of Authors.

Find her on Twitter and her blog, Miriam's Ramblings: www.miriamwakerly.blogspot.com